the Secret

the Secret

BEVERLY LEWIS

DOUBLEDAY LARGE PRINT HOME LIBRARY EDITION

BETHANY HOUSE PUBLISHERS
Minneapolis, Minnesota

The Secret
Copyright © 2009
Beverly M. Lewis

Art direction by Paul Higdon
Cover design by Dan Thornberg, Design Source Creative Services

Published by Bethany House Publishers
11400 Hampshire Avenue South
Bloomington, Minnesota 55438

Bethany House Publishers is a division of Baker Publishing Group, Grand Rapids, Michigan.

Printed in the United States of America

ISBN 978-1-60751-690-3

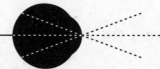

This Large Print Book carries the
Seal of Approval of N.A.V.H.

For
Judith Lovold,
devoted reader and friend.

By Beverly Lewis

THE HERITAGE OF LANCASTER COUNTY
The Shunning • The Confession • The Reckoning

....

ABRAM'S DAUGHTERS
The Covenant • The Betrayal • The Sacrifice
The Prodigal • The Revelation

....

ANNIE'S PEOPLE
The Preacher's Daughter • The Englisher
The Brethren

....

THE COURTSHIP OF NELLIE FISHER
The Parting • The Forbidden • The Longing

....

SEASONS OF GRACE
The Secret

....

The Postcard • The Crossroad

....

The Redemption of Sarah Cain
October Song • Sanctuary* • The Sunroom

....

The Beverly Lewis Amish Heritage Cookbook

www.beverlylewis.com

*with David Lewis

Prologue

························

SPRING

Honestly, I thought the worst was past.

A full month has come and gone since the day of that chilly barn raising southeast of Strasburg. Mamma and I had traveled all that way, taking a hamper of food to help feed the men building the new barn. The plea to lend a hand had traveled along the Amish grapevine, which some said spread word faster than radio news.

There we were, sitting at the table with the other womenfolk, when Mamma let out a little gasp, jumped up, and rushed over to greet a woman I'd never seen in my life.

Then if she and that stranger didn't go

off walking together for the longest time, just up and left without a word to me or anyone.

From then on my mother seemed preoccupied . . . even *ferhoodled.* Most worrisome of all, she began rising and wandering outside in the middle of the night. Sometimes I would see her cutting through the cornfield, always going in the same direction until she disappeared from view. She leaned forward as if shouldering the weight of the world.

Here lately, though—in the past few days—she had begun to settle down some, cooking and cleaning and doing a bit of needlework. I'd even noticed her wearing an occasional smile, a sweet softness in her face once again.

But lo and behold, last night, when talk of my twenty-first birthday came up, silent tears streamed down her ivory face while she rinsed and stacked the dishes. My heart sank like a stone. "Mamma . . . what is it?"

She merely shrugged and I kept drying, squelching the flood of questions throbbing in my head.

Then today, while carrying a thermos

of cold lemonade out to the sheep barn, I saw my older brother, Adam, over in the birthing stall with *Dat.* I heard Adam say in a low and serious voice, "Something's botherin' *Mamm,* ain't so?" My soon-to-be-wed brother must've assumed he was on equal footing, or about to be, to dare utter such a question to our father. Either that or he felt it safe to stick his neck out and speak man-to-man out there, surrounded by the musky, earthy smells, with only the sheep as witness.

I held my breath and kept myself hidden from view. A man of few words, Dat gave no immediate reply. I waited, hoping he might offer a reason for Mamma's behavior. Surely it was something connected to the stranger at the March barn raising. For as long as I remember, Mamma has always been somewhat moody, but I was just certain something had gone off-kilter that day. She kept to herself more and more—even staying away twice from Sunday Preaching. *Jah,* there was much for me to ponder about my mother. And ponder I did.

Now, as I waited stubbornly for my father to acknowledge Adam's question, the only sound I heard was the laboring cry of the miserable ewe, her bleats signaling a difficult delivery. I swallowed my disappointment. But I shouldn't have been surprised that Dat made no response whatsoever. This was his way when cornered. Dat's way in general, especially with women.

I continued to stand motionless there in the stuffy sheep barn, observing my father's serious face, his down-turned mouth. Adam, blond and lean, knelt in the deep straw as he waited to assist the struggling ewe deliver the next wee lamb—a twin to the first one already wobbling onto its feet within moments of birth. Tenderness for my blue-eyed brother tugged at my heart. In no time, we'd be saying our good-byes, once Adam tied the knot with Henry Stahl's sister, nineteen-year-old Priscilla. I'd happened upon them the other evening while walking to visit my good friend Becky Riehl. Of course, I'm not supposed to know they are engaged till they are "published" in the fall, several Sundays before the wedding. Frankly I cringed when I saw Priscilla riding with Adam, and I wondered how my sensible brother had fallen for the biggest *Schnuffelbox* in all of Lancaster County. Everyone knew what a busybody she was.

Now I backed away from the barn door, still gripping the thermos. Perturbed by Dat's steadfast silence, I fled the sheep barn for the house.

Adam's obvious apprehension—and his unanswered question—plagued me long into the night as I pitched back and forth in bed, my cotton gown all bunched up in knots. In vain, I tried to fall asleep, wanting to be wide awake for work tomorrow. After all, it would be a shame if I didn't preserve my reputation as an industrious part-time employee at Eli's Natural Foods. I might be especially glad for this job if I ended up a *Maidel.*

Being single was a concern for any young Amishwoman. But I supposed it wasn't the worst thing not to have a husband, even though I'd cared for Henry quite a while already. Sometimes it was just hard to tell if the feelings were mutual, perhaps because he was reticent by nature. In spite of that, he was a kind and faithful companion, and mighty *gut* at playing volleyball, too. If nothing more, I knew I could count on quiet Henry to be a devoted friend. He was as dependable as the daybreak.

Too restless to sleep, I rose and walked the length of the hallway. The dim glow from the full moon cast an eerie light at the end of the house, down where the dormers jutted out at the east end. From the window, I stared at the deserted yard below, looking for any sign of Mamma. But the road and yard were empty.

Downstairs the day clock began to chime, as if on cue. Mamma had stilled the pendulum, stopping the clock on the hour she learned her beloved sister Naomi had passed away, leaving it unwound for months. Now the brassy sound traveled up the steep staircase to my ears—twelve lingering chimes. Something about the marking of hours in the deep of night disturbed me.

I paced the hall, scooting past the narrow stairs leading to the third story, where Adam and Joe slept in two small rooms. Safely out of earshot of Mamma's mysterious comings and goings.

Was Dat such a sound sleeper that he didn't hear Mamma's footsteps?

What would cause her to be so restless? I'd asked myself a dozen times. Yet, as much as I longed to be privy to my mother's secrets, something told me I might come to wish I never knew.

The holiest of all holidays are those
Kept by ourselves in silence and apart;
The secret anniversaries of the heart.

—Henry Wadsworth Longfellow

chapter

---

one

April in Bird-in-Hand was heralded by brilliant sunrises and brisk, tingling evenings. Every thicket was alive with new greenery, and streams ran swift and clear.

Known for its fertile soil, the idyllic town nestled between the city of Lancaster on the west and the village of Intercourse to the east. In spite of the encroachment of town homes and newly developed subdivisions on nearly all sides, the fertile farmland remained as appealing to outsiders as it did to Judah Byler and his farming neighbors.

Judah's big white clapboard house was newer than most of the farmhouses in the area. Its double chimney and sweeping gables lent an air of style to the otherwise ordinary siding and black-shuttered windows. He'd drawn up the plans twenty-some years before, situating the house on a piece of property divided from a vast parcel of pastureland owned by his father. Judah took great care to locate an ideal sloping spot on which to pour the foundation, since the house would be situated on a floodplain. Together he and his *Daed* planted a windbreak of trees and erected several martin birdhouses in the yard. His married brothers, father, and uncles had all pitched in and built the large ten-bedroom house. A house that, if cut in two, was identical on both sides.

Just after breaking ground, Judah took as his bride Lettie Esh, the prettiest girl in the church district. They'd lived with relatives for the first few months of their marriage, receiving numerous wedding gifts as they visited, until the house was completed.

Eyeing the place now, Judah was pleased the exterior paint was still good from three summers ago. He could put all of his energies into lambing this spring. It was still coat weather, and he breathed in the peppery scent of black earth this morning as he went to check on his new lambs again. He had risen numerous times in the night to make sure the ewes were nursing their babies. A newborn lamb was encouraged to nurse at will, at least as frequently as six to eight times in a twenty-four hour period.

Two plump robins strutted on the sidewalk, but Judah paid them little mind as he walked to the sheep barn, groggily recalling the day he'd carried Lettie's things up the stairs to the second floor. To the room that was to become their own. *As husband and wife,* he thought wryly.

Momentarily he considered Lettie's current dejected state, wondering if he shouldn't stay put today. But on second thought, he could not endure more questions from Adam or furtive glances from Grace. His eldest daughter had slipped into the barn last night and tried to hide in the shadows, as if wanting to inquire about Lettie, too. *Grace is as perceptive as her big brother is bold.*

At twenty-two Adam was the oldest of their four, and then Grace, followed by nineteen-year-old Amanda—their

Mandy—and fifteen-year-old Joseph, whom they called Joe. All of them still at home and mighty Plain clear down to their toes. Adam had joined church two years ago and Grace last September, along with Mandy, who'd always wanted to be baptized with her only sister. He was thankful indeed for his God-fearing offspring, having been privy to some of the fiery trials other parents suffered.

Is Lettie still grieving Naomi? Her sister had died in her sleep several years earlier, within days of Gracie's birthday, as he recalled. A heart attack, he'd heard it was. Poor Lettie had worn black for a full year to show her respect, twice as long as the expected time. There had been other signs, too, that she was locked up in sorrow for longer than most siblings might mourn. Lettie couldn't bring herself to speak of Naomi, which worried her parents, Jakob and Adah, who lived across the wide middle hall on their own side of Judah's house.

Presently Judah looked in on the ewe and her twin lambs, certain that Adam and Joe, with a little help from their grandfather Jakob, could tend to the newly birthed lambs, at least for today. When he was finished checking, he hurried back to the house. He'd seen Lettie stirring up eggs and milk for scrambling as he'd rushed past her to the side door. Disheveled and still in her bathrobe, her fair hair quickly pulled into a loose bun at the nape of her neck, she'd said nary a word.

Returning now, he made his way to the sink to wash up for the meal. Drying his hands, he moseyed over to the table, avoiding Lettie's solemn gaze as she set the table for his solitary early morning breakfast.

"S'pose we ought to have us a talk." Her big blue eyes nearly stared a hole in him.

"Well, I'll be leavin' soon for the animal auction up yonder," he replied.

She grimaced and placed two cups and saucers on the table before preparing to pour the coffee. "It shouldn't take much of your time."

His stomach tensed up and he motioned for her to sit. They bowed their heads for the silent prayer of blessing, which concluded when he uttered a quick amen. Judah reached for the eggs and generously salted them, then spread Lettie's raspberry jam on two pieces of toast. Out of the corner of his eye, he noticed his wife's occasional glance. She was scarcely eating.

When Lettie didn't say what was on her mind, he mentioned wanting to buy another mare for road driving. "I'll know for certain when I see what's up for auction this morning. We'll need another horse with Adam most likely marryin' come fall."

"Can't we rely on his horse later on?" she asked, her voice a thin, sad thread.

"A young man needs his own mare."

"Well, driving horses ain't on my mind today." She sighed loudly. "Judah . . . I need to tell you something."

He braced himself. "What is it?"

A long pause ensued as she attempted to gather herself. He wondered what had caused his wife to go from periodic moodiness to whatever this was. "You ain't sick, are ya, Lettie?"

"*Ach* no."

"*Des gut.*" Yet the tension hung in the

air, nearly visible. Neither food nor drink eased the lingering silence.

"I truly do not know how . . . or where . . . to begin." She did not raise her eyes to meet his as she drank her coffee, not until Judah was done eating and wiping his face on his sleeve. She glanced out the window, eyes glistening. "It's awful hard, really. . . ."

He folded his hands near his plate, waiting. Would she finally tell him what was bothering her—let down this everlasting barrier?

She opened her mouth to speak, lips parted as she turned to look at him. Then slowly she shook her head. "Perhaps it's better this way."

Better what way? Though she'd never before seemed as upset as she had these last few weeks, he'd tried before to pull answers from her but he scarcely ever knew what to say. Truth be known, he'd given up attempting conversation over the years—least where anything sticky was concerned. Nor did he have hope that things would change.

"Ach, you've got yourself a full day," she said again.

He leaned over the table, baffled by her deep sadness. "Keep yourself busy, won't ya?"

She looked his way and nodded. "Jah, we've both got our work. . . ."

He reached for his coffee, taking a slow swallow, and Lettie moved the sugar bowl closer to him. Suddenly, her cool hand was covering his, her eyes pleading. He tensed and withdrew his hand.

"Are you displeased, Judah?"

He saw the deep lines in her sallow face. "Displeased?"

"With *me*." She leaned her head into her hands.

He reached for the sugar bowl, at a loss for words. Then she was on her feet and clearing the table, her face grim as she reached for his dirty plate.

Judah pushed back his chair. "Well, I s'pose I should be goin'." He made his way to the side door, still alert to her presence.

Taking the few steps gingerly, he was conscious of a painful gnawing in his stomach as he headed down the lane past the martin birdhouses. It was then that he realized he hadn't said good-bye.

With a small pang of regret, he was tempted to turn back . . . to say something to smooth things over, if that was even possible.

What good would it do? He stopped for a moment, then resumed his pace.

———

Grace Byler slipped into her cozy gray slippers and put on her white cotton bathrobe. Having awakened before the alarm, she lit the gas lantern on her dresser and set about redding up the room. She made her bed, then plumped her pale green and white crocheted pillows on the settee in the corner, where she liked to sit and read a psalm or two before dressing. Her favorite way to start the day.

She counted two clean dresses and matching aprons left for the weekend, each garment on its hanger on the wooden pegs along one wall. Going to sit on the settee, she reached for the Good Book.

When she finished reading, she dressed, weaving the straight pins sideways on the front of her loose-fitting bodice, hungry for a good breakfast. Last evening's supper seemed far too long ago as she brushed her blond hair away from her face and wound its thickness into the customary bun. She set her *Kapp* on her head, letting its ties dangle free.

That done, she glanced in the dresser mirror and straightened her brown cape dress. Soon it would be time to sew up some new dresses. She yawned as she moved to the window and peered out at the rising sun. Her father stood at the end of the driveway, waving down a van. *Must be he's traveling farther than usual today.* Typically their family preferred to use the horse and carriage for transportation—the team—although Dat frequently used an English driver for longer distances.

Stepping away from the window, Grace was curious to know where he was headed so early, but her father rarely shared his comings and goings. She paused to smooth the lightweight bed quilt, made from an antique pattern they'd copied from Dat's mother. Grace recalled the fun she'd had piecing it together several years ago with Mamma, Mandy, and *Mammi* Adah.

Sweet memories.

On her way to the door, she eyed the braided rug between her bed and the dresser and decided it needed a good beating. She'd do that after breakfast, before Mamma and she took the horse and buggy into town to her job at Eli's. Mamma planned to stop at the general store.

Downstairs, she found her mother frying up eggs and sausage. "Mornin', Mamma," she said, surprised at her mother's already soiled black apron and unkempt hair. Stray strands of blond-gray hair were wispy at her neck, nothing like the neat bun Grace was used to seeing. "How'd ya sleep?" she asked.

"All right, I guess. You?"

"I've had better nights."

"Oh?" Mamma kept her eyes low, but she couldn't disguise their puffy redness.

Grace drew in a breath. Something was terribly wrong.

"You work so hard over at Eli's," her mother said. "You really need your rest, Gracie."

"We *all* do," she whispered. Then, going to the utensil drawer, she said, "I'll be home later than usual today, but I'll get a ride. You won't have to bother pickin' me up."

" 'Tis never a bother." Mamma adjusted the flame under a pot of stew for the noon meal. Quickly, she returned to kneading a mass of bread dough, her lips drawn in a taut line.

Oh, but Grace wanted to throw her arms around Mamma and tell her that everyone knew she was troubled, no matter how much she pretended otherwise. "I saw Dat out early, waitin' for a driver," she said, making small talk.

"Jah, and he was mighty hungry at breakfast." Mamma raised the lid on the pot filled with stew meat and vegetables, and a gust of steam rose out of the top.

"Dat sure enjoys your cooking." Grace was thankful for the gas that powered the range and oven, and the refrigerator and water heater, as well.

The bishop had declared it acceptable to sell the old cookstove and icebox before she was born. That must have been a wonderful-good day for Mamma, who enjoyed working in the kitchen, whipping up one delicious meal after another. All the womenfolk had benefited in scores of ways.

She assumed someone had coaxed Dat to replace their kitchen appliances back then. Most likely her maternal grandmother, Mammi Adah, had stepped in to plead Mamma's case. To this day an unspoken tension over such things continued between her standoffish father and outspoken grandmother.

Grace placed the knives, forks, and spoons around the table, glancing at her tired mother, still so pretty nearly everyone looked at her twice upon first meeting her. The milky blue of Mamma's eyes was remarkable, and sometimes Grace wondered if her mother knew just how striking she really was.

When Grace had poured the juice and milk, she called up the stairs to Mandy, their only sleepyhead. "Hurry, sister . . . breakfast is nearly ready."

At this hour Adam and Joe were out watering the sheep and looking after the newborn lambs, with more wee lambs on the way. Any minute, though, they would be in, hungry as ever, unless they'd eaten earlier with Dat.

"Your sister's ev'ry bit a slowpoke, just as she was as a schoolgirl," Mamma said while pouring coffee. "She's goin' to need more prodding, I daresay."

Grace wiped the counter and agreed. "Mandy's a good help, though, once the sleep's washed out of her eyes."

"Well, she's not near the worker you are."

Grace's breath caught in her throat. She stepped closer. "Ach, Mamma," she said, embarrassed.

Her mother offered a hint of her old warm smile and a good-natured wink. She carried her coffee cup over and sat at her regular spot next to the head of the table. "Best be callin' your brothers."

Heartened by the shift in Mamma's mood, Grace obliged and made her way out to the wide hallway, where pairs of shoes were neatly lined up on low wooden shelves. *More of Mammi Adah's doing.*

Along one wall of the entryway, Dat had positioned pegs for work coats, as well as sweaters, an equal distance apart. The sight of Dat's empty coat peg sobered her, and she wished she might brush away the heaviness she sensed in Mamma. If only Grace could manage the way her father somehow did, letting her mother's sadness slide off him. *Letting everything slide off, really.*

chapter

----

two

Out of sheer habit, Judah hailed the driver when the van was still a good ways down the road. Martin Puckett often came to pick him up, so there was sure to be a comfortable familiarity during the drive to Brownstown today.

Bending down, Judah picked up a pebble and turned it over in his hand, remembering last night. He hadn't known how to tell his firstborn that he had no answers. *This is just how things are. . . .*

He'd done what he did best, sinking within himself, where his son's thorny question vanished away. Where he daydreamed about raising sheep and providing a peaceful place for his family to live and enjoy the good fellowship of the People. Of growing old someday with grandchildren and greats, too, on his knee, all of them resembling beautiful Lettie.

My wife. Things would straighten out as a matter of course. In time, Lettie would return to some semblance of normalcy, just as she eventually had after the death of her sister Naomi. Naomi had never shared Lettie's tendency to moodiness, always behaving like a typical wife. He hoped young Grace, who was the picture of health—both physically and emotionally—favored her aunt in that respect. *Especially if she's headed for marriage.*

The van slowed to a stop. Judah opened the front door and greeted the driver, *"Wie geht's!"*

Martin comically replied with a rather garbled line of Pennsylvania Dutch mixed with English—something about feeling as good as he ought to but not as good as he wished.

Judah reached for the seat belt and managed to offer a cheerful hello over his shoulder to the two middle-aged Amishwomen behind him.

Martin glanced his way. "Pretty soon, I'll have to start hiring *you* to take me on errands," he said, a grin on his ruddy cheeks. "Gas prices and all."

"So I hear." Judah liked Martin's frank way of speaking his mind, his spontaneous sense of humor, too. Martin's jovial nature was one reason Judah contacted the sixty-three-year-old first for transportation, before other drivers on his list. Anymore, the highways were unsafe for horses and carriages with so many impatient motorists rushing along the roads.

Martin shook his head. "Talk has it we'll be paying four dollars a gallon or more by summer."

"Guess you'll have to raise your fee per mile then, too." Judah hoped not. The price of feed and seed and just about everything else made for plenty of worrisome talk at suppertime.

"We'll just have to see." Martin glanced at his rearview mirror. "Where you heading to, ladies?" He tilted his head slightly.

"You can drop us off at market," one of them said.

"Well, I've never *dropped* anyone anywhere," Martin joked.

"Oh, for pity's sake!" the other woman said, laughing.

Judah joined in the frivolity. It felt surprisingly good to laugh again, especially with Martin. An imposing man in girth and stature, Martin had an enormous personality to match, and he had a handshake suggestive of a bear's paw. Talkative, too, he was a teller of often inspiring tales, and one of only a few English folk Judah enjoyed communicating with.

Looking out the window, Judah trained his sights on the splendor of the season on Beechdale Road. He noticed white rose arbors boasting their first coat of paint, accenting soon-to-be colorful flower beds along front and back porches and near small springhouses.

How Lettie loves her roses, he thought suddenly, wondering if their beauty might put a smile on her pretty face once again.

The way he was feeling, he didn't much care what Lettie did with her roses come June. They were her business, after all. But lest Judah allow his aggravation to make a nesting place in his soul, he pushed aside the leftover frustration. He'd had plenty of practice doing so over the past few weeks—no, nearly all their married life. What was another day?

He returned his attention to the road. Presently he would simply appreciate the speed with which he could get to his destination this morning, just as he enjoyed riding by car up to visit his older brother Potato John, near Akron. At less busy times of year, he also made trips south to Bart to see dozens of his father's Stoltzfus cousins. A quick and effortless way to escape concerns about Lettie.

Judah mustn't be gone too long today, however, with lambing well under way, though he was glad for a good excuse to clear his head for a few hours. He was headed to a private animal auction, hoping to purchase another driving horse. The sale would be held in the barn of a Mennonite farmer in Brownstown who'd advertised in *Die Botschaft,* the weekly newspaper for the Plain community. Judah had attended the Mud Sales in Gordonville in mid-March—the fire department–sponsored horse auction—looking for just the right driving horse. He'd come up empty-handed. He knew what he wanted but wouldn't pay top dollar, not with feed prices going through the roof.

Hopefully I'll see something today. With marriage around the corner, it wouldn't be many more months before son Adam would need spirited Sassy, his sorrel, as well as another horse for himself. And their favorite driving horse, Willow—a gentle and big-eyed chestnut mare who was practically a family pet— was getting on in years and soon wouldn't be able to pull her weight around the farm. Or on the road. Judah had often observed Grace in the horse stable, grooming her, feeding her a carrot or apple, and talking up a storm.

Too bad she has to converse with a horse, he thought, wondering if Lettie might ever feel the need to resort to the same.

———

Gripping the banister, Adah moved slowly up the back stairs to Jakob. She'd cooked a hot breakfast—

poached eggs and sausage patties, toast and apple butter—and it was all laid out, waiting for her husband to take his place at the head of the table. He was slower than usual this morning and, since Jakob's hearing had dimmed, she decided to go and find him.

The creaking staircase reminded her of the peculiar talking she had heard in the wee hours. Startled awake, she'd heard someone downstairs on their side of the house . . . jumbled-up words mixed with weeping. She'd sat up in bed, straining to hear. Was it Lettie?

Curious, she'd crept down these steps, their squeaks more pronounced in the dead of night. She had stood in her large kitchen amidst strands of moonbeams, looking past the newfangled stove she'd talked Judah into installing, identical to the one in Lettie's own kitchen. Standing before the front room window, her daughter had been hunched over as if she might be ill. A black silhouette against the white radiance of the night.

Not wanting to make her presence known, Adah had stayed put, not moving and scarcely breathing. A test of her willpower—her muscles, too. She did not want to risk the stairs creaking again. So Lettie was up and restless. Didn't all womenfolk have the sniffles about something at least once during the month?

Surely that's all it was.

"All I hope it is. . . ."

Making her way into their bedroom, she tapped Jakob lightly on the knee as he read from his old, tattered German Bible. "Breakfast is on the table," she said.

He looked up, a twinkle in his eye. "Don't have to ask a hungry man twice." He heaved himself out of his chair and followed her to the stairs.

When they were seated and the silent blessing had been offered, she looked out the window and noticed Adam and Joe—the tall and the short of it— moseying toward the house. No doubt they had been bottle-feeding some of the weaker lambs, those rejected by the ewes. Since Judah had left the house so early, the care of the most recent newborns had fallen to the boys—at least for now.

"Our grandsons are plenty capable of lookin' after things." Jakob grinned at her. He'd caught her gawking and probably looking a bit worried, too. "Word has it Judah's Adam is soon goin' to have himself a farm of his own to look after."

"Oh?" This was news. "But the Stahls don't have land to spare, do they?"

Jakob shook his head, smacking his lips. "I didn't say they did."

So was Priscilla's father handing over the big farm to his son-in-law-to-be? If so, did Lettie have any inkling of this?

Lettie and Susannah Stahl had been friends since childhood, but Adah hadn't heard Lettie mention her much in recent years. Not since Naomi's sudden passing, when Lettie had become hopelessly withdrawn, despite Adah's efforts to get her out to quilting and canning bees.

"The way I heard it, the Stahl farm's bein' divided up again," Jakob explained, shaking pepper on his eggs. "Won't be much of it left if they keep on, but nobody asked me."

"Well, a Mennonite farmer down the way is sellin' off a small section of his land, Marian Riehl says. Four acres or so."

"A small plot like that makes no sense." Jakob shook his head.

"You'd think they'd want to pass it along to family . . . like you say Rudy Stahl's doin' with our Adam and his bride-to-be."

"Well, *that's* a good thirty acres, though. More than enough for a nice truck farm."

"A wonderful-*gut* wedding gift, I'll say."

Jakob chuckled. "Whoever thought a fella could keep his weddin' plans a secret till the time of bein' published never had womenfolk lookin' over his shoulder, ain't?"

They laughed until Jakob had to pull a blue kerchief out of his pocket to wipe his blue-gray eyes.

"I'm guessin' Judah has to know somethin'," Adah said.

"If *we* know, then how on earth wouldn't he and Lettie know, or at least suspect it?"

"Seems to me Lettie has more on her

mind than a weddin' dowry." Adah rose to get more sausage, still warming on the skillet. Jakob liked his meat plenty hot.

"You must've heard her last night, too." Jakob had never been one to beat around the bush, one of the reasons she'd liked him from the very start of their courtship, fifty-some years ago.

Adah stroked the top of his callused hand. "It's just not like her . . . not any-more, at least."

Jakob's eyes searched hers. "*Puh!* She's a woman, ain't she?"

"Oh, go on with ya, Jakob Esh!" She tugged at his cuff.

"Sure hope it ain't something crop-ping up 'tween her and Judah."

Adah's shoulders tensed. "Well, but . . . who's to say?"

"Ain't our business." He paused. "And it never was."

She nodded slowly. "The past is over and done with, thank the dear Lord."

At a loss for how to comfort her daughter, Adah decided to bake a loaf of fresh bread, then take it over to Let-tie. *Poor thing.* A nice warm slice of buttered toast with some brown sugar and cinnamon would surely cheer her up right quick.

————

While she was still carrying breakfast dishes to the sink, Grace heard the side door open. Turning, she saw Becky Riehl standing there, a big smile on her rosy face, her dark hair pulled tight at the middle part. "Ach, hullo. So good to see ya!"

Becky glanced about the room, a joyful light evident in her soft brown eyes. "Are we alone?" she whispered.

Laughing, Grace said, "Sure looks like it." She put down the pile of dishes and went to her friend.

"You'll never believe this, Gracie."

"Jah?"

Becky looked about the room, as if confirming they were indeed by themselves. Then she said, "Yonnie Bontrager asked me to go walkin' with him after the next Singing!"

Grace wasn't at all surprised. "That's just wonderful-*gut,* Becky."

"Do you really think so?" Becky blew

out a breath. "Do ya think I should go along? I mean . . . that makes me, what . . . the eighth girl he's asked?"

Grace suppressed a laugh. According to Yonnie's sister Mary Liz, her brother had made some sort of list of eligible girls from their church district, hoping to get acquainted with each one before deciding whom to seriously court.

"I think you should accept," Grace said.

"Honestly?"

Becky's dark eyes widened as Grace revealed what she'd heard from Mary Liz. "He made a *list*?" she exclaimed. "That's lots different than the way we do things here, jah? Do you suppose he got that idea from where he grew up in Indiana?"

Grace shrugged. "He'll likely run out of girls to choose from," she said. "The longer he takes to decide, ya know, the more girls'll get snatched up by other fellas."

Becky paused, her eyes wistful. "Mighty puzzling, 'tis. If he wasn't so interesting, I might just decline."

Grace remembered Yonnie's appeal all too well.

"So, I guess I'm one of the last ones on that list of his," Becky said, shaking her head. "What do you think the chances are . . . ?"

It was clear to Grace that no matter her hesitance, Becky was indeed smitten. She smiled at her dearest friend. "You have every bit as good a chance of stealin' his heart as the next girl, Becky."

"Well, I don't know . . ."

Grace reached for her hand. "I'm tellin' ya, you *do*." She motioned for her to sit on the wooden bench. "Have a cinnamon bun with me," she coaxed. Secretly, she was surprised it had taken this long for Yonnie to work through his supposed list. As for herself, she was in love with Henry Stahl, who stuck closely to their courting rituals. Her Henry had a good head on his shoulders, and he was hardworking, too.

Just like Dat!

chapter

-----

three

Judah was mighty glad the auction's makeshift registration window had opened early. He'd waited only a short time for his ID number, enjoying a cup of coffee and briefly chewing the fat with several Amish farmers. He'd even become acquainted with one intriguing *Englischer* from out of state—a friendly man in his early fifties or so who was sniffing out the area for a gentleman's farm to purchase. He'd given Judah his business card, but it was only printed with the man's name, *Roan Nelson,* and his email address. The man had immediately apologized, pointing out Judah was most likely not in a position to contact him that way. "Not without a computer," Roan had quipped.

Laughter followed, and for a time Judah and Roan strolled the grounds together, talking about the morning's offerings. Judah had been glad to oblige when Roan had asked more than a handful of questions about what qualities to look for in a good horse.

Presently Judah found himself shoulder to shoulder in the buzzing crowd, vying for the fine mare on the auction block. He caught the auctioneer's eye and then twitched his eyebrow—his preferred way to bid. The mare, a young black Morgan named Maddie, had already stepped out nicely to demonstrate her road trot. This was one slick auctioneer, and Judah had to stay alert. Tough when his mind kept wandering.

Judah arched his eyebrow to the auctioneer, raising the bid. . . .

This morning's exchange with Lettie plagued him. He'd witnessed her occasional moodiness from early on in their marriage, although she'd done her best to conceal it. But in the past weeks her gloom had been more pronounced, and he had no idea what to do to make things better. He'd never had a good understanding of womenfolk.

The auctioneer looked to him for a

third bid, and he nodded his head. He was staying in and soon would be the happy owner of this horse if the farmer over yonder bowed out. Even if the other bidder kept going, Judah was willing to go a bit higher. It wasn't that he was suddenly willing to pay a pretty penny for a horse, but he knew the value of a good mare.

His thoughts returned to Lettie. There had been times in the past when he'd wondered if her thinking was askew. After Naomi had died so unexpectedly, she'd gone to Ike, Naomi's husband, asking to go through her sister's personal effects. For a reason unknown to Judah, or even to Ike, Lettie had been particularly interested in some poetry books. She'd said merely that she wanted to have them, and she'd brought a collection of them home, placing them in the bedroom bookcase Judah had built as her engagement present. He knew the books were there, but he'd never looked at them. Never cared to. She was, after all, entitled to a measure of privacy.

Eventually, though, as time had

passed, Lettie became less sorrowful, apparently accepting her sister's untimely death. And once again, all seemed to be well.

But then came this year's blustery month of March, with its early spring barn raising down south. He had been too tied up to attend as he worked through his detailed records on his flock and plans for the year's breeding pairs—instructing Adam about the paper work involved. But looking back, he never should have allowed Lettie to go, because his wife had not returned the same woman.

He raised his eyebrow at the auctioneer yet again. Then came a pause as the auctioneer looked about the crowd, waiting for one more bid.

At last the wood gavel pounded. "Sold! To number eighty-three!"

Rejoicing with a nod of his head, Judah made his way to the cashier's table to pay for and claim his new horse. He spotted Roan Nelson on the fringe of the crowd. When he saw him, the man waved and called, "Did you get your horse?"

Judah nodded, surprised the Englischer thought enough to ask.

"Congratulations!"

"Denki," he called over his shoulder. While making his payment, he recalled hearing that a small parcel of land was up for sale—by word of mouth only—a mere two miles from his own farm. "Say, Roan," he said, turning, "if memory serves me, there's a piece of land available over on Gibbons Road, not far from the one-room Amish schoolhouse. A small swath is all, but it might serve your purpose."

Roan's eyes lit up. "Wonderful . . . thanks for the tip!"

Judah gave him directions and said if he ended up with it, they'd almost be neighbors. "There's no house on that property, though," he added.

"Oh, that can come later." Roan was making note of the directions on a square-shaped gadget that looked like a small calculator with letters. "This sounds great. . . . I'll follow up today."

Mighty friendly for a city slicker, Judah thought, tipping his hat.

"It's s'posed to be nice all week." Grace smiled at her mother, who sat beside her on the right side of their family carriage, holding the reins. They'd chosen their gentle trotter, Willow, for the trip, and Grace was delighted to slip her some sugar cubes right after hitching up the buggy.

"Well, lookee there!" Mamma pointed to the purple ground cover near the neighbor's mailbox as they rode. "In full bloom already."

"Reminds me of my English lavender," Grace said.

"You and your herb garden." Mamma laughed softly, glancing her way. "You remember where your fascination with herbal remedies came from, don't ya?"

She'd heard it many times before, but she listened attentively now, because it had been a good while since her mother had been this talkative.

"Mammi Adah was the one who first taught you 'bout growin' herbs. I think you were around nine."

Grace cherished the memory. "I remember sitting beside Mammi out on the front porch swing on that hot and muggy summer day. Then, when it was close to sunset, we walked hand in hand around her herb garden, and she named off each plant . . . and described the medicinal properties, too."

"That's right," said Mamma, a faraway look in her eyes. "And you were just ten when the two of you concocted a special tea for sore throats. Do you recall?"

"Jah, had some chamomile in it." Grace smiled to herself, tempted to lean closer to Mamma.

Maple Avenue was coming into view, and soon they made the turn east toward the store. "Denki for droppin' me off." Grace jumped down from the carriage, her apron floating up slightly.

"When did ya say you'll be home?"

"In time for a late supper." Grace held on to the buggy door, searching her mother's face.

"All right, then. I'll keep it hot for ya."

Reluctant as she was to end this pleasant interlude with Mamma, Grace turned toward the store. She wanted to be on time and preferred to be a few minutes early.

She looked back and noticed Mamma still sitting in the enclosed buggy, unmoving, like she was daydreaming. When at last Willow pulled forward and the black spokes on the buggy wheels turned, Mamma straightened to sit taller in her seat, her Kapp strings floating in the breeze.

Why's she sometimes so dear and other times so distant? Grace shook her head. If there was a way to make things better, she would certainly try.

———

As he was headed back toward Bird-in-Hand, Martin Puckett received a call on his cell phone. An Amish family of six needed a ride down to Paradise. More than anything, Martin enjoyed driving Amish children, with their happy chatter in Pennsylvania Dutch. The things they said often brought a smile to his face.

"Okay. Off to meet the Zook family in front of the general store," he muttered to himself, thankful his Plain customers were becoming dependent on his transportation service. *Like a taxicab without the meter,* he thought, remembering what Judah Byler and he had discussed earlier that morning. The way the economy was heading had become the hot topic of conversation in households around the country, and his home was no exception. These days his wife was limiting her driving to only twice a week. Surprising, because she had been known to gallivant some with their married daughters—frequenting Root's Country Market and traveling nearly every Tuesday morning to Central Market at Lancaster's Penn Square. Before the gas crunch, they'd made a habit of driving up to the Green Dragon for Amish baked goods or homemade candies on Fridays.

Turning into the parking area in front of the general store, Martin spotted a vacant spot and pulled in. Next to him, a solemn-faced middle-aged Amishwoman stepped down from her buggy and went to tie the horse to the hitching post. She looked familiar, but not wanting to stare, he looked the other way as he turned off the ignition.

Martin leaned back on the headrest, twiddling his thumbs. Semiretirement was working out well, despite its coming on his doctor's orders. *"If you want to die of a heart attack, keep doing what you're doing."* His wife, Janet, was all for his switching gears from his former hectic job as an electrician to providing wheels for the "People," as some referred to Amish and "team Mennonites." Both Plain groups set themselves apart from the modern world. Who else could pull off living and dressing like it was the 1800s while surrounded by all the modern trappings of the twenty-first century?

All of a sudden another Amishwoman came rushing out of the store, waving her hand in greeting to the woman tying up her horse. "Lettie . . . ach, is that you? It's been ever such a long time since you've come to quilting bees and whatnot all." The woman sounded as though she was a close friend or relative.

Lettie? Of course—he recognized her now. He'd driven Lettie Byler and her pretty blond daughters—Gracie, they called the older, and young Mandy—at least a dozen times in the past year. On occasion, Martin had even taken the whole family to see relatives southeast of Strasburg, near Bart.

While the two women visited on the porch of the store, he realized it had been weeks since he'd received a request for transportation from Lettie Byler and her girls.

But he *had* seen Lettie heading somewhere on foot. He'd observed her twice recently as she walked south on Church Road, past his own house. He would never have been up at that hour had he not suffered from insomnia and been doing a bit of walking himself—the full length of the first floor—waiting for his sleeping pill to take effect.

Watching her now, as Lettie stood silently listening to the other woman, her face impassive, he couldn't help but notice how ashen she was. Her vacant stare reminded him of his own sister's; she had seemingly walked in a daze for a year before a doctor prescribed depression medication.

Just then, the Zook family emerged

from the store. Sadie Zook herded her brood toward his van, carrying a large sack.

"Hello there!" he greeted her and opened the passenger door for them, waiting as they climbed in. "Going to Paradise today?"

"No, no . . . I've changed my mind." Sadie fanned herself with a handkerchief after she got settled into the second seat with her youngest two, the sack of purchases on her lap. "Ain't much use runnin' ourselves ragged. We're all but tuckered out."

"*Un hungerich,*" the smallest boy declared, rubbing his stomach.

"Then to home it is. We'll have us a nice hot meal," said Sadie. Glancing up, she gasped when Lettie Byler hurried back to her carriage and climbed in. And she was openly staring at the sad-eyed woman as Martin pulled the door closed for her.

Martin was taken aback—even embarrassed—by Sadie Zook's gawking as he went around and got in behind the wheel. In his rearview mirror, he could see her craning her neck, eyes positively fixed on Lettie as he backed up and turned around to merge into traffic.

Has she also seen Lettie Byler out alone at night, walking? he wondered.

chapter

....

four

Heather Nelson sat on the lone chair across from the oncologist's desk. The room was spinning and she focused on her every breath. How many times had she walked into this doctor's office in the last six weeks? She'd come secretly, so as not to alarm her father, not wanting to burden him with this impossible situation.

Dr. O'Connor was talking again, but she had difficulty following him, especially after hearing the initial comment. "I'm sorry to tell you this. . . ."

Other worrisome phrases intermixed with his medical jargon: "lymph nodes . . . stage IIIA . . . radiation . . ."

Her lab results had come back startlingly bleak—a diagnosis precipitated by a physical after she'd discovered a couple of painless nodules in her right armpit.

Completely stunned now, she un-crossed her legs and leaned forward. She looked the doctor in the eye as he ceased his discourse. "This may sound presumptuous, but how can you be so sure, Dr. O'Connor? You say the areas of swelling in the lymph node regions have spread, but I have no symptoms." She made herself slow down. "I mean, I feel perfectly fine."

Am I making any sense?

Dr. O'Connor wore an annoyed look, as if he'd heard this rebuttal before and did not appreciate being questioned. But didn't he understand she'd just had the living daylights knocked out of her?

He folded his well-manicured hands and leaned forward at his desk, more solemn than before. "There are four lev-els of this disease. And with each of the first three stages, many patients have few, if any, symptoms." He shook his head gravely. "After all the tests, Heather, I'm afraid the reports are quite conclusive."

You're afraid?

He continued on—something about a "nodular sclerosis variant in the late stage." He sounded too clinical . . . detached.

He must tell hundreds of patients similar news.

She wanted additional information, the kind that wasn't so quantifiable . . . and cold. Perhaps if she focused on the medical jargon—assuming she could— it would help her to make some sense of it. What exactly *had* the PET scan detected? Was it enough to know the medical imaging had shown increased glycolytic activity . . . and blood tests had found elevated levels of eosinophils?

She wanted to see these reports for herself, even though her brain was currently in freeze-up mode. *Was this how Mom felt?*

"Would you mind . . . starting over?" She blinked back tears.

The doctor nodded, offering a considerate smile. "I'll go over the initial biopsy results again and then the PET scan." He turned a light on behind him and dimmed the canned lighting overhead.

She stood up to watch the screen, listening as her plans for a career, her perfect wedding, her future with the only guy she'd *really* loved—all of it—slipped away.

How can this be happening?

She was too young and too healthy—only twenty-four. The staggering news seemed far too pessimistic. Heather had always lived life with a cheerful outlook, even in spite of her darling mother's passing. She had been perpetually upbeat most of her life, even without the benefit of a serious date for high school prom or college sorority events. While she had a few casual friendships with a handful of girls, truly connecting with anyone, especially with guys, had always been difficult . . . if not impossible. But all that had changed when Devon Powers stared her down during an English Lit class in her final semester of undergraduate work. She'd promptly decided he was her one and only heart mate. Never before had she so thoroughly latched on to another human being, aside from her mother.

She had struggled through a challenging double major—sociology and English—at the College of William and Mary, near historic Williamsburg. The school was also her parents' alma mater, where they'd met their junior year and fallen in love, and within easy driving distance of Heather's childhood home. But she had spread her wings and lived in the dorm her freshman year, moving to a sorority house for the next three. Not so fond of hanging out with elitist roommates, she'd longed for her own place. Mom had always said Heather was happiest with her own company.

As eager as she was to make her way in the world following her four-year degree, after a year's break Heather had opted to continue on, content to remain enmeshed in the academic mind-set as she worked toward a master's degree in American studies. She'd managed to work part-time all the while, editing web content for a large telecom firm, not willing to mooch off her too-generous father, who'd received a significant sum from Mom's life insurance policy.

She jerked to attention. Was this a cruel twist of fate? *First Mom, now me?*

My poor dad, she thought as Dr. O'Connor droned on. Inhaling slowly, she folded her hands, as if clasping them together might help her through this painful maze. She paid close attention now: He was saying that medical imaging did not lie, walking her through even the smallest details as though trying to convince her things were as serious as he'd first said.

This doctor could definitely use some work on his bedside manner. *The grim reaper . . .*

In the midst of her fog, a tiny thought burst through: Maybe he was wrong. Shouldn't she get a second opinion? Or even a third? After all, she couldn't let this news destroy her dreams.

Dr. O'Connor had definitely made a mistake. But it wouldn't make sense to argue with him. He was obviously convinced of the diagnosis.

When the lights came up again, she could see the concern on his face. "I wish I had better news, Heather," he said, his mouth a tight line.

How old was this guy? Not much older than she was.

"But . . . I've got big plans." A surge of adrenaline made her feel lippy. She was going to marry her fiancé one year from next month. "This isn't going to happen, okay?"

The doctor nodded as genuine relief spread across his face. "I wholeheartedly agree. You're a fighter, Heather. And this disease is highly curable." Pausing to shuffle through some papers on his desk, he quickly turned to his laptop. "I'll see about an opening for your first round of treatment."

Treatment? The word stopped her heart. She was well acquainted with the word and what it entailed—a combination of chemo and radiation. Her mom had endured the effects nobly, and according to her doctors it had extended her life a few months. But from what Heather had witnessed, the results had been dubious at best as her mother's quality of life dropped drastically. "Uh, no . . . I'm not interested in nuking my insides."

His look of astonishment was off-putting. "Well, let's talk about survival rates—"

"My mother was promised four more years."

"Your mother's cancer was quite different from yours. And she was twice your age." He drew a long breath, holding her gaze. "Why don't we set a time to discuss this further . . . perhaps after you've slept on it?"

I'm supposed to sleep?

"I don't think you understand, Doctor. I watched my mom die. I'm not sure what killed her, the cancer or the treatments."

He flinched at her comment. "Heather, I urge you to take some time to think about this. Without treatment the disease *will* progress . . . and you'll become very sick. Eventually it will take your life." He paused, his eyes small slits. "Of course, if you're worried about fertility, most centers offer some preservation procedures."

She reached for her purse and slung it over her shoulder. As she got up, the floor seemed to slip from beneath her, and she leaned down to grip the chair to steady herself.

"Are you all right?"

"I'm fine." She forced a smile.

Perfectly fine.

"You're strong, Heather . . . and in otherwise good health," the doctor emphasized. "Every patient responds differently—there's no guarantee you would react to radiation the way your mother did."

There's no guarantee I'll be cured, either.

"Thanks anyway." *I'd rather not die before I'm dead.*

She didn't bother to pull the door shut behind her. Let him get up from beside his high and mighty desk and close it himself.

What must it be like playing God? The thought lingered as she hurried past the receptionist's desk where she'd made her co-pay.

They should be paying me! Glancing up at the clock, Heather was suddenly unable to suppress the lump in her throat. Overwhelmed, she pushed open the door, helpless to stop the tears spilling down her cheeks.

———

"Why, sure, we stock a large variety of herbs to help with digestion," Grace told her customer. She led the woman to the tonics and tea section of the store. "Here's what we have." She reached for a popular herbal combination. "This one has a nice blend of herbs . . . it's helped lots of folk."

"Is this something you drink?" The woman turned the package over in her hands.

"Oh jah, and real tasty, too, I'm told. You can mix it with any kind of juice."

The dark-eyed woman took a moment to read the ingredients and compare the first suggestion to several other options, including bitter orange tea leaves. "Have you ever tried this?" she asked. Then, sputtering, she retracted her question. "Oh, well, I doubt *you* have stomach upsets."

Grace hardly knew what to say. There had been several times recently when she'd experienced queasiness, but it had nothing to do with indigestion. "You might want to just try one of these and see how it works for you."

The woman's face creased with un-certainty. "It's hard to decide."

"You're welcome to try one, and if it doesn't help, bring it back," Grace of-fered.

"Fair enough." The woman followed her to the cash register.

"Remember, if you have any ques-tions at all, just ask. If I can answer them, I will. And if not, I'll find out the answer for you." Grace made change and counted it into the woman's hand. "Now that you know where we are, you'll have to come again."

The woman smiled. "You're very kind." She looked at Grace, her gaze drifting up to the head covering of white netting she wore from morning to night. "I've often wondered what it would be like to live as you do," she whispered.

Grace laughed softly. "Well, we're not as strange as you may think."

"But you don't drive cars or have electricity, do you?"

"Neither one, no."

"No phones or radios, either?" Looking chagrined, the woman said, "I don't mean to pry. Your ways *are* fascinating, though. You see"—and here she stepped closer—"I've always felt drawn to a simple life."

Grace rarely encountered this sort of open admiration among the English customers here or while tending the roadside vegetable stand in front of her family's house. Most Englischers were proud of their complicated lives with televisions, computers, cars, electricity, and whatnot. Uncertain how to reply, she only nodded in agreement.

"Oh goodness, I hope I didn't offend you, miss. I would just love to know more about Amish folk."

Grace thought of suggesting a book, but she certainly wasn't ready to offer the woman a tour of her father's house. "We live as our Anabaptist ancestors did." She suddenly remembered the cell phone one of her aunts was permitted to use for her quilting shop over in Honey Brook. "With some slight modifications."

"Oh really? Like what?"

The woman's fascination struck Grace as comical. She wondered, for a fleeting moment, if this customer with all her questions was somehow related to nosy Priscilla Stahl. "There are plenty of differences 'tween churches amongst the People. What's allowed from district to district is entirely up to the voting membership."

"Members are permitted to give their input?"

"Jah, we vote twice a year on our *Ordnung*."

The woman's bewilderment registered in her big brown eyes.

"The church ordinance," Grace added. "Our rules."

Another clerk came over to ask Grace something, and she was secretly relieved. "You'll have to excuse me." She smiled and scurried off to the other side of the store.

Such a curious soul!

She'd heard plenty of stories about pushy Englischers. But this woman had been the first Grace had ever met who'd seemed genuinely interested in their way of life. Of course, that didn't mean she was ready to join their ranks. All it took to discourage some outsiders was the thought of rising at four o'clock to milk a herd of dairy cows . . . *before* a hearty breakfast. That and having to learn the language of their forefathers, Pennsylvania Dutch.

Grace located the item the other clerk had wanted and wondered what might have prompted the customer's preference for all things simple. She recalled something Mammi Adah often said with a knowing smile on her wrinkled face: *"When you get what you want . . . do you want what you get?"* Grace assumed it was merely human to crave a different situation in life and not something unique to fancy folk.

———

Adah stood out in the middle hallway and knocked and yoo-hooed to Lettie, the newly baked bread warm in her hand. She'd tried to make a point of respecting Judah and Lettie's privacy but knew she hadn't always succeeded since she and Jakob had moved into their side of the roomy house.

Lettie called back for her to let herself in. "You can just come over without askin', Mamm, you know that." Lettie had her hands in a wash pail and was down on the floor on all fours, looking up at her.

"I baked you some bread." Adah placed it on the table and sat down with a grunt as she observed Lettie wash the floor by hand. "Your Mandy ought to be helpin' with that."

Lettie kept on, her head down. "Sometimes doin' the work yourself is better."

"Does help occupy one's mind."

Lettie nodded slowly. "At times, jah . . ."

Not knowing how to broach the subject that nagged at her, Adah rose and walked to the side door, opened it, and looked out. She'd never been one to get anywhere with *this* daughter by making small talk. No, she had always had to take matters into her own hands . . . her own way. "Did I hear ya wanderin' the house and talkin' to yourself in the wee hours?" she asked, eyes still fixed on the pastureland to the south.

"Why do you ask?"

"Well, your father and I were talkin' and—"

"You know there's nothin' to gain from that."

Adah turned to see Lettie sitting upright in the middle of the floor, her bare feet peeking out from beneath the green choring dress spread out all around her. "I meant no harm, Lettie."

"Then say nothin' further." Lettie wiped her forehead with the back of her hand. "I have enough to think about just now."

She means without me poking my nose in. "All right, then." Adah glanced at the loaf she'd placed on the table. "I just thought you might like some fresh bread this morning. Would you want me to slice a piece for ya?"

Lettie shook her head. "Denki, but I'll take a break when I'm *gut* and ready."

Adah forced a smile and said she had work to do, then left for her own kitchen. No matter her hopes, the tension between Lettie and herself had never lifted despite the passing of years. She could only wonder when, or if, her daughter might open up to her ever again.

chapter

five

Today the doctor informed me I'm dying. Someday, he's going to feel foolish for having ruined my day.

Heather stopped typing in her laptop journal, resting her fingers on the keyboard as she stared at the screen. She sat high on a barstool at the kitchen counter, one of several favorite spots in the house she'd shared with her parents for so many years. Pulling up her file of personal photos, she smiled as she stared at the most recent pictures of her and Devon, taken at Busch Gardens. *Before* climbing aboard the Loch Ness Monster, the most intense ride ever. She studied herself carefully. She looked exactly the same then as now, the picture of perfect health. Her shoulder-length brown hair with golden highlights gleamed in the sunlight, and her blue eyes sparkled with anticipation. Sure, she was tall and slender, but that was nothing new for her.

"See?" she said to a pair of matching black Persians. "I'm absolutely fine."

The cats had been a gift from her parents to each other on their twenty-fifth wedding anniversary. The big silver year was celebrated by most couples with a trip to Hawaii or Cancun . . . or silver jewelry and other finery.

But in spite of their practical approach to marriage, her parents had always been anything but typical. For their special anniversary they'd dipped into their savings and bought the pure-bred kittens.

As cat lovers, they had already owned three beautiful cats since saying "I do." Tiger's and Sasha's lives had been short-lived . . . but the sweetest cat of all, Kiki, had surprised even the vet by living seventeen years before succumbing to old age. Mom had been too heartbroken to replace Kiki right away, so they'd waited a couple years to purchase the black feline siblings.

Heather nuzzled her face into Moe's

gleaming fur. He always seemed to know her mood and liked to meow-talk when alone with her. She sighed and turned to scowl at the computer screen. "Starting over." She selected what she'd just typed, then pressed Delete. "Hypothetically speaking, if I *were* as sick as the doc seems to think I am, what would I do?" She floated the question to the air.

Meow . . . mew.

She reached for Moe and held him close. "You silly cat."

What would Mom advise?

She recalled her mother's calm, sensible response to her own diagnosis. While she had gone the route of modern medicine, in the end she'd wished there had been time to pursue an alternative treatment method. *But Mom didn't have the luxury of time. And she had numerous symptoms,* Heather thought, wanting to quell the memories.

Still holding Moe, she got online and found a bunch of emails from friends. The only one she really cared about was from her fiancé, who was still frustrated about having been sent to Iraq. Looking on the bright side of things, though, to-day Devon had some good news. His tour of duty would be completed by Thanksgiving!

She hadn't forgotten the night six months ago when he'd made the upsetting announcement about his deployment. Back in his college days, he had thought it a good idea to join the National Guard and had assumed he'd only be gone on some weekends. But when his unit was called up and he was shipped off to Iraq via Texas, she'd inwardly recoiled, not wanting him to know how frightened she was.

Now she kissed Moe's furry head and decided not to tell Devon about her recent trips to the doctor. In fact, the more she considered it, the less she wanted to tell anyone. *Especially not Dad.*

He was still struggling over his grief—her depressing news would surely send him spiraling back down into a black tunnel of despair. She must spare her father that if possible.

Getting up, she went to pour some apple juice from the fridge and noticed a picture of the three of them, a magnet framing her parents and herself on the occasion of her college graduation. The grand brick buildings of William and Mary created an idyllic collegiate backdrop. The second-oldest school in the nation, it counted Thomas Jefferson among its distinguished graduates.

She flashed through her memories of her first year. She'd been so wet behind the ears and unsure of herself, looking back made her cringe at times.

"You never know what you'll accomplish if you don't take the first step." That was her dad's mantra, and a good one to live by, too. Heather had succeeded as she lived out her academic dream at the challenging college. How she'd loved the feel of the old campus and the engaging professors—so much so she sometimes fantasized about becoming a perpetual student, maybe working toward her doctorate.

But then her mother had gotten sick . . . really sick. Heather had deferred her admission to the master's program and managed to get out of her apartment lease and move home, driving to and from work near Williamsburg.

Based on the oncologist's prognosis, she'd had high hopes for her mother's recovery. All three of them had.

Even now, reflecting on the past, a plan began to churn in her head. The idea was quite appealing, actually. Why couldn't she simply drop out of her world for a while? With Devon serving overseas, who else would really notice?

Well, there was Dad, of course. He might notice if she disappeared, even though he was always preoccupied with work now that Mom was no longer around. He and Heather rarely bumped into each other at the house, which was just the way she liked it.

Frankly, her biggest obstacle to running away from it all was the timing. She was so close to the end of her final semester—just another week away. It would be smart to finish her work first, to keep her credits.

I'm fine, she reminded herself. *They just got my lab results mixed up.*

Second-guessing was her forte. What if someone else had gotten *her* report by mistake? She'd read about the frequency of misdiagnoses enough to know she wasn't borrowing trouble, yet . . .

Me and my overactive imagination. Most likely, they'd only misinterpreted her lab results . . . the other tests, too.

But what if they hadn't?

I have plenty of time to sort this out, she decided. Besides, from what she'd observed with Mom, if dying prematurely was absolutely in the cards, you couldn't argue with fate anyway. When your number was up, it was up.

Setting Moe down, she closed her laptop and headed outside to the two-tiered deck. She moved down the stairs to the large water feature her mom and their landscape architect had decided on before Mom died. The cascading mini falls reminded Heather of their many visits to Pennsylvania Amish country, where they had loved walking the back roads, stopping in at roadside stands, and enjoying the sound of gurgling creeks. *"Cricks,"* one Amish girl had called them, and Mom had looked at Heather with a twinkle in her eye, a smile on her pretty face. The three of them had frequently vacationed there, soaking up the tranquillity offered by rolling, picturesque farmland stretching in all directions.

I need something like that again.

Sipping her juice, Heather strolled through the grass, past the patio gardens and around to the front of the grand old colonial where she'd grown up.

"I miss you, Mom," she whispered.

She walked around to the opposite side of the house, taking her time as she pushed dry leaves out of the empty birdbath, wishing she could talk to her mom about Dr. O'Connor's diagnosis. The last thing she wanted was to be unreasonable. Maybe there was something else she could do . . . perhaps she could look into some naturopathic treatment alternatives in Pennsylvania. There was a woman specialist somewhere in Lancaster whom Mom had wanted to see—Dr. Marshall, she recalled. According to the information Mom had jotted down and stuck on the fridge, her expertise was in stress relief, sleep disorders, cancer, headaches, and emotional well-being. Heather thought the list was still around.

Her mind was in a whirl as she slipped back into the house. Inside, she wandered down the hall to Dad's den. Somewhere in a drawer, waiting to be inserted into a photo album sleeve, there was a handful of brochures she and Mom had picked up and collected the last time they'd done something impulsive. They had planned the last-minute trip together, anxious to get away from the anxiety-ridden worlds of school and job and housework. Maxed out on stress, both of them had craved a serene spot that summer.

It would be like old times, visiting there. Heather recalled that her mom hadn't had a clue about her cancer then, though she'd been experiencing some weight loss and a puzzling lack of appetite. Her mom had been focused on nothing more serious than her obsession with heirloom quilts. While she'd never sewed herself, she loved seeing the quilts up close, even talking with expert quilters. On the final day of their trip, her mother had taken the plunge, purchasing the handmade Amish quilt that now adorned the guest bed downstairs.

"Think. Where *are* those brochures?" she muttered, aware of Moe's padding close behind her. Of the cat duo, Moe was more eager for company, following her from room to room as if he were her assigned shadow. "My constant companion, huh, Moe?"

She pulled out the top drawer of Dad's custom maple built-ins. Beneath a road atlas, she found the pamphlets wrapped with a rubber band. "Jackpot!"

Heather curled up in her dad's recliner next to the bay window. Moe waited until she was settled, then jumped into her lap. "Well, aren't *you* needy," she joked. She flipped through flyers touting the Amish Farm and House on Route 30, J & B Quilts & Crafts, a strolling tour of Strasburg's historic district, and Wheatland, the historic mansion residence of President James Buchanan. She studied the words *Mennonite Information Center—welcome, let us help you feel at home*—and was captivated by the large barn and silo on the front of the brochure.

A page fell out onto her lap. It listed tourist homes in Lancaster County. She slid her finger down the list of people offering lodging in private family homes: Benners, Groffs, Rohrers, Wengers . . . Many families offered places to stay, some suggesting a "hands-on farming experience."

She sighed. "How cool is this? I might actually get to stay with an Amish family. That's something we never got to do. What do you think, Moe?"

The cat meowed twice loudly, and Heather gave him a pat. "Hey, now . . . I wish I could take you and Igor along, but I don't think any of these places accept cats." *Besides, there are probably zillions of Amish barn cats running around.*

The tilt of Moe's head seemed to indicate his displeasure. He was never too keen on sharing her with his brother, let alone anyone else.

Sighing, she decided to leave her father a note about her plan to take a break before working in earnest on her thesis . . . something vague like that. No need to concern him. And anyway, he'd understand; lately he'd talked of getting away for a while himself.

"Terrific." She looked down the long list of accommodations, wondering how many phone numbers she'd have to try—didn't these people have Web sites or email?—before she landed a place to call home. *A place to defy gravity.*

Moe leaped off her lap, a black streak across the floor, and dashed into the hallway and out of sight. Headed for what, she had no idea. Maybe to find Igor, who was undoubtedly asleep on Dad's bed down the hall. Cats were weird like that, but these two were definitely family to her and Dad.

The elegant photo on Dad's desk caught her eye, and she leaned down to gaze at it. *Christmas past.* She'd had no problem returning to live at home, putting off her master's studies. Someone needed to be with Mom those final months and then keep Dad from becoming a total recluse during the first shock wave of grief. The emotional anesthesia they'd initially felt wore off quickly, following the funeral.

Then, a year or so ago, she'd moved into the spacious loft over the garage that connected to the rest of the house. The living arrangement allowed her to come and go as she pleased, which suited her need for seclusion.

I'm like Dad. We need our space. Lately, though, her father had begun to rally some, but just about the time you thought you were home free, waves of grief had an uncanny way of creeping up, building until they overtook like a tsunami. She'd discovered over the long months that one never fully recovered from losing a parent. And although Dad rarely talked about Mom's passing, she assumed it was even worse to lose a spouse.

Turning her attention again to the many addresses, she enjoyed the quirky names of the towns—Ronks, Gap, Strasburg, Kinzers. Each had its own wonderful personality.

"Which one . . . and which host family?" Heather tried to imagine what it would be like to live with strangers, even for a few months.

What about Amish farmers? Maybe

she'd help with the chores and get a re-
duction in boarding costs. She laughed
at the image of herself perched on a
stool beside a cow, bucket in hand.
Yeah, that'll be the day.

She stared at the brochure, tracing
the words with her finger.

*Mom would never let me get away
with this.*

Her dad might not, either. But then, he
wouldn't know. . . .

Her breath caught in her throat. It was
one thing to talk bravely to herself or to
a cat. But what if the diagnosis was correct? What if she *was* dying?

With just the end of this semester left
to complete her M.A. course work,
Heather decided to forge ahead and finish up. Nothing must keep her from that.
Sick or not, she'd worked too hard to
quit now. Meanwhile, she would take
her exams next week, then go north to
Lancaster County for some rest and re-
laxation before fall. If she felt up to it,
she could work on her thesis there.

The list of names and addresses
blurred suddenly. She'd held her emotions in check for this long since this

morning's appointment. Wasn't she entitled to a good cry?

The tears fell fast, dripping onto the
page . . . landing on the names Andy
and Marian Riehl, who lived in a town
called Bird-in-Hand. When at last
Heather pulled herself together enough
to call the number, a woman politely answered what she later referred to as
their "barn phone." And Marian's warm
assurance that they had a place for her
seemed like a sign.

———

Judah hired a Mennonite farmer to
haul the new mare back to the house
later that day, then bummed a ride with
another English fellow heading his way.

During the drive, they traded stories
of past auctions and talked some of a
man near Gordonville who was doing a
brisk business selling solar panels to
Plain folk. "I've heard more and more
these days that people see solar as an
alternative to gas-powered generators,"
the Englischer said.

Judah nodded thoughtfully; he knew
of the man, as well, and imagined the

panels were fodder for discussion among the brethren of Bird-in-Hand.

They passed a sign advertising a new residential development, and the Englischer asked how Judah felt about the encroaching neighborhoods around his farmland.

"Well, none of us likes it," Judah said. "And we're losin' too many of our young folk to upstate New York and other areas round the country—Kentucky, Indiana, Virginia, and even farther south. Not sure where it'll end, all this movin' out to buy more land."

"Will the Amish end up being squeezed out of Lancaster County?"

"I'd hate to see it. But the reality is the outlet malls and the nursing homes are takin' over." He'd been hearing it for years already. If anything, more developers were building town houses and such than ever before.

The driver had a big talk going, but Judah preferred to mull over the failed breakfast conversation with Lettie. *"S'pose we ought to have us a talk,"* she'd said. Despite his wife's behavior over the past month, he now realized there had been something different about her manner today, something more defined in her attempt to share whatever she'd had on her mind.

Yet he'd pulled his hand away when she'd clasped it, seemingly eager at last to open up. *Why now?* he wondered. He recalled finding her shivering downstairs in the front room on the hand-me-down sofa, all bundled up in quilts from her wedding hope chest. Other times, he'd seen her out walking through the corn-field, awake all hours. What was behind her apparent struggle?

He was pulled out of his musing when his driver asked, "Did you happen to no-tice that guy all dressed up in a sports coat and tie, walking around at the auction?"

"Jah—got his card right here. Name's Roan Nelson."

"That's right," the driver told him. "Ev-idently he's looking to buy a small hobby farm somewhere in the area."

Judah nodded. "That he is."

"He must not have heard of the land shortage here . . . that even some Amish farmers are going door-to-door asking if land might soon be available."

"Some folks inquire if the owner has passed away," Judah said.

The driver glanced at him. "That happened to my uncle and aunt. A young Amish farmer came knocking, said he'd heard the husband of the house was awful sick."

Judah shook his head but didn't mention the available plot, lest the Englischer have designs on it. For some reason, he didn't want Roan Nelson to miss out. "The man's a bit overzealous, I daresay. Now, if he wanted to buy a bed-and-breakfast or a house without acreage, there are plenty of those for sale."

"A glut, I'd say."

They discussed the housing situation and how terrible it was for people to have the bottom fall out of what had previously been a thriving market. " 'Specially painful if you were hopin' to turn a profit right quick," Judah said.

"You can say that again. People used to be able to buy a house and flip it nearly right away."

They drove silently for a time, and then the driver spoke up again. "I don't know about you, but this Nelson fellow strikes me as odd."

"How so?" Judah looked at him.

"I just don't see how he's goin' to find what he's looking for round here. The way things are goin', it'll take a miracle."

Judah knew without a doubt the driver was quite right. Then, thinking once more of his wife, he wondered if it might not take another such miracle for Lettie to truly love him again.

chapter

....

six

Thursday morning, Martin pulled into the Bylers' driveway and parked, waiting for Grace. She'd called last evening to say almost apologetically that she wanted to go to Belmont Fabrics in Paradise to purchase dress material—and would it be all right if he picked up her friend Becky, too? She, like her mother, always planned multiple stops to accomplish more errands in a given day.

He found it curious how the Amishwomen expressed themselves and wondered if this tendency to overclarify was their way at home, as well.

"Good morning," he greeted Grace as she met him on the right side of the van.

"Hullo." She touched the top of her white head covering lightly as she got inside. He waited for her to put down her purse and get settled in the seat.

"You won't forget to pick up Becky, will ya?" she asked, turning to smile at him.

"That's our next stop," he said and pulled the door shut.

On the short drive to the Riehls' dairy farm, he noticed Grace was jotting down a list of sorts on a piece of paper. He wondered if it might be a shopping list—he'd known Amishwomen to go to that large fabric store and fill up the entire back of a van with dress material. Since there were only two of them shopping, he supposed that might not be the case today.

When he pulled into the Riehls' lane, he spotted Becky waiting near the sidewalk behind the house. She was wearing a blue dress and apron identical to Grace's. He wondered if they'd planned to match.

"Ach, looks like Becky needs plenty of sewing notions and whatnot," Grace said, probably because of the large, homemade bag flung over her friend's shoulder. "That or her Mamma does, maybe." She let out a little laugh. "Guess we'll be havin' us a big sewing frolic pretty soon."

"Before canning season?" He glanced back at Grace, who nodded before he got out to help open the heavy door.

Once Becky was buckled in, the girls spoke in whispers, mostly in their first language. Becky brought up a relative newcomer from Indiana, and a Yonnie Bontrager's name was soon accompanied by titters and soft laughter.

But the most remarkable comment of the trip was overhearing that this Yonnie was supposedly so smart he could "do crossword puzzles in his head." According to Becky, the young man had no need to ever fill in the blanks. The girl seemed quite taken with his intelligence and playful personality.

Martin smiled and glanced in the rearview mirror as the doting friends talked, their heads occasionally touching as they went from the topic of Yonnie to Grace's upcoming birthday next week.

Oh, to be young again, he thought with a quiet chuckle.

———

On the day before her birthday, Grace hurried downstairs to help with breakfast and found Mamma cooking up some potatoes in a large kettle. A heaping bowl of potato salad was a birthday tradition. No doubt her mother was off-kilter, perhaps thinking the birthday supper was this evening instead of tomorrow.

"Makin' boiled potatoes for the noon meal, perhaps?" she asked, cracking eggs into a bowl to make scrambled eggs.

Her mother looked momentarily confused. Then she let out a disgusted laugh. "Well, puh! I must've jumped ahead a whole day."

Grace frowned. It wasn't like Mamma to be so forgetful.

Shrugging, her mother continued. "Ach, my mind's on other things." For a quick moment, she looked at Grace—really stared—like there was something burning within her, something she needed to say. But when had Mamma taken anyone into her confidence? Other than Aunt Naomi, that is. Word was that her aunt had sat and listened to Mamma pour out her heart weeks before Aunt Naomi had died. Becky's mother, Marian, had bumped into them sitting in front of the springhouse, both Mamma and Aunt Naomi in tears and holding hands.

Grace felt terribly hesitant to pry but felt she had to make an attempt. Gently, she asked, "Mamma, would you mind terribly if I asked . . ."

Mamma shook her head, eyes misty. "What?"

Breathing in her courage, Grace looked up for a moment, staring at the day clock high on the shelf. "I hear ya walking round sometimes in the hallway," she said softly. "And down the stairs, too . . . late at night."

Her mother sighed audibly. "Now, Grace, is this anything to talk with your mother 'bout, really?"

"No, Mamma." It tore at her heart, knowing her parents must be at odds. Why else would Mamma be so out of sorts? And Dat wasn't one to say anything. Why, he hadn't budged an inch to answer Adam's inquiry out in the barn last week, either, and she doubted he'd said a word on that since.

Mamma glanced at the window, as if

concerned someone might interrupt them. "After your birthday, we'll talk, all right?" She paused, making a slight movement toward Grace, like she might embrace her. Then she stepped away. "Isn't that soon enough?"

Grace nodded, more hopeful. "All right, then." She turned her attention to the meal planned for tomorrow. If the gathering turned out to be anything like last year's, it would resemble a party. Becky Riehl had given two quilted potholders for Grace's hope chest, and their English neighbors to the west of them had come to surprise her—childhood playmates Jessica and Brittany Spangler. The girls had brought yellow roses from a nearby florist and put them in a pretty blue vase. *"Cut flowers, indeed!"* Mamma had said, startling Grace. Her mother preferred to leave flowers in the ground, where the Lord intended them, but there was no sense in hurting their neighbors' feelings over that. To help smooth things over, Grace had thanked the girls repeatedly, admiring the pretty blooms and wondering what had come over Mamma to say such a thing.

With Mamma so distressed, who knows what tomorrow might bring? Grace thought now as she turned on the gas and found the frying pan for the scrambled eggs. Then, pouring the egg and milk mixture into the pan, she hurried to set the table.

———

Adah placed a full glass of water on the small table next to Jakob's chair, smiling at him even though he did not look up from reading the Good Book. She reached for her tatting, glad to rest here in their cozy front room after supper. The days were lengthening quickly now, and in two months they'd enjoy the longest day of the year. But late June was not the only thing she looked forward to in this fine season of newness. Tomorrow was Gracie's birthday.

She raised herself up a bit to glance out the window, noting Lettie out on the porch. *Des gut . . .*

"Gracie's friend Becky was over this

afternoon, askin' for her," she said softly, eyes still on the window.

"What'd she want?" Jakob seemed preoccupied with his reading.

"They had themselves a phone call from a young woman in Virginia, Becky said. Lo and behold if she ain't comin' clear up here to stay for the whole summer."

"That's what happens when ya open up your house to strangers," said Jakob, looking up at her briefly before returning to the Bible.

"It does seem as if they have folk in all the time . . . some from even farther away." The Riehls had started doing this sort of thing a few years ago to bring in extra income. " 'Specially during the summer months, they're perty much full."

"But someone's staying all summer long?"

"That's what I heard," said Adah.

"When's this here woman s'posed to arrive?"

"Sometime next week." Adah picked up her tatting hook, intent on finishing the pink edging on the pretty hankie for

Grace. "The young woman's named for a flower, Becky said."

"Iris, maybe?" Jakob tilted his head down and looked at her over the top of his bifocals. "Black-eyed Susan?"

"Oh, for goodness' sake, Jakob . . . it's Heather." She couldn't help but laugh and wondered when he'd be saying she ought to hush now so he could read to her, like he always did in the evening.

"That *is* a nice name." He had his finger in his German Bible now and was eyeing her but good. "Ready to listen awhile, love?"

How well she knew him. Smiling, she nodded as he opened to the page he'd marked with his finger and began to read. Adah continued tatting as fast as she could, enjoying the sound of Jakob's dear voice and the way he shaped the words of the Lord.

———

Grace eagerly turned in her time card and headed for the door to meet fellow Eli's employee Ruthie Weaver, a sweet Mennonite newlywed who'd offered to give her a ride home. She was conscious of the warm evening sun on her back as she hurried toward the waiting car.

Ruthie sat there behind the wheel, her window all the way down. "It was the nicest day so far this spring," she said, smiling. "And to think we spent it mostly indoors."

Grace could hear the redwing blackbirds congregating near the mill creek across the way. The air was so fresh, if not fragrant, and it held the promise of summer.

Ruthie offered Grace some raw nuts from a small plastic container as she got in the front seat. "If you prefer salty snacks, you might not care much for these." Ruthie shifted the car into gear and pulled out of the parking lot.

"They're fine with or without salt. Denki." Grace took three. "My mother, though, loves her salt."

"Oh goodness, and so does my husband." Ruthie giggled, her face aglow. "He's downright dangerous with a salt shaker."

"I wonder if he craves iodine." Grace

had read this sometimes explained people's hankering for salt.

"Wouldn't be surprised." Ruthie
turned on the car radio and a clear so-
prano voice came through the speakers.
"Oh, I've heard this woman before . . .
wish I knew her name. Some folk say
she has a special anointing."

Grace listened intently, soaking in the
soul-stirring melody and the meaningful
lyrics. "I see what you mean. 'Tis won-
derful-*gut*."

Settling back, she enjoyed the lush
landscape as they traveled past newly
plowed fields and the wide millstream.
Willow trees gracefully hovered near its
banks, and cows dotted the pastureland
in all directions. Such a short ride home
by car, but she was glad not to have to
walk today. Though she wouldn't dare
complain, her feet hurt.

"You worked extra late, didn't you?"
Ruthie said, reaching for more nuts.

"So I can take off a little early tomorrow . . . my birthday."

"Well . . . happy almost birthday!"
Ruthie smiled. "And let me guess . . ."

Laughing, Grace waved her hand.

"No, I didn't tell ya for any special attention."

Ruthie looked her way again. "Well,
I'd say you're not a day over nine-
teen . . . if I was to try and guess."

"That's close enough."

"So, will there be a family get-
together?"

"Just a few of us for supper, is all."
Mamma most likely had invited Becky
again, as well as the Spangler sisters
from up the road. *Will Jessica and Brittany bring a plant this year?*

"Hope you have a real nice time."

Grace was relieved to see the house
coming into view. Birthday or not, she
was rather uncomfortable talking about
herself.

"Here we are. Need a ride tomorrow?"

"Only if you'll let me help with gas."
She pulled out several bills from her
wallet.

"Thanks, but really, you're right on my
way home, Grace."

"Won't ya please let me this time?"

"Put your money away." Ruthie
pushed her long auburn hair back over
her shoulder. "See you bright and early."

Grace opened the door, thanked her again, and said, "So long, then."

As she turned, she saw her mother standing on the front porch, near the mailbox mounted to the railing. Grace hoped for a smile or a wave, but Mamma appeared to be immobile, like she was glued to the porch.

"Hullo, Mamma!"

Slowly her mother turned. "Gracie? Aren't you home awful late?"

"I worked overtime to make up for to-morrow . . . remember?" She headed up the steps to the porch and opened the front door. "Come . . . let's go inside."

"No . . . no, you go on ahead."

Grace closed the door and touched her arm. "You all right?"

"I'll just sit here awhile." She smiled weakly and went to sit on the old wooden porch swing. Grace saw her chin quiver. "There are leftovers. . . ."

Grace went to sit beside her. "What's wrong?"

Mamma placed the mail in her lap and shook her head. "There's nothin' you can do. Nothin' at all."

"Well, no—not if you won't talk to

me." She felt the sting of guilt for having spoken so bluntly. She'd never done so before to anyone, let alone to a parent.

"Go now and warm up your supper."

"But, Mamma . . ."

"I'm fine." Her mother added, "I just need some time alone."

Torn between obedience and concern, Grace rose and turned to look down at Mamma, sitting there so pitifully on the swing, completely still. She recalled how they'd swung there together, back and forth, free from all cares, so many summers ago, when Grace was little. Mamma looked as forlorn now as the day her sister had died.

Grace hadn't realized it, but she was holding her breath. Her mother seemed to look right past her, alert to something far beyond the porch. Grace felt compelled to turn and look, as well, but she saw only the first iris spears in the side garden near the springhouse and, farther away, Dat's flock of sheep. The new lambs followed the ewes ever so close.

Turning back to her mother, she noticed tears spilling down her face. "Aw,

Mamma, won't ya say what's makin' you cry so?"

For a second, her mouth opened slightly, and Grace thought her mother might respond. But all she said was "You go on ahead now, Gracie."

"All right, then. I'll leave ya be." Despairing, she opened the screen door and slipped inside.

chapter
seven

Lettie watched her daughter go, her heart breaking. She pressed her bare feet against the wooden slats of the porch, painted white every year by dear Mandy, who had plenty to do since Grace had begun working at Eli's. The swing squeaked its familiar sound, bringing a sense of solitude to her mind, pushing her thoughts back to happier days.

We were happy . . . weren't we?

She'd sat on this swing—in this very spot—to rock tiny Gracie when she was brand-new. Oh, that first summer following her birth was a jumble of smiles and tears . . . and precious moments holding her daughter near, letting tiny Grace nurse at will. So happy she was to have another cuddly babe in arms. Adam, already a towheaded toddler of eighteen months, often crawled up and planted himself next to them, his sweaty little head against her arm, his skin nearly sticking to it at times, so close he was. The three of them swinging on the porch, waiting for a breeze.

Sometimes the neighbors would come bearing sweet, ripe watermelon. Thoughtful Marian Riehl had heard that Lettie was suffering from the baby blues, no doubt. Marian and her husband, Andy, would cut generous slices of the cold fruit and perch themselves on the porch steps or the railing and eat clear down to the rind. Sometimes Judah and Andy would joke to see who could spit the seeds the farthest.

She smiled, remembering the fun they'd shared together, surrounded by laughter and stories. Marian's little Becky hadn't even been born then.

Becky, she thought now. *Not Rebekah, as anyone would have supposed.* Marian had come calling to ask her opinion on the name when the wee babe was just three days old. It seemed Marian and her husband were at odds on a name, and Marian wanted Lettie's say-so, too, which at the time had seemed downright comical to her. Less comical, though, was Andy Riehl, who all too often looked for opportunities to dig in his heels, much to Marian's dismay. Lettie found little to like about the man. *Theirs is a thorny marriage,* she thought.

Shrugging the memory aside, she heard Grace's voice, mingled with those of her parents. And with a push of her big toe against the porch, she made the swing move faster and wished the crickets were out in full force this evening. Their refrain was sure to drown out any inside talk among Mamm, Dat, and Grace. Soon, very soon, the insects' chorus would return . . . come summer.

Lettie breathed in the cool evening air. How she needed solitude, craving it even more with Grace's coming milestone birthday.

Where have all the years flown?

Oh, but she knew. They'd vanished into the seasons, year after year . . . going the way of all good and lovely things.

Like love . . .

She could not even remember the last time she and Judah had given affection—not even a peck on the cheek. It wasn't that they'd meant to come to this place in their marriage; she guessed they'd simply fallen out of each other's hearts.

She covered her face with her hands, knowing what would happen if she was bold enough—and insensitive, too—if she were to reveal her heart to Grace. But no, her daughter couldn't begin to understand. And Judah? Doubtless her husband would simply view her revelation as yet another reason to retreat deeper into his own skin.

Judah's own world . . .

So, even though she'd given it great consideration since the barn raising last month, there was no question in her mind that she would be on precarious footing with everyone if her well-guarded secret was unveiled.

No, she must not take a risk like that.

Her husband, Jakob, wasn't but ten minutes into the reading when there stood Gracie in the doorway to the hall, coming slowly toward them.

"Just a minute, Jakob." Adah leaned forward in her chair, slipping her tatting behind her. "Gracie? You hungry, dear?"

"Mamma says there are leftovers. . . ."

Pity's sakes, the girl looked like she might cry.

"Aw, why don't you just have some of ours?" Adah reached for the nearby pillow and stuffed it behind her to better conceal the birthday hankie. She rose and motioned for Grace to follow her to the kitchen. "Your *Dawdi* was just reading Scripture, but maybe he'll come join us, so you can hear, too." She said this louder than usual, hoping Jakob might take the hint.

When he did, Grace brightened and pulled out a chair. She sat down and leaned into her hands as Jakob came along and placed his big leather Bible on the table. "Haven't seen much of yous lately," Grace said, looking up at him.

"You're such a busy girl . . . all that workin' over at Eli's." Jakob sat down, giving her a sidewise smile. "What'd you bring me this time?"

"Oh, go on with ya," Adah said. "She doesn't have to bring free samples every day."

Grace was now smiling to beat the band, which pleased Adah. "I doubt you'd have wanted what they were samplin' today, Dawdi."

He looked at her, mischievous as all get out. "I guess I'll bite. . . . What was it?"

"Spicy beef jerky, the hottest you've ever tasted."

Jakob's head pushed back with laughter. "Well, you just never know till ya try something, ain't?"

Grace shook her head. "I spared you, Dawdi. I can guarantee you'd be havin' yourself a terrible sour stomach 'bout now."

"Then I guess I oughta be thankin' you, jah?" He reached for Grace's hand and squeezed it quickly, then let go, still beaming.

Adah reheated the tuna macaroni casserole and warmed up the remaining buttered peas in a smaller saucepan.

From where she stood at the gas range, she could no longer see Lettie outside on the swing, but she would have heard her if she'd already come inside.

Stirring the macaroni, Adah wondered what it would take to get things back on an even keel. Looking fondly at her granddaughter and husband sitting so comfortably, surrounded by the golden circle of light from the gas lamp over-head, she felt a little lump rise in her throat. Jakob's hair was peppered with gray, and these days he had to stand gingerly for a few seconds before proceeding to walk, his legs a bit wobbly after getting out of his chair. And their dear Grace, so full of youthful energy, surely ought to be getting married before too long.

She'll follow in her brother's footsteps, no doubt.

This minute, the warmth of family spread its wings over her . . . over the three of them. And Adah did not want a single thing to spoil its sweetness.

"You're comin' for supper tomorrow, jah?" asked Grace, breaking the stillness.

"Couldn't keep me away," Jakob said, looking at Adah.

"I'll bake your favorite dessert, Gracie," said Adah. "Carrot cake with butter frosting."

"Mamma doesn't like to make much to-do 'bout birthdays, ya know," Grace said unexpectedly.

"Well, if you could mark the day however you'd choose, what would ya do?" asked Adah.

Grace stared down at the table. "Well, let's see. You'd all sing the birthday song, for sure." She raised her head slowly. "I do like hearin' Mamma's perty voice rise up above all the others. Oh, ever so much."

That joyful side of Lettie's rarely seen anymore, thought Adah.

"And, without thinkin' too hard, I'd prob'ly like to spend a good part of the day with Becky." Grace squinted her eyes, as if expecting a retort. "And with Adam."

"In other words, with your closest friends," Adah said.

"Jah." Grace smiled warmly at them

both. "But don't misunderstand, I'd take yous along, too, if I could."

"Take us where?" Jakob leaned forward again.

"To the ocean. Someday I want to see it for myself . . . not just in books." Grace glanced toward the window. "There must be something mighty special 'bout the roar of it, ya know?"

"And the extent of it," Adah added.

"To think you can see nearly forever . . . well, out to the edge of the world, so to speak." Grace was lost in a daydream, something Adah had never noticed before. *Thank goodness she's not the dreamer her mother always was!*

Jakob waved his hand. "Well, maybe that driver could take you to see that there horizon line you're talking 'bout. What's his name?"

"Martin Puckett?" said Grace. "A right cheerful fella, I'll say."

"Jah, that's who. Maybe Martin'll drive you, Becky, and Adam out to the ocean one of these days."

That brought the biggest smile to Grace's face, but it didn't last long, because just then Adah heard the front screen door smack shut. Grace's face paled, and her gaze found Adah's and held it awkwardly for a long time.

chapter

eight

Grace's birthday began like any other day except for one thing: She was awakened by Mandy, who slipped into the room and planted a kiss on her cheek. "Happy day . . . happy year, sister!" Mandy announced, all smiles.

Squinting up at her, Grace stretched and yawned. "Ach, you're up even before me."

Mandy sat on the edge of the bed, her long, reddish-blond hair flowing over her round shoulders, clear to her chubby waist. "I wanted to be the first to wish you a happy birthday, Gracie." She tried to suppress a yawn but did not succeed. Laughing softly, she said, "We have something special planned."

"Honestly?"

Mandy bobbed her head up and down, eyes shining. Then, pretending to seal her lips, she whispered, "That's all I'll say."

Grace loved her playful sister, who always seemed to have something interesting or mysterious up her sleeve. "Well, the day will go by quickly, I'm sure." She sat up and looked at the wind-up alarm clock on the small table next to her bed. "I best be getting ready for work."

Mandy stood up, still clad in her long white cotton nightgown. "And must you work tomorrow, too?"

"*Nee*—no, not that I know of."

"Well, *gut,* then . . . we'll have us some sister time, jah?" Mandy's sleepy eyes sparkled.

"What were ya thinkin'?"

Mandy walked to the doorway and turned, her face beaming. "How 'bout if we take Willow out to the meadow and ride her bareback? That'd be such fun!"

Their horses were meant for pulling carriages and market wagons, not riding, as Mandy well knew. Some bishops were rather opposed to the latter. "What would Dat say to that?" asked Grace.

Mandy wore a mischievous grin.

"Well . . . if you must know, I already said something to Mamma."

"Jah? And?"

"She doesn't think it's anything to worry 'bout, as long as we aren't out on the road . . . ya know, showin' off."

"All right, then . . . if Mamma says not to flaunt, we won't."

Mandy fluttered her fingers in a little wave and left the room.

Grace jumped out of bed and closed the door. She picked up her brush and began counting the strokes as she brushed her hair. *What will come of this day?*

She knew one thing: She didn't feel a speck older than yesterday, even though the calendar said otherwise. She pulled on her robe and raised the green shade all the way, then sat near the window to read from the Psalms. When she was finished, she prayed a blessing on the day and for all those she might encounter, gathered up her clean clothes, and headed downstairs for a warm bath before the rest of the family awakened. Her father had spent a lot of time and money putting two modern bathrooms in the house. One on their side and one over where Dawdi and Mammi lived. She sometimes wished for a washroom upstairs, as well . . . just down the hall a few steps from Mandy's and her bedrooms. But Dat had said they must make do with what they had. As it was, Mammi Adah was mighty happy about having a fancy indoor bathroom. She enjoyed the convenience of a nice big tub and modern facilities, especially during winter months.

Grace reached for the shampoo and lathered up, taking special care with her hair, eager for it to be shiny and clean.

What will Henry do for my birthday?

She hurried along, stopping herself each time she felt the urge to hum, holding back. Truth was, she wondered if Henry's shyness, even awkwardness, might hinder him from wanting to celebrate.

Today she wished to get a head start on breakfast, even though Mamma might surely have something planned already. Still, Grace wanted to get the day off on the right foot to make certain things were just as they should be.

Several other years, on landmark birthdays such as sixteen—the start of courting age—her mother had surprised them with homemade waffles and specialty soufflés or, Grace's very favorite, cinnamon rolls and a spritz of chocolate syrup in her coffee.

Such happy memories of gathering round the table for a delicious birthday breakfast. She allowed herself to hum. *A few more minutes won't hurt,* she decided.

She thought again of Henry, who was the most handsome of all the fellows she'd known. So much so, she sometimes pinched herself. *Why did he pick me?*

She had been told by several young men that she was pretty. "*Mighty pleasing, in fact,*" Yonnie had once said right to her face during one of the three short evenings he had gone walking with Grace last year, before Henry had asked her out riding. Such compliments were foreign to the Plain way . . . leaving room for vanity to grow.

She had to smile as she recalled Yonnie's peculiar ways. Even then, he'd never bothered to take a horse or court-ing buggy to Singings or other youth gatherings; they'd walked everywhere. Never had she gotten more exercise in her life. Grace had sometimes thought that if the Lancaster bishops ever got wind of it, they might want to encourage this rather irregular way of courting— perhaps it might keep young folk more attentive to the youth in their own church district.

Plenty of stories floated around about young men who were sweet on several girls, so she supposed Yonnie wasn't unusual in taking his time to choose. And from what Mammi Adah had once hinted about Mamma's own courting days, Grace wondered if Yonnie and her own mother had something in common.

Dear Mamma . . .

Grace stepped out of the tub and dressed, then wrapped her hair in a towel. She opened the door, nearly bumping into Adam, who stood right outside. "Ach, you scared me . . . for goodness' sake!"

He grinned, his sleepy eyes meeting hers.

"Time to rise and shine." She moved away.

"I've risen . . . just not shinin' yet. 'Twas a rough night in the sheep barn." He wandered in and shut the door, and she heard the water running for his shave. Then, nearly as quickly, the door opened and he poked his head out. "Someone's a year older, and it sure ain't me!" With a sleepy-sounding chuckle, he again closed the door.

Grace felt warmed by her brother's humor as she rushed through the kitchen and sitting room toward the center hallway, making her way to the stairs. She flew to her room, needing to towel dry her hair before winding it into a bun. Letting it down long past her waist, she was glad it wasn't as thick and hard to untangle as Becky's or even Mandy's, who had the prettiest color she'd ever seen—like sun-kissed strawberries and harvested wheat all mixed together. Her sister certainly stood out in a crowd. Years ago, when Mandy was only fourteen, Mamma had complained about the number of times Mandy had sneaked away to Singings, hoping to pass herself off as older. *"All in harmless jest,"* Mandy had assured them when she'd been caught. Still, both Mamma and Dat had given her a good talking-to.

Even though Mandy presently had several nice fellows interested in her, Grace wasn't entirely sure whether her sister cared for any of them, or vice versa. She only knew what she'd observed at Singings, where the boys sought Mandy out. Her sister's popularity was no secret, but despite her cheerful birthday greeting, Mandy's pensive brown eyes revealed an uneasiness. One Grace had observed often lately.

She dealt with an uneasiness of her own. Life just felt so unpredictable. *Between Dat and Mamma, especially.* As much as she wished they'd be more content with each other, she'd seen similar signs of aloofness in Becky's parents. She'd begun to worry that many married couples were equally distant.

I'd like something far better . . . if I ever marry.

when she heard Mamma cooking downstairs, Grace hurried back down, aware of the tantalizing smell of chocolate as she came to the landing. *Can it be?* She went through the sitting room, to the kitchen.

Seeing her, Mamma quickly attempted to hide the package of unsweetened chocolate.

"*Gut* mornin'," said Grace, trying not to smile too big.

"You weren't s'posed to sneak up on me," Mamma said, a sparkle in her eye. Gone was the sadness of the days before.

"I sure like your chocolate waffles."

Mamma gave a nod, her eyes still on Grace. "I made some peach delight for you to take with you to work, for your lunch today."

Grace was relieved that her mother was sounding—and acting—more like her old self.

"That'll be ever so tasty. Denki, Mamma."

So, Mandy was right—surprises a-plenty!

———

It was midmorning when Grace glanced up from the cans she was shelving and spied the top of a man's head. Rising to her tiptoes, she was startled to see Henry Stahl entering the store, his light brown hair combed ever so neatly.

She looked down at her hands and wondered what to do with the tins of tea. And why on earth was she shaking so?

Quickly placing the cans on the shelf out of order to be free of them, she moved down to the end of the aisle, near a display of the *B* family of vitamins. Her heart sped up as she watched him move through the store.

Of all things, he's come to see me here!

"Oh, Grace ... there you are." He glanced about, his eyes darting nervously. Standing there, she couldn't help wondering why he'd worn his for-good black trousers and vest for this unexpected visit. All that was missing from his regular Sunday Preaching attire was his thin black bow tie.

"What a nice surprise," she said softly.

He inhaled and straightened to his full

height, squaring his shoulders—a tall man at six feet two. "I'm here to say happy birthday." He leaned closer and, lowering his voice, said, "Somethin's waiting for you . . . in the buggy." He moved his head slightly toward the door. "All right?"

Oh, this was beyond her expectations!

She glanced toward the counter and saw the manager give her a quick nod. "If it's just for a minute."

Henry's grin made her blush even more.

Outside, he led her around to the other side of the buggy, where they could escape the prying eyes of the other clerks. She was mighty sure if she glanced at the store window, Ruthie and the others would be watching. "I've got a present for ya." He raised the lap blanket and there, beneath it, was an unwrapped box with the words *chime clock* printed on it.

"Goodness, Henry!" She couldn't believe her eyes. A young man didn't give his girl a gift like this unless he was on the verge of proposing marriage.

Grace's heart flew into her throat, and ✝ for a moment she had trouble gathering her thoughts.

"I'd be happy to open it for you." He reached for the box, turning it around to show her the picture of a beautiful golden clock with moving chimes encased in glass.

"No . . . let's keep it all wrapped up and safe." She shook her head as she looked at the picture of the lovely clock and then up at him. "It's ever so perty. I can't begin to say—"

He reached for her hand, the first time ever. Oh goodness, the feel of his warm, callused fingers made her smile right back at him.

She was suddenly too aware of the daylight. Had they ever been so close on their nighttime rides? She was quite sure they hadn't. But she liked the way their fingers entwined and being able to look into his gentle brown eyes. Well, up . . . up into them, as he was at least a half foot taller.

"Denki . . . I really like the clock, Henry," she said, still feeling awkward

about anyone's witnessing their affection.

His eyes lingered on her. "You have a
place for it?"

She paused, wondering what would
be most appropriate to say. "Well, more
than likely, it'll go in my room."

Till later . . .

He fell silent, looking down at her,
more serious again.

"I'll hope to see it, then . . . one day."
His face lit up.

She thrilled to his words. So he *was*
going to shine his flashlight on her window and come calling. If he did, they
would not remain alone in her room for
more than a few minutes, as Mamma
had always urged her and Mandy to entertain serious beaus in the kitchen,
near the heat of the corner stove. Other
families allowed courting couples to
spend hours talking in the girl's room.
Yet even as some church districts encouraged such activity, others frowned
on it. Such distinctions in the Ordnung
from church to church could be ever so
confusing. Grace was glad she'd grown
up in this particular district, where cau-

tion in courting was urged and where folk spoke openly about the Lord, even offering prayers aloud at times.

She suspected she knew the reason why there was an emphasis on pure motives and holy living in their house church, which met every other Sunday. But she wouldn't give those rumors about other youth another thought. Not on this, her special day.

"Henry . . . I'm more than pleased. Truly, I am." She scarcely knew what to say to open his heart wider, if that was even possible.

He nodded and smiled warmly.

Glancing toward the store, she explained that her clock was ticking. Then she suppressed a laugh—that had not come out at all the way she'd meant it! "Ach, I hope you understand what I'm tryin' to say."

Again, he nodded. His eyes were merry, but he said nothing. Oh, how she would love to hear him laugh heartily.

Awkwardly, Henry climbed into his black open buggy and picked up the reins. "Have a nice day, Grace."

She blushed as she waved good-bye

and returned to the store. The other girls attempted to keep from grinning but failed miserably. Ruthie was the worst of them, too cheerful and trying hard to bite back a smile. Surely every one of them knew that it was her soon-to-be-intended—her handsome Henry—who'd just visited.

chapter

nine

Grace counted the hours till she could head home, still delighted by Henry's visit and his generous gift. She couldn't possibly know when he might drop the chime clock off at the house. Since he wasn't one to make a spectacle, she doubted it would be in the daylight.

To contain her excitement, she kept busy with her store inventory list, documenting each item among all the varieties of food supplements and arranging them in alphabetical order. She smiled when she came to zinc, an essential mineral for building a strong immune system. It also helped reduce acne, according to Ruthie, who'd struggled with pimples—*"too much chocolate,"* she'd admitted, though after taking zinc for three months, her complexion now looked as clear as Grace's.

Mamma often said, "You are what you eat." Grace considered the kinds of fried foods and soda pop the Spangler girls preferred, yet *they* had perfect complexions. Did that alone refute Mamma's words?

Grace was not overly strict about her diet, as some were who now advocated eating only vegetables, grains, and legumes. *"Rabbit chow,"* Adam had jokingly said when she told him about some of the health fads making the rounds.

Thinking of vegetables, Grace missed helping with the gardens as much as she always had. The smell of freshly plowed soil was invigorating . . . that and deciding where to plant the various vegetables. She loved spending early morning hours weeding and harvesting a good variety of produce to eat, sell, and put up for the winter. Since starting to work at Eli's, she'd largely had to assign the weeding and tending of her herb garden to Mandy, though sometimes Becky came over to help on Grace's days off.

All the hot, humid hours of hoeing and

watering rows of lettuce, snap beans, radishes, tomatoes, and squash were also times of laughter. But Mamma wasn't usually the one smiling—not lately. Oh, Grace could see that she attempted to enjoy herself and enter into the fun, but when all was said and done, Mamma seemed to hold back.

Presently, Grace moved on to the next shelf and began to alphabetize the many kinds of herbs, beginning with alfalfa, aloe, angelica, and anise. She refused to think about dismaying things, especially on such a fine day. Fretting over bygones had never proven to be helpful. Besides, Mammi Adah said dwelling on the past could become obsessive, even destructive.

Today, however, Grace had awakened to birdsong and brilliant blue skies—such a bright way to begin the day. The birds had come right up to the feeders she and Mandy had placed in strategic spots around the back and side yards. Avid bird watchers, the whole family enjoyed the robins, finches, blue jays, and chickadees that found sanctuary close to their house, though it was Mamma who loved observing them most of all, especially from the back stoop. Her favorite was the gray-brown mourning dove, which produced multiple offspring each season. Mamma had taught her children to listen for the fluttering whistle its wings made when taking flight. *"But only the male makes the mournful-sounding call,"* her mother had said.

Recently there had been a good amount of rain, and robins could be seen searching for worms, making their songs even more plentiful. Or so Grace liked to think. Considering how the rain had greened the grazing land for Dat's sheep, she was doubly thankful for the ample moisture.

Grace had never questioned why her father was one of only a handful of Amish in the area who wasn't a dairy farmer. An exceptionally private man, her father's dawn-to-dusk approach to raising sheep earned him admiration from other farmers. Grace liked to observe his interaction with other men, because she gleaned more insight into her own father's thoughts than when he engaged in most family conversations. His tongue just seemed to loosen up as Grace listened in sheer amazement.

Now she'd come to the *G* herbs, including ginseng—one of Mammi Adah's favorites. She continued lining up the bottles in perfect order, hoping all would go well this evening. Secretly she once more pondered Henry's visit. *Of all things, coming here!*

When it was time to leave for home, Grace spotted her younger brother, Joe, waiting in Dat's buggy in the parking lot. Joe waved to her, a piece of straw dangling from his mouth as he sat on the right side of the family carriage. He often came to pick her up, relishing the freedom of driving, as if impatient for his own courting buggy once he turned sixteen next year.

The afternoon had been rather mild, with only the slightest hint of a breeze. She glimpsed through the stately trees a buildup of dark clouds in the west. Tossing her purse on the seat, she hopped into the carriage and noticed her favorite horse hitched to it. "Nice ya brought Willow," she said, smiling.

"Well, it was either her or Sassy, 'cause Dat's gone to the blacksmith with the new mare. And Adam put his foot down on usin' *his* horse."

"Why's that?"

"Said he needed to run a last-minute errand." Joe put on a straight face and looked back at the road.

"Wouldn't have anythin' to do with tonight, would it?"

Joe didn't flinch. "Why, what's goin' on?"

"Oh, you . . . don't ya know?"

Still keeping his face forward, he said, "You speaketh in riddles, Gracie."

Stifling a laugh, she turned to look at the landscape. She was ever so sure Joe and Mandy and Adam, too, were all in cahoots.

A sudden rumble of thunder caught her attention, and she leaned forward to survey the ominous sky. "Looks like a storm's comin'."

"A nice soaker would be right *gut,* 'specially since we just planted corn."

Joe craned his neck to survey the wall of clouds.

Hope the rain's gone before supper. Grace envisioned the extra people who would gather at the table tonight. She looked forward to seeing Becky and the Spangler sisters again.

Joe clucked his tongue. "Seems Willow's out of sorts today."

"Just today?" She grimaced. "She's always slow, ain't so?"

"Well, she's got ev'ry right to be, old as she is."

She smiled and watched Willow's head rise and fall with each trot, her long, thick mane waving in the breeze. "She's been the best driving horse ever." Grace remembered Dat first bringing her home with an enormous smile on his ruddy face. They were having a picnic on Ascension Day, and here came Dat leading the beautiful young mare, showing her off. *"Lookee at what I've got,"* he'd said. *"This one's as gentle as they come."* Within days, the chestnut-colored horse had endeared herself to the entire family.

"Why'd you name her Willow back

when?" Joe tossed the piece of straw onto the road.

"Because she was always graceful, whether she was trotting or eating feed. Like willow branches movin' in the wind."

He pulled on the reins to make the sharp right onto Church Road. "Jah, I guess I can see that."

"Willow just seemed like the perfect name—"

"For a perfect horse," Joe finished. They laughed at each other because this happened among the four siblings too often to ignore. They were all so closely linked as sisters and brothers and friends.

She'd often wondered about Becky's relationship with her brothers and sisters. Did most Plain families have such a close bond?

When Joe guided the horse and buggy into the driveway, everything looked to be ready for company. The lawn had been carefully mowed and manicured, and the pasture fence freshly painted white, thanks to Mandy and Joe.

Out front, Mamma glanced up from the porch, waving at them. Seeing everything looking so spiffy—and Mamma waiting for them—was heartening to Grace.

"Mamma waits for the mail nearly ev'ry day," Joe said softly as they headed up toward the horse stable.

"How do you know?"

"Well, I ain't blind, am I?" He leaped out of the buggy and began unhitching Willow. Working around the horse, Joe said with a grunt, just like Dat might have, "Happy birthday, by the way."

Grace laughed out loud. What an unpredictable brother!

Lettie eyed the front porch swing, wishing she had time to sit awhile. *Before the house is all filled up.* Sighing, she moved toward the swing, thinking if she could just rest a bit, she might feel better. *I'm so weary.*

More than anything, she wanted to reread the latest letter from her Indiana cousin Hallie Troyer, who had scarcely a care in the world. Or so it seemed from her frequent correspondence. Lettie stared at the return address: *Nappanee, Indiana.*

She was thankful Adam had run to pick up a birthday card for all of them to pass around and sign. She'd also asked him to purchase some nice writing paper and two pretty pens for Grace's gift.

Dear girl.

There was some indication from across the wide hall that Mamm had made a small present for the birthday girl. *Why must my mother spoil her so?* Lettie wondered, thinking Grace was much too old to be given many gifts. But old-school though Mamm was bred to be, she was also one to push the line, inching toward it until it almost felt sometimes like they behaved like fancy folk.

"I mustn't let her get the upper hand ever again," Lettie muttered, pushing Cousin Hallie's letter deep into her pocket. She wished she might simply sit and write Hallie another note right back. But first things first.

She rose. Joe had arrived with Grace from work, and they were probably wondering why the table wasn't even

set. No doubt, Grace was already tin-
kering around in the kitchen herself, if
she wasn't upstairs brushing her hair
and pinning it up fresh. It wasn't that
Grace was known for vanity or putting
on airs—far from it. She was one of the
sweetest girls around, living up to the
promise of her name early on.

Looking longingly at the porch swing
again, Lettie knew she must make a
quick phone call. Did she have time to
hurry up the road to the community
phone shanty? Hopefully the gloomy
skies would hold off their rain for a few
minutes yet.

Ach, I should've called sooner, she
thought, knowing full well why she'd put
it off this long.

She breathed a prayer for strength . . .
both for the birthday feast and for whatever lay ahead.

For all of us.

chapter

ten

Judah removed his straw hat in the hallway and plopped it down on his own wooden peg—one he'd used for twenty-some years. He smelled the pot roast cooking and a thought crossed his mind: How had Lettie ever managed before the bishop gave the nod for them to get a gas range and oven? It was hard to remember the days before that time, although he was mighty sure his wife remembered quite well. Adam, too, since he'd had the daily chore of hauling in the wood for the cookstove.

He walked around to the kitchen, glad to see Mandy helping. *Where's Lettie?* he wondered, not bothering to ask Mandy or Adam, who just that minute had come indoors. Adam's unruly bangs were all combed down for a change. Seeing the washroom door standing open, Judah made his way inside and closed the door.

Removing his glasses, he filled the sink with warm water, grateful for the hot water directly from the spigot. Long gone the days of carrying water from the springhouse and waiting around for his parents to heat it up for baths and whatnot.

He splashed water on his face and lathered up with the homemade soap Lettie purchased from Preacher Josiah Smucker's wife, Sally. The industrious woman had herself a small shop right in their house, out near the utility room. Being that she was married to one of the brethren, she'd gotten permission from the bishop himself to run the business. The man of God understood their plight.

The plight of many Amish . . . With farming land dwindling and being divided up among marrying-age sons, no wonder folk kept moving out of Lancaster County to other counties and states—some even out of the country to Canada. A good many, in fact, over the years.

He suspected several families in the

church of scouting out places like Kentucky and Virginia to obtain farmland, places where Amish had already established small communities. Some had talked privately about starting a new church district down as far south as Georgia, and not only in Macon County. These days, it seemed there were Amish and Beachy Amish branching out nearly everywhere.

But for Judah's needs, Lancaster County was just fine. Really there was nowhere he'd rather be. Besides, with word from old Rudy Stahl that Adam was going to be given a good portion of Rudy's land, Judah had only to be concerned with young Joe's future land options.

Won't be long and I'll be turning my pockets inside out for yet another courting-age son, he mused. Truly he didn't mind seeing his offspring grow up and look ahead to starting their own families. And, just maybe, once he and Lettie had themselves an empty nest, they'd somehow manage to get things back on an even keel.

He dried his face and put his glasses

back on, glancing in the square mirror above the sink. "Goodness, but you're gettin' old," he muttered.

"Someone talkin' in there?" Adam called through the door.

"Can't a man have some peace?"

Adam chuckled. "Take your time, Dat. I just wondered . . . when's supper?"

Judah checked his watch. "Should be now." He opened the door. "Better ask your Mamma, though."

Adam shook his head. "Joe said he saw her out front on the porch a little bit ago, but she's not there now."

It wasn't like Lettie to invite guests and then dillydally about getting the table set and all done up. "Could be she's helpin' bring Dawdi Jacob over for supper," he suggested as they stepped into the kitchen.

Adam nodded thoughtfully, then showed him a birthday card. "Want to sign this now, before Gracie sees it?" Glancing over his shoulder, Adam indicated he should hurry.

Judah noticed the pen stuck atop Adam's ear and reached for it. *Happy birthday, Grace, from Dat,* he signed simply.

Adam retrieved the card and pen when Judah was done. He dashed out of the kitchen, leaving Judah there with Mandy, who was bustling about, checking on the roast and baked potatoes, carrots, and onions. Such tantalizing aromas—but where *was* Lettie?

Going to the side door, he looked out and saw, in the near distance, the English neighbor girls walking this way, each carrying a present, an umbrella at the ready. Becky Riehl was coming up the driveway, too. Had Lettie invited others besides these three?

He turned away from the door, wishing his wife were there to greet the young women. Feeling awkward, he was glad to see Adam returning and Jakob hobbling over from the other side of the house, through the sitting room. "Hullo there, Daed," he greeted him.

Adah and Lettie were right behind them, as was Joe, who sniffed the air, clearly ready to dig in to the delectable meal. "Looks like nearly all of us are here," Adam said, trying unsuccessfully to slip Grace's birthday card under her plate before she noticed. Mandy's eyes were wide with disapproval, but Grace flashed him a smile.

"Oh look! There's Becky . . . and the Spangler girls, too!" Grace rushed to the door and ran down the steps to greet them.

Judah looked at Lettie, who caught his eye and gave him a small smile, as if to say, *It's our daughter's birthday . . . let's be merry.*

He returned the smile, aware of a curious new light in her eyes.

Soon their guests were welcomed by Lettie herself, who stepped into her comfortable role as hostess. She and Mandy carried the food to the table in Grace's honor. They'd changed the normal seating arrangement considerably for the evening, putting Becky on one side of Grace, and Brittany Spangler— the darker haired of the two sisters—on the other side. Lettie, as always, sat to Judah's right.

"Time for the blessing." He bowed his head and remained so for longer than usual, adding a special silent prayer for good health for Grace—and for a hard-working husband for her someday, too. Then he made a little cough and raised his head as he always did to signal the end of the prayer.

Lettie reached immediately for the large platter and sliced an ample portion of roast for him first. Then she asked Grace to hold her plate and served another smaller portion to her. The two English girls glanced at each other, and Becky engaged them in casual conversation as Lettie saw to everyone's plate, making sure each one had plenty.

Seeing her so caught up in her hostess role, Judah couldn't help wondering how long it might be before she grew weary of wandering about at night. How long before Lettie behaved like a good wife?

He picked up his fork and cut the roast with it, so tender it was. Focusing now on the delicious meal at hand, he dismissed his scattered thoughts, falling into the pleasure of this fine feast.

The talk around the table quickly caught Grace's attention. Becky hadn't waited long to begin describing several new quilts she'd put in the frame with her mother. Neither of them cared much for finishing off quilts, sometimes letting several sit around before finally stopping everything to sew the binding at last—"all at once, to get it over with."

"Oh goodness, I don't mind doin' bindings," Mandy spoke up.

"Well, piece work's more fun," Grace said, glad for Becky's presence.

"Hard work, though," Becky replied. "But I like choosin' the colors."

"Me too." Mandy leaned over the table. It was obvious from her attempts to be part of the conversation that she wished she'd been seated closer to them.

After a short lull, Jessica Spangler announced her plans to marry her college sweetheart during Christmas break. "A festive time for a wedding, don't you think?" At that, all the women at the table, including Mamma and Mandy, nodded in agreement. Adam, Joe, and Dat continued eating as if merely onlookers, present only in body.

Then Mammi Adah surprised Grace

by talking of Grace's childhood and "her many firsts," as her grandmother liked to refer to her little-girl antics. Grace cringed a bit, hoping Mammi would not take this too far. "The first time Gracie ever went off to school, her Mamma and I stood like two protective doe on the porch, creepin' down the steps, then eventually out to the lane . . . watching our Gracie walk up the road with her big brother. She looked awful tiny to be a first grader."

"Too tiny, really," Mamma added.

"Kids *all* look that small when they first start out," Joe piped up.

"Did ya take a lunch bucket to school?" asked Becky, her brown eyes curious.

Brittany laughed. "Sure she did— Grace used my old one that whole year." She covered her mouth, trying to subdue her giggle. "Remember it, Grace?"

"How can I forget?"

"It was one of those funky California Raisins lunch boxes, and Grace couldn't part with it when she came to play at our house." Brittany leaned forward next to her sister, who was also nodding. "So I let her keep it."

Jessica continued. "It pictured a raisin singing into a microphone, and three girl raisins singing backup. It was too cute."

Half the table was snickering, and Grace couldn't help laughing herself. When she looked toward the hushed end of the table, she noticed a small smile on Mamma's face, but there was no hint of the same on Dat's. His attention appeared set on the spread of food before him—all that mattered.

As for Grace, she had two birthday wishes: She wished that the evening might last long past the supper hour. And she wished that Mamma might remain as happy as she seemingly was this very moment.

———

The sky hung low in the trees bordering the side yard and the pastureland where Judah's sheep grazed all day. Now that the rain had passed, a dark blue band lined the horizon to the east.

Lettie forced her gaze away from the

window as she helped Mandy clear the table. Grace's friends had left for home, and Lettie wanted to give her birthday girl some time to do as she pleased.

Mamm and Dat had surprised Lettie by staying around longer than usual following such a big gathering. Lettie felt both appreciative and perturbed. Glad, because her mother had an uncanny way of drawing any attention away from Lettie, and fairly annoyed because more than a full hour ago she'd hoped to write another letter.

She assumed Grace's supper had been everything her daughter had hoped for. Grace had been so cordial, accepting the tatted hankie from her grandmother with a pleasing smile, and later, offering plenty of *oohs* and *ahs* when the Spangler sisters each presented a gift—a floral-covered book of blank pages and a long, thin case of colored pencils. The latter was something Lettie could not imagine Grace using, or even wanting.

Becky had held to tradition, giving Grace a simple homemade card, just as Judah and the boys and Mandy had—

except their card had been store-bought. Regrettably Lettie had failed to sign it, thanks to her ill-timed phone call. She hoped Grace hadn't noticed . . . but then, Grace noticed nearly everything. That was precisely why Lettie felt so anxious now as she inspected the kitchen and went to the next room to pull out a writing tablet, one of three she stored in the corner hutch drawer. She'd always kept stationery there, as well as a few nicer pens.

The pretty yellow lined paper would help to keep her hand straight. Truth be told, she had much to make up for with dear Grace. *With all of them, really.*

Grace and Mandy were curled up on the floor in the front room, playing checkers. Judah and the boys had naturally been in a big hurry to return to the barn, what with more lambs on the way. It was something of a rarity to have the kitchen table all to herself.

Sighing, Lettie thought again of Cousin Hallie and the appealing way she described her loving marriage in her weekly letters. Was it truly possible for anyone to be so happy?

———

Heather carried her laptop out to the deck and settled into her mother's comfy chaise. She yearned to be close to nature, already anticipating the upcoming Pennsylvania trip. Opening her laptop, she began to write.

> *Seven days have passed since my diagnosis, and I still feel perfectly fine. The whites of my eyes haven't turned yellow, no fever yet, and I have zero pain.*
> *Hard to believe I'm supposed to be dying.*
> *Well, we're ALL dying, aren't we, from the second we're born. But only some of us get to actually live a full life. . . .*

She glanced up and watched a bird in flight, its wings seemingly so fragile. Yet the delicate creature managed to fly using the wind current and its own strength.

"Flying strong . . . just like me," she

whispered, although that wasn't even remotely true.

Her stuporlike cloud of denial had finally lifted that morning, and Heather wanted to know what she was up against. If she procrastinated on getting her treatment started, what symptoms had the doctor warned might develop?

She typed in the address for WebMD, a credible online resource, and soon discovered her symptoms might someday include weight loss—up to ten percent of her total body weight—heavy night sweats, fevers with no apparent cause, itching, and a cough or breathlessness.

She was confused because she had none of these symptoms, even though the oncologist had told her she was in stage IIIA. That meant the disease had spread to three lymph regions in her body, though the nodes remained small and painless.

One thing led to another, and soon Heather was reading Web pages for holistic alternative treatment centers around the country, and even one in Salzburg, Austria. Wow, there was one situated on a private island in the Caribbean, too. *Who wouldn't feel better just being there?* She spent the next hour online, viewing sites for fasting weekends, day spas, Candida cleanses, and alternative treatments ranging from detoxes to therapeutic massages and thermal water cures.

Quite the gamut, she thought, baffled. One YouTube clip actually featured a man vowing his water diet would cure anyone of anything.

Heather shook her head, sighing. Some of this was almost laughable. But people did impulsive things when their life was in jeopardy. How was it possible to sift the scams from what was legitimate, especially when so many of these places were charging an arm and a leg? *They're certainly not covered by insurance.*

She closed the laptop and stared at the sky. Despite her initial denial, she was ready now to make some choices based on her diagnosis. Closing her eyes, she reveled in the springtime sounds and smells. Didn't she owe it to herself and to her family to give natural methods a try, at least for the summer?

Yes, she definitely wanted to experiment with a natural approach before getting a second opinion from a medical doctor later. The Lancaster naturopath came to mind once again, and she decided to call Dr. Marshall's office for an appointment.

She might've helped Mom, if it hadn't been too late. . . .

———

While Grace waited for Mandy to determine the next move of her king on the checkerboard, she admired again the cute card from Becky. A hummingbird fed from a single pink flower, a vibrant sea of flower cups opening to the sun in the background. A legend she'd heard as a girl said that a hummingbird's flight was unfettered by space and time . . . and carried all one's hopes for lasting affection, greatest joy, and merriment. Grace paused to consider it, looking fondly at the expertly rendered likeness.

Becky's a wonder. . . .

It was evident how many hours her

friend had put into the picture. Grace almost felt guilty for having received the many multicolored pencils in the fancy case from Jessica. Surely they were something Becky might better enjoy.

"Your move." Mandy looked up, eyes mischievous.

Grace laughed. "Nice try. I see you're goin' to double jump me!"

"If you're not careful."

She smiled at her sister, then made her move.

"You're partial to board games, ain't?"

"Any time you want to play, I'm willing." Grace also enjoyed cross-stitching and tatting, just as Mammi Adah did. And, on occasion, she liked to spin wool on an old treadle wheel Brittany and her mom had purchased at a flea market— a most unique hobby.

"Are we still taking Willow for a ride tomorrow?" Mandy asked.

"Fine with me." She waited for her sister to move her checker.

Mandy folded her arms, grinning because she'd made the perfect setup to block Grace. "There . . . how'd ya like that?"

Not ready to be outwitted, Grace leaned closer to the board, studying her options. "Do you think our grandparents had a *gut* time tonight?" she asked.

"Jah, why?"

Grace shrugged, reaching across the board to move her king backward. Truth was, she worried all the foolish bantering at the table had not been overlooked by either her parents or her grandparents. But each year they put up with it, and rather graciously at that. Next year, though, things would be different with Jessica Spangler married and living elsewhere. And who could know about Becky? Mandy, too, for that matter.

Grace did not include herself in the group of potential brides, although she wondered if she would still be residing in her father's house on her twenty-second birthday. Would Henry decide to make her his wife at last?

Mrs. Grace Stahl . . . She considered Henry's family name. There were plenty of Stahls locally, but they weren't Amish, except for Henry's extended family. His grandfather had settled in Bird-in-Hand from south of Somerset County, where

Stahl was a common Amish name. Sighing while Mandy decided where to move her only king, Grace was drawn to the card Adam had slipped under her plate before supper. A placid ocean scene with a lone seabird walking the shoreline. He knew well her desire to see the ocean for herself one day. She hadn't paid close attention to the inside of the card, at least not until now. Adam's note made her smile: *If you keep having birthdays, you'll soon catch up to me. Your older brother, Adam.*

Joe had made a squiggly, smiling figure beside his name, and Mandy had signed, *With love to my best sister, Mandy.*

"How silly," she said, showing Mandy what she'd written. "I'm your only sister, in case you forgot."

Mandy pulled a face, which made Grace laugh even more. Then, looking for her grandparents' names, she was delighted to see Mammi Adah's shaky hand. *Yet the Lord will command his loving-kindness in the day time, and in the night his song shall be with me, and my prayer unto the God of my life.*

"My favorite verse . . . she remembered," Grace said, showing Mandy. "Psalm 42:8."

"Mammi Adah always writes Scripture in her cards," Mandy said, all smiles. "What did Mamma write?"

Grace searched the card, blinking . . . looking. "Well, that's odd."

Mandy reached for it. "Let me see."

"She must've forgotten," Grace said, befuddled.

Mammi Adah had once told her, during last September's walnut-picking time—their hands stained brown from the nuts—that it wasn't what you intended to do in life that mattered, but what you actually did. "I'm sure Mamma meant to sign it," she said.

"Ain't *gut* enough." Mandy got up, waving the card.

"What're you doin'?"

Mandy marched straight to the kitchen. "Mamma?"

"Ach no . . ." Grace's voice faded to a whisper, her heart sinking. Mamma had seemed so content earlier. She hadn't wanted anything to ruin this day.

chapter

eleven

Grace had just curled up on her little love seat to write in the pages of her new blank book when her mother knocked on the slightly open door.

"Come in, Mamma."

Her mother wore a tentative expression as she lingered in the doorway. Then she slowly moved toward the dresser, where the birthday cards were lined up, returning the card given to Grace by her family.

That done, she made her way to the bed and sat down gingerly, drawing in a long breath. "I'd planned to sign your card before supper," Mamma said softly, a little hitch in her voice. "Truly, I did."

Grace suddenly felt sorry for her. "You had a lot on your mind."

"Well, seems the time got away from

me." Her mother looked as embarrassed now as Grace had been earlier at the thought of Mandy's bringing the card to Mamma's attention.

"The supper was wonderful-*gut*," Grace said, changing the subject. "Denki, Mamma."

"You certainly seemed to enjoy yourself."

Grace smiled. "Mammi Adah told some stories on me, jah?"

"We all have stories. . . ." Mamma paused and a frown crossed her brow. "Gracie, there's something I've been wanting to ask you."

Grace caught her breath. Never had Mamma looked so serious. Was she about to reveal her heart at last?

Mamma straightened and folded her hands. "I don't mean to seem nosy, dear. But I've guessed that Henry Stahl might be courtin' you."

Grace didn't feel comfortable letting on that the hunch was correct, but she was curious as to what her mother might say.

"Now, I know he's a nice boy . . . his

parents are hardworkin' and God-fearin' and all, but—"

"But what, Mamma?"

Her mother looked down at her hands for a moment. "It's just that . . . well, have you thought what it might be like, marryin' someone so reserved?" Mamma brushed her hand against her face, her expression sad. "I've noticed he's awfully quiet—even awkward—around everyone. Is he that way with you, Grace?"

"Ach, Mamma . . ."

Her mother's tone was almost apologetic as she continued. "I know it's awfully bold of me. Mind you, I don't mean to criticize Henry in any way. I'm just lookin' out for you . . . making sure you're thinking things through, is all."

She should've been glad for this mother-daughter talk, but Grace was more bemused than happy—there seemed to be much more on Mamma's mind than Henry. Her blue eyes were too solemn.

"A reserved man can be hard to live with," Mamma said softly. "A woman might never know where she stands."

Grace sighed sadly, reading between the lines. She had worried that Mamma's melancholy—and her nighttime wanderings—had something to do with Dat and the state of their marriage.

" 'Tween you and me, Mamma, I care for Henry," she whispered. The past eight months together had been pleasant and a longer time than most couples spent courting.

Mamma blinked her eyes, then rose. "Just please think 'bout it, won't ya?" With that she kissed Grace's forehead and patted her face. "Sleep well, dear one."

Her mother left the room, and Grace heard the familiar footsteps in the hall. Out of curiosity, she got up to look at the now-signed card standing next to Becky's hummingbird on the dresser. Opening it, she was surprised to see what Mamma had written: *You came into my life just in time, Grace. I will always love you. Your mother.*

Tears sprang to her eyes. "Oh, Mamma . . ." Struggling not to weep, she placed the card in the center of the birthday wishes.

I will always love you, too.

Slowly, she began to remove her hair-pins, one at a time. When she'd fin-ished, she shook out her long tresses, the length falling around her like a thick shelter. Reaching for her brush, she be-gan to count the strokes. Soon she would dress for bed, but tonight she wanted to burn the lamp oil a bit longer.

It's my birthday, after all.

She paused her brushing and glanced out into the hall, noting her parents' door was closed.

How long before Mamma goes walk-ing tonight?

Grace resumed brushing her hair until her scalp tingled. Then she settled back down on the settee to write, still pon-dering the surprising things Mamma had said.

———

Judah sat in his chair near the bed-room window in his pajamas, the old German *Biewel* open on his lap. He looked out at the moonlit sky and heard Lettie open, then close the door behind her.

Without acknowledging her, he turned back to the Good Book. Quietly, she moved to sit across from him. "Judah . . . I don't want to interrupt your reading, but . . ."

He raised his head to see the dark circles beneath her tearful eyes, her face so drawn. Another moment passed as Lettie appeared to gather herself.

Judah felt the old, familiar tension in his gut. How long had their conversations been something akin to the birthing of a stillborn lamb? Without thinking, he said, "Whatever's wrong . . . well, it's awful hard on the children, Lettie."

She frowned, her hands folded on her lap. "What is?"

"The past month."

She seemed to bristle. "Well, I've tried to explain, Judah. Truly, I have."

"You've tried, jah. Perhaps you might try talkin' to someone besides me."

Instantly, he regretted his words. He didn't wish to speak harshly—her pained expression bored a hole into his soul. She withered before him, and he felt guilty again. Guilty for every conversation that had gone miserably awry. And yet, hadn't he waited in vain for her to speak her mind, only for her to shrink back time and again? He'd learned as a young husband that his bride harbored something deep within, something she could not seem to share.

Now, quietly, he waited again, searching for the right words to make things easier for her. But the moment was tense, even draining. He leaned forward. "What is it, Lettie? What's botherin' you?"

She fixed her eyes on him, her words coming with slow deliberation. "I want you to hear this from me, Judah. . . ." She paused again, and Judah felt the blood drain from his face. After weeks of wandering the night, was she finally about to say what troubled her?

Suddenly, a series of loud thuds came from downstairs. He jerked his head toward the door.

"Judah . . ." Lettie whispered, her pretty eyes brimming with tears.

Adam's voice rang out. "Dat, *kumm schnell*—come quick!"

Judah turned back to his wife. "Ach, the ewes!"

"Dat! You awake?" Adam's voice was closer now, his footsteps in the hall.

"Let Adam manage for a few minutes," she pleaded. "Won't ya hear me out, Judah?"

He stood up, pulled away by his own insensible need to go. "I should see about this."

"Please?" Her voice was a mere whisper.

Swiftly, he pulled on his work trousers over his pajamas. "I'll be right back," he said, dashing out the door.

Downstairs, he cringed at his cowardly reaction but hardened his resolve, hurrying outside. Whatever was on Lettie's mind could wait till morning.

Tomorrow, he promised himself. *We'll get to it then.*

Lettie closed her eyes as she lay in bed. She should have gone out to help her husband. More times than she could count, she'd assisted with pregnant ewes struggling in their labor. But now she felt depleted of energy, too exhausted to walk across the room, let alone to the barn.

"It's awful hard on the children," Judah had said, referring to these recent weeks.

"Ach, such trouble in my spirit," she whispered.

The memory of Judah's fiery eyes remained before her, yet her own emotions were torn between what she recalled of their former love and the present reality. Oh, she knew he'd cared for her early on. But now?

Still fully dressed, Lettie lay there, waiting for her husband's return.

———

Along about ten o'clock, when she'd filled several pages of her new journal, Grace was startled by a bright light climbing slowly up the windowpane, then swimming crazily across it. As the light moved in a circular motion, she realized what this might be. Going to the window, she raised it high enough to poke out her head.

She looked down and saw Henry

standing far below, shining the light on his face.

"I've brought the clock," he whispered, cupping a hand around his mouth. Then, catching himself, he added, "Hullo again, Grace."

"Henry?" She hardly knew what else to say. He was standing clear down there, directly below her window. Chime clock aside, that could only mean one thing.

Glory be! Is this the night?

"Is now all right . . . I mean, for a visit?"

Goodness, he could scarcely get the words out. Was he that nervous?

"I'll meet you at the side door," she said, then slowly closed the window.

Heart in her throat, Grace wound her hair back up into the best bun she could manage quickly, her hands trembling. Her mind raced as she twisted the sides of her hair and pinned it quickly, then secured her reverent white Kapp. As excited as she was for this moment, she worried Henry had arrived too early, before everyone was sound asleep—especially Mamma.

She looked closely at her room, glad she had not put on nightclothes or rumpled her bed just yet. Oh, to think Henry had come calling here!

Scarcely able to believe it, she took the stairs quietly, then once she was down, she flew through the sitting room and into the kitchen.

She opened the side door and stood waiting as he carried the chime clock up the steps. "Please, come inside," she said, unsure of herself.

"I best be takin' the clock out of the box first," he said, and she wondered if he was concerned about the chimes making a ruckus. As was the age-old custom, they mustn't draw any attention to themselves whatsoever—all of it an overture to the most wonderful-good part of all.

Soon . . . very soon!

———

Heather finished studying for tomorrow's exam and decided to incorporate some additional ideas into her master's thesis, titled *Patriarchy in the Writings of Colonial Williamsburg.* Her fingers tapped

out her thoughts, racing over the keyboard as she added a few more pages.
Soon she would have to begin the
dreaded chore of double-checking the
latest footnotes.

Stretching, she looked at the digital
clock on the microwave. *Dad should be
home by now.* She hadn't expected him
to call; he rarely did. She assumed he'd
picked up dinner or ordered take-out for
the office. *"Eat on the run or go hungry,"*
he'd once said in reference to his de-
manding schedule.

She thumbed through two research
books—one focusing on the patriarchal
ideal and reality, and the other on the
function of the colonial family—making
sure she'd accurately documented
everything. A desire for top marks had
always been her priority, and that had
not changed, even with Dr. O'Connor's
words still ricocheting in her head. *Even
now,* she thought, shrugging away the
dreadful diagnosis. *I've no time for
doom and gloom.*

For the time being she was determined to cap off her last semester by
acing her exams. After that she would

head to Amish country for a great escape, leaving next Tuesday—in six days. She hoped to further her work on her thesis and oral presentation at the Riehls' quiet tourist home.

When she'd tweaked the first twenty pages for the umpteenth time, Heather was satisfied . . . for now. Tomorrow she would print out what she had and work off the hard copy, obsessing as always. After all, anything written late at night often looked entirely too disappointing in the daylight.

She was tempted to call it a night and head off to bed, but something urged her to check her email . . . see if Devon had written. She still was not totally clear about what the time difference was between Virginia and Iraq. She was sure he was in Baghdad, but his company was constantly moving, and for security reasons he wasn't allowed to disclose his location.

Her heart slammed hard when she saw who'd written: Devon's battle buddy, he'd called him. *If anything happens to me, you'll hear from Don Hirsch first,* he'd written soon after deployment. The words had sounded so ominous.

And now here was Don's email address showing up like a bomb in her inbox. She could hardly breathe as she read. *Hey, Heather, don't freak. . . . Devon's sick, but he's gonna be okay.*

She squinted back tears to read more. *There's a weird virus floating around,* Don explained.

"Aw, poor guy . . ." she groaned.

They'll keep an eye on him at the military hospital for a few days, so he won't be online for a while. He says not to worry and sends his love "to his sweet babe"—and I quote.

"Um, how do I not worry?" she sputtered, and Moe meowed loudly. She leaned down to pick up her favorite cat. "Devon's real sick," she whispered. "Can he get well fast without us, huh?"

Moe began to purr, rolling over on his back as he lay on her lap. She rubbed his tummy, thinking all the while about her fiancé's being so ill he had to go to a hospital. *Where?* She felt helpless not knowing . . . not being able to visualize any of it. She really wanted to hop on a plane and fly over there.

Shoot, he'd signed up for guard duty and gotten *this*? It still baffled her why he'd signed up at all.

Hey, Don, she began to type, expressing her gratitude for his email, jarring as it had been to receive it. *Tell Devon I love him, and I'm really sorry he's sick. Please keep the updates coming. Thanks!*

She stopped typing, frustrated with the immense distance between them. *My incredible guy . . . so ill!*

She wished she could do this entire year over, starting from the day Devon had held her in his arms at the airport. She'd gotten a gate pass so she could go with him through security to his departing gate. In the end, it might have been easier if they'd said their *good-bye*s and *I love you*s a dozen times in the terminal. But no, she'd had to see him off completely.

"I really despise this war," Heather muttered, hitting Send. She shut down the laptop and shuffled off to her room. *I'll be lucky to get any sleep tonight.*

Henry carried the clock up the stairs without the chimes ringing even once. Grace shyly led the way to her room, leaving the door slightly open as Mamma would expect.

Whispering now, she moved the birthday cards off the dresser. "For the time being, it can go here."

Henry placed the small, gleaming clock in the center, in front of the mirror on her long doily runner. He seemed stiff, standing there in the middle of her room.

She felt just as ill at ease—so much so that she nearly forgot what to do next. Thankfully, Henry motioned toward the hope chest at the foot of her bed. "Oh . . . jah," she said, still concerned their talking might disturb the family. "Would you like to see what I've made?"

He moved to the padded settee and silently sat down.

"I embroidered these pillow slips," she began, wondering if he expected her to describe each item. She'd never done this before. Of course, neither had he, and she smiled at the lovely thought.

Next came the woolen shawl she'd made several years ago, when she'd first learned to spin wool with Jessica. And the woolen lap afghan for chilly days.

Henry regarded each item with seeming interest, and Grace hurried along, showing him the four winter-weight quilts she and Mamma had made, and another one made by Mammi Adah. There were quilted potholders and placemats, too, and dozens of linens—many of which were treasured family heirlooms—towels, bed coverlets, and even a cradle quilt done in lovely pastels. She told him about her sewing equipment and cooking utensils, all packed away in boxes in the attic for now.

When she'd displayed everything, she carefully returned the items to the chest and closed the lid. She sat there, heart pounding as Henry gave a slow smile and held out his hand. She rose and went to his side.

"Sit here . . . with me." He released her hand. "Denki for showin' me all your nice things."

She nodded, still feeling awkward and shy. "Happy to."

He faced her, his dark eyes serious. "You must know I'm quite fond of you, Grace."

She looked into his face, smiling . . . soaking up his attention. "I love you, too," she said in a whisper.

" 'Tis mighty *gut,* then." He lifted her hand to his lips and held it there, eyes fixed on her. Then he kissed her hand. "Will you agree to be my bride?"

My bride . . .

She could hardly keep from bursting out in laughter . . . no, in tears. This was the most wonderful moment ever. "I'd be honored to marry you, Henry. Jah!"

Still clasping her hand, he nodded his pleasure, and she cherished the feel of her small hand in his big, work-roughened one. "We'll tie the knot sometime this fall."

She gave him her sweetest smile. "All right."

His eyes searched hers and his head tilted sideways for a moment, as if he might say more. But when his gaze became uncomfortable, she looked down, not sure what to say next. She didn't want to rush him out in an unfeeling sort of way, yet their time here together should come to an end.

"God be with ya, Henry," she said kindly, hoping he'd take the hint.

He did. He rose and walked to the door, turning briefly to look once again at the chime clock. "Looks right nice there," he said.

She agreed and followed him downstairs, both of them tiptoeing as they went.

When they were outdoors, she saw that he had not parked his buggy in the lane. "It was awful nice seein' you twice in one day," she ventured, hoping it didn't sound forward.

He leaned down and kissed her cheek. "Good night, Grace."

"G'night." She broke into a smile as the feel of his kiss lingered on her face. Waving now, she watched him hurry away, out to the road.

Good-bye, my love . . .

Reluctantly she turned and walked toward the dark house.

chapter

twelve

Grace dropped off to sleep after lying awake for a short time, reliving the last hours of this wonderful-good day. Later, she dreamed of walking with Henry along a path strewn with bright yellow rose petals. She could not, however, hear what he was saying no matter how she strained to listen.

Eventually the dream floated away to nothingness and she slept more soundly. But in her haze, she sensed someone kissing her cheek.

It was still dark out when she awakened. She had not heard her mother's footsteps in the night, and Grace marveled at how soundly she must have slept.

Turning over, she looked at her dresser and saw what appeared to be an unopened envelope propped up against her dresser mirror, to the left of the chime clock. She leaned up, rubbing her eyes. The house was still quiet; it was too early to get up.

Lying back down, she glimpsed the small alarm clock on the bedside table and saw that it was only ten minutes before five. She looked again at her dresser, wondering where the envelope had come from—had someone placed it there while she slept?

Her curiosity got the best of her, and she went to look. She carried the letter to the window and opened the shade slightly, letting in the waning moonlight. The words *To Grace* were written in her mother's handwriting on the envelope.

Quickly, she tore it open.

My dear Grace,
You looked ever so happy tonight on your birthday. I know you enjoyed the supper and your time with our family and the neighbor friends.
I promised to tell you what is bothering me, but now, frankly, I can't find the words in me. I've

*seen the concern on your face
since we helped at the big barn
raising last month—heard your
gentle prodding, too. Your caring
heart is such a dear part of who
you are.*

*It's very late, and all of you are
sleeping as I write. I trust you will
share my thoughts here with your
brothers and Mandy, as well as
with your father. I know if I'd told
all of you my plans in person, I
would not have had the courage to
leave.*

"What on earth?" Grace whispered,
her breath coming in short, panicked
bursts as she read on.

*I fear that what I'm writing
makes little sense and will change
your birthday joy to sadness. For
that, I'm very sorry, Grace.*

*You see, there's another whole
side to this, and such pain comes
with all of it. But I cannot spell it
out just now. In time, you will
understand, I promise. Perhaps all*

*of you will. Even so, my leaving will
bring shame to my family . . . and
sorrow, too.*

 *I hope you will not despise this
hard thing I must do. My heart is
ever so tender, if not breaking. Yet
go I must. I love you.*

Always,
Mamma

"She's leaving?" Clutching the letter,
Grace fled the room, peering first
through her parents' open door. Dat lay
crosswise on the bed, sound asleep.
Rushing downstairs, she looked everywhere for her mother, including the cold
cellar in the basement, then clear out to
the barn, near Willow's stall.

Not finding Mamma, she went all the
way around the house to the front
porch, still pondering the strange letter . . . ever so mysterious. She turned
and looked toward the field, where
Mamma often walked. How many times
had she seen her out there, wrapped in
moonbeams, her arms tight around her
middle, as if she were holding herself
together?

Breathlessly, Grace returned to her room, where Henry had proposed just hours before. *Does Dat know any of this?* Looking at the letter again, she read it more slowly and began crying.

Baffled and confused, she rose once more and headed for the hallway. This time she stopped to look in on Mandy, her arm flung over her head, sound asleep.

Poor sister, what will she think?

And what about Dat? Apparently Mamma had written a letter only to *her* . . . but why?

Walking to the dormer windows, she peered out and, to her fright, saw what she hadn't seen before—a faraway dark figure walking briskly from the house, heading west toward Route 340. *Can it be?* She leaned forward, squinting to see.

Grace darted back to her room and tossed the letter onto the bedside table, atop the envelope. She yanked her bathrobe off the wooden peg and put it on, not bothering to tie the belt. Then, rushing outside, she dashed past the well-groomed lawns and the pasture fence near the road.

Grace stumbled and caught herself, running as she tied a knot in her robe. She was gaining some ground, getting closer, desperately hoping that the distant black silhouette was *not* her mother. That this whole thing was some horrid mistake. Surely her mother wouldn't just up and leave while everyone was sleeping. Would she?

Through a blur of tears, she saw a car heading this way, then slowing and coming to a stop.

There's another whole side to this, Mamma had written. Grace couldn't imagine what that meant, or even what it *could* mean.

The moon moved out from behind a cloud, making it easier to see more clearly now. The figure was definitely a woman. Suddenly it was unmistakable: Mamma was practically running toward the car, her head covered by a heavy black outer bonnet, something bulky at her side.

The car door opened. Grace sucked in her breath and nearly choked when she realized what was in her mother's hand. Their old brown suitcase!

"Mamma!" she called, gasping for breath. "Come back! Please, come back!"

Slipping inside the car, her mother did not stop or even turn to look back. *Can't she hear me?*

The door slammed shut, its echo reaching Grace with a final thud. *No, this can't be!* Stunned, she slowed to a walk, holding her sides and breathing fast . . . then she stopped completely, unable to go on.

I hope you will not despise this hard thing I must do, Mamma had written.

"No, Mamma . . ." wept Grace as the vehicle sped away. "Why must you go?"

Judah awakened with a jolt. He thought he'd heard someone rushing about. Alarmed, he pulled himself out of bed to flounder down the hall to look in on the children.

Strange, he thought, *I still think of them that way. Especially the girls.*

He peered through the open door at Amanda, who was softly snoring in her sleep, recalling that it was Lettie who'd always done this sort of checking. He would sometimes awaken as she returned to bed.

Before she started wandering all hours, he thought, still feeling guilty for his own cowardice last night. He headed slowly up the narrow staircase that led to the boys' rooms on the third floor. All was well.

Back on the second floor, he noticed Grace's door ajar, and when he looked in, he saw that her bedclothes were thrown back. "Odd," he said, but on second thought he wondered if she'd gone out to meet her beau.

He was about to head to the main floor and have a look outside when he noticed a letter lying close to the edge of Grace's bedside table, as if flung there. Not given to reading other people's mail, he hesitated. Then, thinking that it was out in the open, he looked at it more closely and immediately recognized Lettie's handwriting. He shrank back then, thinking of just leaving it there . . . letting it be.

But something stirred within and he

reached for it. He carried the letter back to his room, scanning the first line as he went. Then, with a great sigh, Judah closed the door and sat down to read what appeared to be Lettie's farewell to them all.

Grace trudged along the road, her mind in a dither. She was scarcely able to see the road through her tears as she made her way home. And she found herself wrapping her arms around her stomach, just as she'd seen Mamma do.

In the midst of her grief, her favorite psalm came to mind—the one Mammi Adah had scrawled on Grace's birthday card. *In the night his song shall be with me. . . .* The words went round and round in her head as she plodded toward the house.

What will Dat say? she thought, at a loss for how to tell him.

None of the family would believe it. Even Mammi Adah would look at her askance if Grace was brave enough to reveal what she'd just witnessed.

Had Mamma been rehearsing her

quick escape those other nights? Had she been getting up the courage to walk away . . . escape from her family, maybe?

Escape? It was downright strange to be thinking of such a word. "Escape from what?" she said into the chilly air.

Plain wives and mothers simply did not leave their families. Even when there was trouble in marriages, divorce was unheard of among the People. Only on rare occasions were there even whispered comments about legal separations. No, married folk somehow made do, or they found a way in spite of their difficulties.

Surely Mamma has only gone to visit someone. Surely . . .

But the words of her mother's own heartbreaking letter belied Grace's hopes, and she trembled.

———

Martin Puckett had been somewhat surprised by Lettie Byler's call early yesterday evening. She'd sounded distraught as she asked him to pick her up at an appointed spot and time.

"Just before 5:00 AM tomorrow . . ."

He'd had a hard time convincing his wife that it wasn't out of the ordinary to leave the house when it was still dark to pick up an Amishwoman. "She needs to catch a train," he'd explained.

So here he was, behind the wheel of his car, with Lettie sitting in the front seat, a position she'd never occupied while traveling with either Judah or the rest of her family. She'd hopped right in, as if eager to get to her destination.

He could hear her muttering in *Deitsch* as he drove toward Lancaster, something about being worried she was doing the right thing by Judah. "I tried to tell him," she said in her first language. The children, too, were apparently heavy on her mind.

"Are you all right, Lettie?" He glanced at her.

She waved her hand. "Ach, don't mind me."

He'd never thought twice about driving the Amish, least of all at an hour when it would seem dangerous to travel with horse and buggy. "You'll be mighty early to the train station," he mentioned.

"I don't yet have a reservation."

He hoped she would be okay traveling alone, as bleak as her face looked. But it was not his place to pry. *Unless she is in danger . . .*

When he arrived at the Amtrak station in Lancaster, he stopped in front and got out to retrieve her suitcase. She stood at the door, waiting. "I'd like you to keep mum 'bout this, if you don't mind," she said.

He'd never heard her, or any Amish-woman, speak so pointedly to a man. Nor speak with such determination.

"You mean Judah doesn't know about your trip?" he asked, suddenly more concerned.

She hung her head. "I best not say."

"Lettie," he pressed her, "does *any-one* know of your travel plans?"

Her desperate look when he set the suitcase down told him all he needed to know. "Have you thought this through?"

"Ain't anyone else's business. Please keep this mum."

At a complete loss as to what should be done, Martin stepped back. "Now, you know I can't do that," he told her.

"In fact, I have a mind to take you right back and—"

"No . . . please." She shook her head. "Someone's meeting me . . . where I'm goin'. Not to worry."

Relatives? he wondered. But it wasn't his place to ask.

"As I said, please keep this hush-hush, Martin."

"Well, your husband is a friend of mine. If he asks me whether I drove you here, I won't lie."

Worry swept her face and she held out his pay for the trip in rolled-up bills. He stepped forward to take it, then withdrew quickly. "Have a safe trip . . . wherever you're going."

"Ever so kind of you."

He offered to carry her suitcase inside, but Lettie declined. "No need, but thank you." Then she said a quick goodbye.

Her dejected tone made him shudder as she clutched her suitcase and resolutely walked into the station.

chapter

thirteen

As panicked as she was at the sight of her mother's leaving, Grace was also terribly upset at not finding Mamma's letter in her room when she returned. Mentally retracing her steps, she remembered staring out the hallway window, seeing her mother's dark silhouette. . . . Then hadn't she tossed it into her bedroom?

But rechecking her room—and the hallway—the letter was nowhere in sight.

She made her way downstairs and looked in the front sitting room, searching even on the china hutch, where Mamma displayed her prettiest teacups and saucers and plates. Breathlessly she hurried into the kitchen to look on the table and counter—every imaginable spot she might have inadvertently left it during her rush out the door.

Could it have been taken? But who would do that?

And anyway, everyone was sleeping.

She crawled into bed, still wearing her robe, shaking with a bad case of nerves. She'd witnessed her mother leaving, carrying a suitcase . . . getting into a car even as Grace pleaded for her to stay. Was it possible to ever wipe away that image?

Doubting she would fall back to sleep, she prayed. Only the dear Lord knew what she should tell Mandy and the boys at the breakfast table, when they discovered Mamma gone. And Dat? What could she possibly say to him?

She rolled over and covered her head with the quilt. *What would cause Mamma to do such a thing?* It was incomprehensible, and now she couldn't even reread the letter . . . unless it had fallen under the bed.

Tossing off the covers, she got out of bed and peered beneath. Not finding the letter there, either, she opened the narrow drawer on the small round table next to her bed, her heart racing.

She slipped her hand inside but found nothing.

Reaching under the bedside table, she discovered only a coating of dust— she must remember to push the dry mop under there later. Weeping silently, Grace returned to bed and curled up in a tight ball as she recalled the dear way Mamma had signed off: *My heart is ever so tender, if not breaking. . . . I love you.*

Oh, Mamma, she cried silently, *but it's* my *heart that is breaking now.*

Judah's hand trembled as he held the letter. He hadn't been able to put it down.

"Lettie," he whispered, head throbbing. "Why?"

He stared at the bare wooden pegs on their bedroom wall where her dresses and black aprons had been and remembered their awkward discussion last night. Something compelled him to open her dresser drawers, though he felt oddly intrusive about that. Each one was empty.

Earlier, he'd searched the house and outdoor perimeter for her, shining his lantern over the pastureland, spreading its light over the area. He'd walked the road, too, heading north, thinking surely she would not go on foot out toward the highway. Route 340 was much too dangerous.

He'd wanted urgently to call out her name, but that was impractical. Besides, he didn't want to raise the neighbors. They'd all know soon enough, come daylight.

Bad news travels faster than good.

For now, though, his knowledge of her intentions belonged to him alone. Or to him and Grace, if she'd even read her mother's letter yet. Most likely she had been out with her beau. If so, Grace knew nothing of Lettie's leaving . . . or the letter.

Assuming he was correct in his thinking, the best thing to do was to keep the letter hidden for now. That way Grace would be spared having to read it, although Lettie's words to her daughter were as tender as any he'd heard uttered from her lips.

"She's miffed at me," he said. Maybe she'd simply gone walking in the wee hours and would return when she was ready to forgive him. Certainly, he had offended her.

After daylight, he thought, *I'll go and find her . . . bring her home.* In his bewilderment, he read the letter again, searching for a clue—anything at all.

But as he reread the puzzling words, it seemed even Lettie was unsure about her destination. Her desperate plea last night rang in his ears. *"Won't ya hear me out, Judah?"*

No, this letter was no mere attempt to get his attention.

———

Martin Puckett hadn't driven but two miles when he noticed something Lettie Byler had dropped on the floor. At the nearest stop sign, he leaned down to get it and saw several phone numbers— all outside the 717 area code. Just what part of the country they were from he did not know. But they were undoubtedly important to Lettie, so he turned around and headed back to the Lancaster train station.

Under different circumstances, he

would have enjoyed seeing the historic
station again. Now, still pensive about
Lettie's troubling request, he almost
timidly entered the nearly palatial-look-
ing terminal. The place seemed to be in
the process of restoration. He recalled
having read something about the
restoration online, as well as in the *Lancaster New Era.*

The ceiling soared to a glass-paned
insert high overhead, and the words *To
Trains* were engraved on the wall over a
portico. Even at this hour, the waiting
area was scattered with would-be trav-
elers, and he spotted Lettie over in the
far corner, sitting alone on a tall-backed
wooden bench. She was crocheting a
scarf. He considered her forlorn state
momentarily, noticing the streaks of
gray in her blond hair for the first time.
Then, pulling the piece of paper from his
pocket, he slowly approached her. "Excuse me, Lettie." He reached down to
give her the paper.

She started, obviously surprised to
see him.

"I found this in my car. Is it yours?"

A light came into her sad eyes. "Ach,

I would be a cooked goose without it."
She smiled broadly. "Ever so *gut* of you
to bring it."

Still anxious about her safety, he felt
compelled to sit with her. "I thought it
might come in handy," he said.

She nodded, obviously pleased. "Oh
my, you have no idea. . . ."

"Well, I'm glad it's helpful." She hadn't
invited him to sit, but there he was all
the same. "Lettie . . . I . . ." He paused,
cautious as to what he should say. "I'm
concerned for you."

She looked down at her hands, the
crochet hook poised to make the next
loop. "You mustn't be. Really."

He noticed her sack lunch and the
book she'd brought. "I don't wish to
meddle." He assumed Judah and Lettie
Byler were as amicable at home as they
appeared to be in public. Yet if so, why
was she here in secret?

She smiled weakly, then began crocheting again. Instinctively, he sensed
their conversation was over.

Not thinking, he touched her arm. "If
you ever need help—from either my wife

or me—please don't think twice about calling."

Slowly, as if painfully, she nodded, lifting her eyes to his. He saw tears wetting her cheeks and took his handkerchief from his pocket and handed it to her. "You're very kind," she said, accepting it and dabbing at her face. "Very kind."

"I mean it . . . no matter where you're going," he emphasized. Then, when she'd returned his handkerchief, he remained there awhile, temporarily unable to say yet another good-bye.

At last he rose and walked across the marble floor. It was then he recognized Sadie Zook's cousin among those waiting for trains. Pete Bernhardt traveled weekly to the Big Apple on business and was sitting across the way, his briefcase propped near his feet.

Because he'd known Pete for many years, Martin was about to head over and say hello, but Pete glanced up furtively and quickly looked away. Confused by that, Martin hesitated. *Why so distant?*

Then it struck him—had Pete witnessed his exchange with Lettie Byler?

Offering a wave, Martin felt quite embarrassed by what Pete might presume to have seen. He made his way out the door and down to the parking lot, mortified for having taken even the most benign liberty with Judah's attractive wife—sitting beside her, offering his handkerchief.

Martin opened his car door and got in. Janet would be up making breakfast before she put the finishing touches on their packing. They were eager to get an early start to their own out-of-town trip today. He needed to do his part in fueling up and having the car washed, the reason he'd chosen to drive the car instead of his usual van.

As he turned the key in the ignition, he found himself breathing a prayer for Lettie, a vulnerable Amishwoman traveling quite alone.

chapter

fourteen

Grace awakened with a jolt, having fallen back to sleep. Still wearing her robe beneath the covers, she was vaguely aware of the sound of steady rain on the roof. She stretched but instead of relief came a profound feeling of melancholy and fatigue. Bits and pieces of the predawn hours slowly emerged in her memory. *Finding a letter from Mamma . . . racing down the road . . . watching helplessly as Mamma stepped into a strange car.*

Grace sat up in bed, her heart pounding. Had she simply dreamed this nightmare?

Moments passed as she attempted to sort through the panic. But no, it was true. She hadn't imagined it at all.

Grace peered with one eye at her exquisite chime clock. Seven o'clock. *Ach, I overslept.*

Leaping out of bed, she nearly tripped on her robe and could not find her slippers. *I'm misplacing too many things.* She thought again of Mamma's letter as she moved to the window and looked out on a dim and foggy morning. It was impossible to see even to the edge of the yard, let alone out to the road. She pressed her fingers against the pane, feeling the chill through it and remembering Henry's visit.

How overjoyed she had been. Now she felt so grief stricken in comparison as the recent events of her life mingled—Henry's proposal and her mother's departure—like the intricate weaving of a variegated rag rug.

Grace felt terribly out of sorts. Something had gone completely off beam for Mamma to pack a suitcase and leave.

After forcing herself to go through the motions of getting dressed, she hurried downstairs to start breakfast, late as it was, and realized Mandy was still asleep. A glance around the corner into the front hall revealed her father's and brothers' work boots were missing. The men had already gone to look after the baby lambs. New ones were arriving every few days now, just as Dat had planned it. The round-the-clock checking on the expectant ewes kept him and the boys up off and on during the night.

Didn't they wonder about breakfast— why Mamma wasn't up and cooking? She found it curious no one had even called to awaken her for the task. What did they make of Mamma's absence? Did they assume she, too, had overslept?

Hearing sounds coming from the kitchen on the other side of the house, she guessed Mammi Adah was making eggs for Dawdi Jakob. The air caught in her throat as she thought how saddened they also would be by Mamma's disappearance.

Once it's known.

Turning on the faucet, Grace filled the kettle, thinking that on such a dismal and rainy day the men would want coffee. The mid-spring day more resembled autumn in temperature and dampness.

Glad that Mandy had gathered the eggs yesterday, she brought out the bowl filled with fresh ones and set it down on the counter. She turned on a burner and set the frying pan on the stove, plopping a chunk of butter in the center. Dat's stomach would be growling and so would Adam's and Joe's. They liked scrambled eggs made with bits of bacon and cheese, but today she wouldn't take the time for any of that. *Fried eggs are quicker.*

Still in disbelief, Grace gritted her teeth and wished she might know what to say when they came in. Suddenly she realized she'd stepped immediately into Mamma's role without even considering it.

She set the flame to a gentle heat, then cracked the eggs against the edge of the pan before dropping them in. Placing a lid on top, she turned to stare out the window. Still not hearing Mandy, she walked to the bottom of the stairs. "Daylight's a-wastin'!" she called, waiting to hear the thud of her sister's feet on the floor before she resumed cooking.

In a few minutes, Mandy came dragging down, barefoot and in her bathrobe. "Why'd ya let me sleep in?" she asked, sounding nearly accusing.

"I overslept, too."

Mandy slumped onto the bench next to the table, leaning her head into her hand. "I'm so tired . . . can't seem to wake up."

"Jah, the weather's downright gloomy."

Mandy looked out the window. "It's really makin' down."

"Well, we need rain." Bracing herself for the question that was sure to come, Grace faced the stove, putting salt and pepper on the yolks, which were now nearly done. Dat liked his slightly runny, but everyone else wanted their yolks firm. "Would you mind toasting some bread right quick?" she asked Mandy. "Wash your hands first, though."

"Ach, you sound like Mamma." Mandy sauntered to the sink and turned on the water. "Why're you cookin' breakfast anyway?"

"Why not?"

Just then, Adam and Joe came in through the side door, even though Dat always urged them to use the front door that led to the hallway, with its specified places for work boots and outerwear.

"Is Dat with you?" Grace asked, glancing toward the door.

"He took off with Sassy and the buggy earlier . . . didn't say where he was headed," Adam said, referring to his own driving horse.

"He was in a big hurry. Must be an important errand," Joe said as he clumped over to the sink, where Mandy was standing, drying her hands.

"So early?" Mandy said. "What's open this time of day?"

Grace cut in, "Better take off your boots. Leave 'em outside."

"They'll get rained on," Joe said, removing his and leaving them on the oval rug near the door. He looked up at the three of them . . . minus their mother. "Where's Mamma?"

Grace glanced at Adam, who seemed oblivious. "Well, she's not here," she said, heart sinking.

She's left us. . . .

"So *you're* makin' breakfast?" Joe said. "It better be *gut*."

She took the spatula and lifted the eggs out of the pan and set them on plates. "How many eggs can ya eat?" she asked Adam, then Joe.

They each claimed their usual three, along with two pieces of the buttered toast that Mandy provided.

"Maybe Dat went to fetch Mamma," said Mandy out of the blue as they all sat down.

Grace was caught by surprise. What did her sister mean?

"She's not in the barn," said Adam. "Has *anyone* seen her?"

"Not this mornin'," Mandy said.

"Could be Dat's taken her to visit one of her sisters," Joe suggested.

Grace squeezed her hands tightly beneath the table and looked to Adam for the table blessing, since he was the oldest male present. She bowed her head when he did, praying the silent rote prayer she'd learned as a child.

"Why would ya say that . . . what you said before?" Joe asked Mandy when they started eating. "That Dat went to fetch Mamma?"

"Because," Mandy replied. "Don't ya know she goes out walkin' at—"

"Mandy, you'd best be eatin'," Grace interrupted.

Her sister frowned, clearly resenting Grace's rebuke. "We *all* best dig in now," Grace suggested, feeling sick to her stomach.

————

Judah was on his third pass down the road and garnering stares from the neighbors. He'd even ventured as far east as Monterey Road, near Eli's Natural Foods store and back, keeping his eye out for any sign of Lettie. He'd driven past several of her cousins' houses, as well as all of her siblings', not stopping to inquire after her . . . not wanting to worry anyone needlessly. But he assumed if Lettie had gone merely to visit, someone would've come out to hail him.

Feeling mighty weak now, he knew he ought to head home. Yet he was hardly ready to face questions from Adam or the others, and surely there would be some.

Waving at the neighbor up the way, Judah tipped his hat when he was greeted with *"Guder Mariye"* and a big wave.

If Lettie's gone, my children won't be the only ones asking questions.

"And I have nothin' to appease their curiosity." He clucked his tongue to spur Sassy onward, observing his fine sheep grazing in the distance.

He waved to the next neighbor, Marian Riehl, who was out on her porch, beating rag rugs. He'd heard from someone, he didn't recall who, that the Riehls were getting a long-term paying guest. This struck him as both curious and practical. Andy and Marian were hard-pressed to make ends meet, as many were. Plain folk were thinking twice these days about having gas-run appliances—some wished they could return to wood-fed stoves.

He wondered how his mother-in-law must be feeling *now* about her doggedness in wanting more modern kitchen appliances.

Shaking his head, he also considered what Adah Esh would think if she'd received the kind of letter Lettie had written to Grace. Perhaps Lettie *had* shared her plan with someone besides Grace.

If Naomi were still alive, she *would undoubtedly know.*

As Judah surveyed the rain-drenched landscape, he could see patches on the ground where samara had fallen last year and were already beginning to take root. He was anxious for the sunny days of May, another week away.

Lettie will miss watching her beloved mourning doves if she stays away too long. He recalled her fascination last spring as she'd observed the males accompanying their mates to possible nesting sites, the male birds gathering twigs and other material for the female that built the nest. Lettie had stood and watched at the kitchen window for nearly half an hour just after dawn one day. Judah had offered to make a ground feeding tray for them, since they weren't hoppers like some birds, and Lettie had been so pleased, giving him a rare smile.

Will she miss the late-blooming honey

locust? he wondered. *Surely she'll return for harvesting elderberries and peaches. Surely . . .*

He rubbed his neck and shoulders—the pain at the nape of his neck had become a searing ache. No more putting off the dreaded breakfast scene. It was past time to head home. By all indications, his wife had flown the coop. For how long, Judah did not know.

———

Dat took his time unhitching Sassy from the family buggy, then headed toward the house, cutting across the drive and through the side yard. Grace noticed he'd worn his winter hat instead of the straw one and was all dressed in black. *Like for Preaching service,* she thought, stepping away from the window, her heart pounding.

He looked ashen as he came into the kitchen. Grace had cleaned off the table and washed the dishes, not knowing when he might return. With Mandy upstairs making her bed and straightening her room and the boys back in the barn monitoring the new lambs, the house was uncomfortably quiet. She felt ever so strange, knowing all she did about Mamma . . . wondering what her father knew, if anything.

She moved silently to the cupboard and again took out the frying pan, ready to make breakfast for Dat if he wanted it. Mandy would be down soon enough, she was sure, which would help things along, as well. Unless Mandy once more brought up Mamma's absence.

Dat had broken his own rule about not using the side door. He'd come in stocking footed, having removed his work boots and left them outside since the rain had stopped. "Am I too late for some eggs and toast?" he asked, his face angst ridden.

"Not at all." She turned and set the gas flame where she liked it. She longed to fill up the dreadful void, the aching emptiness between them, but she knew better than to ask where Mamma was. That would be deceitful. Yet, because he didn't utter a word about her taking over the cooking duties, she guessed he knew something. Perhaps they'd had words in the night?

Dat went into the washroom and decisively closed the door. She heard the click of the lock, as well, which was not at all like him. He—all of them—simply shut the door. The whole family respected a closed door, no matter the room. *"A closed door is closed for a reason,"* Mamma had often said when they were little.

By the time Dat appeared again and took his place at the head of the table, Mandy reappeared in the doorway of the kitchen, wearing a scowl. "Did ya find her?" She planted herself next to their father.

"Your Mamma, you mean?" Dat eyed them both.

Grace carried the food over, the eggs cooked to Dat's liking, and put the plate in front of him. She waited, wondering what more he might request. And if he might say where he'd gone.

"She's nowhere to be found." Mandy leaned forward, her elbows on the table, hands supporting her chin. "Where on earth could she be?"

"I don't know," Dat muttered.

"She's not usually gone first thing in

the morning," Mandy declared, turning to look at Grace.

Dat bowed his head for the blessing, squeezing his eyes tightly shut. When he'd said amen and picked up his fork, he whispered, " 'Tis a mystery."

"Well, where do ya *think* she is?" Mandy folded her hands on the table.

Grace gently touched her shoulder. "Let Dat eat in peace."

Mandy frowned at her, getting up. "Sorry," she muttered and left by way of the side door.

Dat continued eating, his eyes fixed on his plate while Grace went to scrub out the frying pan for the second time. In spite of her father's blank expression, she sensed he knew something.

She turned, her hands still in the sudsy water. "Mamma wrote me a letter 'bout her leaving." Pausing, she quickly dried her hands and crossed the room to him. "She must've left it on my dresser in the wee hours."

A flicker of surprise crossed Dat's face, and then he nodded. "I saw it."

"You read it, then?"

"Jah."

He must've taken it.

Grace sensed how awkward he surely felt. "Well, I never would've known how to share it with you, Dat, anyway. None of it made sense."

His eyes were sad, and she lowered herself to sit on the wooden bench to the left of her father, in Adam's spot. "I went lookin' for her right away, all through the house."

"So did I," he said.

"And then I saw her running up the road. A car stopped to pick her up. I could hardly believe my eyes."

At that, he frowned and ran his hand over his untrimmed beard. He sighed ever so deeply.

"Where do ya think she went, Dat?"

He sat motionless. "Haven't the slightest notion."

She heard him breathing, yet he said no more. So many questions ran through her mind, but he was clearly in no shape to tend to them just now. Surely he had dozens of his own.

Getting up, she returned to the sink.

"A reserved man can be hard to live with. . . . A woman might never know where she stands," Mamma had said. At the time, Grace had hoped her mother was referring only to Henry.

chapter

fifteen

When Adah wandered across the down-stairs hall and into the kitchen through Lettie's sitting room, she was surprised to see Grace wiping off the counters. "A bit late to be cleanin' up after breakfast, jah?" she teased.

Grace nodded and kept cleaning.

"Is your Mamma around?" Adah asked, then noticed her granddaughter's peaked face. "Ach, girl . . . are you feelin' all right?"

"Just a little tired, I guess."

"Well, if you see her, tell her I'd like some help with a quilt top I've been puttin' off."

"Mamma's not here." Grace's lower lip trembled. "She's gone."

"Gone where?"

Grace stopped scrubbing and folded her dishrag. "Wish I knew."

Has Lettie taken one of her long walks? Adah wondered. "Come, sit . . . let's talk." She gestured to Grace.

They moved into the cozy sitting room. Grace sat on one of the hard cane chairs, while Adah sank down into an upholstered one. The spacious square room was darker than the kitchen, which gave it a feeling of confidentiality. "Why do you say your mother's left?"

Grace inhaled slowly. "I saw her go."

Adah had known Lettie to traipse around outside after Judah was sleeping. Why would Grace think this was different from other nights?

"You saw her . . . just like other times—is that what ya mean?"

"No, I don't think you understand, Mammi. I saw her get into a car."

"Maybe you were dreamin', dear," suggested Adah.

"Honestly, I might've thought that, too . . . 'cept Mamma left me a good-bye note."

A note?

"Ach, we'd best slow down." Adah fanned herself with the white hankie she'd pulled from beneath her sleeve.

"You have something from your Mamma in writing?"

Grace nodded, explaining also that she'd seen her mother running away from the house, carrying a large suitcase. "She went down toward Route 340."

This made not a whit of sense. *Lettie left?*

"I wish I'd imagined it," Grace said softly, her eyes moist.

"Has your father gone looking for her?"

"Jah. Adam and Joe said he left early this morning, even before takin' his turn with the newborn lambs. He didn't find her, though."

Adah had a dark, sinking feeling and leaned her head back against the wing of the chair for a moment.

"You all right?" Grace came to kneel beside her.

"The room's turnin' awful fast."

"You take it easy," Grace said. "I'll get some water."

Adah took several slow, deep breaths. "If I can just sit here quietlike . . ."

She fanned herself, trying to remain

calm. Truth be told, Lettie's disappearance was the last thing she'd expected from this daughter.

The very last thing.

Grace hurried to get a glass from the cupboard, letting the water run. *I could get cooler water from the springhouse,* she thought. But no, her grandmother shouldn't be left alone. Not as dizzy as she was.

The pain and fright of early this morning came rushing back. Tears sprang to her eyes, and she leaned her head against the cupboard. She struggled to control her emotions, wanting to be strong for her grandmother, who was clearly as distraught as Grace herself.

Not willing to be gone for long, she wiped her eyes and dabbed at her wet cheeks with her apron hem. Taking a long breath, she carried the glass of water back to the sitting room.

Adah was relieved when Grace returned. Merely seeing her granddaughter again helped Adah regain her own composure, and she accepted the water. "Denki, Gracie."

"You feelin' a little better now, Mammi?" Grace asked once Adah had taken a few sips.

Adah finished a long drink, then said, "You're not to worry, dear." She leaned forward to look in the direction of the kitchen but saw no one. "Where's your father now?"

"Must be out with Adam in the barn," Grace said softly, appearing very much as though she was trying not to cry again.

Adah reached out her hand. "Everything's going to be just fine, ya hear?" Grace came over and took her hand, regarding her with those tender eyes. Adah recalled having to help Lettie through the dreadful loss of Naomi. How difficult that had been to bear! "We'll be all right," she said again, assuring herself as much as her granddaughter.

Grace's lips parted, but she looked away, falling silent.

"What is it, dear?"

Shrugging, Grace hesitated at first. Then she knelt beside Adah's chair, her hands on the upholstered arm. "I wanted to share somethin' wonderful-*gut* with Mamma. Something important." Tears welled up in her eyes. "And now I can't."

"Aw, honey-girl." She was fairly certain Grace's news involved a serious beau, but she wouldn't think of assuming Lettie's rightful place as confidante. "Your Mamma will be delighted 'bout your news when she returns. Whatever 'tis."

Shaking her head, Grace wiped away her tears. "I don't want to foster unkind feelings toward her, Mammi. Never . . ."

"Of course not." The sound of the day clock in the kitchen, its pendulum ticking, was unmistakable in the quiet. Adah's heart was ever so heavy for Grace . . . and for her daughter, too. "I'm sure she'll return right quick."

After a time, with Grace's help, Adah got up from her chair. She made her way to Lettie's gas stove and set the teakettle on the burner. "Would ya like some tea?"

"No." Grace said she had work to

catch up on. "If you'd like, I'll help finish
your quilt top later, though."

Adah nodded. "That'd be mighty
nice."

"All right, then." Grace headed for the
arched doorway and out into the hallway.

Adah heard the front door open and
close. *Poor, dear thing.*

Pushing her hankie back up her
sleeve, she was nervous about Lettie's
rash decision. More than anything, she
hoped Lettie hadn't gotten a bee in her
bonnet and let her curiosity overtake
her. She'd been known to be an impulsive sort. But now Lettie was older . . .
and a good deal wiser.

———

Moving through the morning like a
swimmer in a pond, tangled up in willow
roots, Grace longed to be free of the
mental weights—the wearisome questions. All of them devoid of answers.
She could not voice her concerns further to Dat or to Mammi Adah. She
worked quickly, yet carefully, on the quilt
with Mammi, glad her grandmother was

also silent. Deep in thought, no doubt, as they sat together in the cozy third-floor sewing room on Mammi's side of the house.

Later, when it came time to put food on the table at noon, Grace carried the baked chicken and rice casserole from the counter. She placed it near Dat's spot, the way Mamma always served the hot dish.

After the blessing, Mandy spoke up about Mamma again. "It's not like her to disappear in the daylight, too," she said once they'd helped themselves to the large casserole.

"Sure ain't." Adam looked up, then back down at his plate.

Dat said nothing, his eyes vacant as he occupied himself with buttering his bread and salting his green beans.

It wasn't until close to dessert that Adam asked, "Haven't we all known Mamma wasn't herself lately?"

Joe and Mandy nodded. "Jah, like she's not feelin' so well," Joe suggested.

Adam turned toward Dat. "Could she

be visitin' one of her sisters . . . for a bit of rest?"

Dat nodded slowly. "Might be."

"Did she say anything to you, Dat?" asked Mandy, her fork clinking on the plate as she set it down. "She would, wouldn't she? I mean, if she was goin' to go off visiting somewhere?"

"You'd think so." Joe glanced at Mandy while Adam's face grew more flushed by the second.

"None of us knows where Mamma is . . . or when she'll return," Grace intervened, studying first Adam and then Dat. She felt she must interject lest the talk get out of hand. No need to jump to conclusions.

"What should we tell our neighbors . . . our friends?" asked Mandy, her face knit into a tight frown. "With Preachin' being held here, everyone will know come Sunday . . . unless Mamma returns before then."

"I doubt she'll be back anytime soon," Dat surprised them by saying.

Grace gripped her fork. She'd assumed as much from the size of the suitcase Mamma had hauled up the road.

Dat continued. "Your mother wrote a note . . . to Grace."

Startled at having this dumped in her lap, Grace stiffened.

Mandy shook her head, as if uncomprehending. "Well, what did it say?"

Quickly, Grace replied, "Mamma didn't reveal where she was going or why . . . something 'bout not having the courage to leave if she talked with Dat . . . or us."

Grace saw her father's pained grimace.

Adam leaped up from his spot on the wooden bench, glaring at Dat. "Mamma didn't tell *you*?" He wore a fierce frown. "Why not?"

Their father shook his head.

"Was it 'cause she didn't think you'd listen?" Adam was red in the face now, his right foot planted on the bench as he bent forward.

Grace cringed, her feet curling tightly beneath the table.

"What'll we do without her?" Mandy sniffled.

"Oh, for pity's sake, Mandy," Adam said, raising his voice. "Ain't like you need takin' care of . . . or do ya?" He ran his hand through his thick shock of blond hair. "You're grown now. We all are."

Grace saw her opportunity. "Adam's right." She directed her comment to her sister. "Besides, this isn't the time to worry 'bout ourselves, jah?"

Dat set down his knife and fork and folded his hands as he would if he were ready for the final prayer. Yet they hadn't finished the main meal, let alone dessert. Leaning back in his chair, he slowly spoke in a low, measured tone, ignoring Adam's accusations. "Above all, we must pray for your mother's safety. That is what the Lord requires of us."

Mandy's face clearly registered her pain.

Dissatisfied with Dat's lack of response to Adam, Grace felt only frustration with her father's suggestion that they commit Mamma into Providential care. She wanted to know when their mother was coming home, for goodness' sake!

When they were washing dishes— Mandy was drying and chattering anx-

iously about where Mamma might be—
Grace merely listened to her sister, lost
in thought. Had her father no opinion
about what had transpired to make
Mamma leave?

Throughout the meal, Grace had noticed how he'd often stopped to swallow before speaking. That and the unmistakable misery in his eyes combined
to encourage Grace somewhat. In a peculiar sort of way, Dat's struggle gave
her heart. *He's missing Mamma, just like
the rest of us.*

She lifted the last plate out of the hot,
soapy water and began scrubbing the
large pots and pans, glad this chore was
nearly done.

The minute the last pan was dried,
Mandy flew out the door, not staying to
help sweep the floor or gather up the
trash. Secretly, though, Grace was
pleased to be alone.

She went to get all the throw rugs on
the first floor and lugged them out front,
draping them over the porch railing.
When they were lined up, she beat them
with the broom. With each blow, she
contemplated Henry's marriage pro-

posal, his reticent manner even at this most joyful moment.

"I'm fond of you," he'd told her.

Oh, how happy she'd been last night. Any thought of being passed over as a bride had vanished with his visit. And then, within hours, so much had changed. Now she pondered whether it wasn't best to talk to Henry about postponing the wedding, at least till Mamma could be present. Yet the wedding season was some months away. Surely her mother would come to her senses before then. Grace could only hope for that, but the contents of the letter—and Dat's bleak outlook—made her wonder.

As for Adam, she was sure he hadn't meant to lose his temper at the table. *So unlike him.* The whole family was on edge, and no wonder.

Yearning for peace, she remembered Becky's hummingbird birthday card, drawn with such care. She dried her hands and ran upstairs to look at it once again.

Unfettered by the earth and its woes, hummingbirds fly free.

Upstairs, she was surprised to see

Mamma's letter lying on her dresser.
She sat down with it, anxious to read
her mother's words yet again, searching
each one for an answer.

———

The rhythmic sway of the train lulled
Lettie into a more restful state than
she'd experienced since first boarding.
Closing her eyes, she attempted to
block out the memory of Grace's cries
on the road. *"Mamma, please . . . don't
leave!"*

She shuddered. She'd refused her
dear girl, of all horrid things. Grace
would surely question everything Lettie
had written in the hasty letter, based on
her apparent rejection. And how un-
thinking she had been, failing to write in
Grace's birthday card till Mandy had
come waving it at her, all upset. To think
she'd chosen to run off to the phone
shanty to call for a driver instead of
staying put at home, where she could
have signed it.

What's come over me?

She dared to think of her husband;
she hadn't even taken time to write a

good-bye note to him. She'd simply run out of time . . . and felt helpless to put her thoughts into words. Well, on paper anyway.

She pressed her book—a collection of favorite poems—close to her heart. She'd been ever so nervous about not having made a reservation ahead of time for the 1:52 PM departure for Pittsburg. How could she, without causing more of a ruckus than she already had? And dear Grace had seen her go— unthinkable!

I never wanted that.

Suddenly she felt lightheaded—she'd allowed herself only a few hours of sleep, then sat in the train station for hours, eating her sack lunch there, too, and reading from the poetry book. More than six hours of waiting in all—simply because she could never have slipped away with a suitcase in broad daylight.

Even now, rest was elusive. Weary from planning this day, Lettie offered a prayer for strength. *Help me, Lord, to do this difficult thing.*

She had a long trip ahead. Sighing, she opened the book to its flyleaf and read the inscription written so very long ago. *On your sixteenth birthday.*

She pressed her lips firmly together to keep them from trembling. To keep the tears in check.

Gently she placed her hand on the precious words: *To my dearest Lettie . . . with all my love, Samuel.*

chapter

sixteen

Heather detested the evening rush hour, but she made good use of her time while sitting in bumper-to-bumper traffic, typing out a text message and sending it to Devon's email address. He'd get it later, once he was released from the hospital.

Not hearing anything more from his buddy Don was both nerve-racking and reassuring. Heather hoped her fiancé would defy the viral infection and soon return to health once again.

As terrific as I feel . . . She was still baffled by her energy level and good appetite. Mom had always said you were healthy if you were hungry.

The traffic inched forward and she flicked on the radio to drown out her worry for Devon . . . and her own insidious apprehension.

She'd hung around longer than she'd planned after her exam and now it was close to five-thirty. No wonder she was parked here on I-64. She'd run into several classmates and had mentioned her plans to go north next week, instead of sticking around for the summer to finish her thesis, like most students in her program. Despite their pleas—*"Aw, stay with us ... we'll do the beach and boardwalk scene"*—she dug in her heels, not wavering.

She didn't have the heart to dampen their enthusiasm by dumping the terminally ill news on them. Who would believe it anyway? Heather was having a hard time buying the doctor's diagnosis herself.

When she finally arrived home, tired of fighting traffic, she called for her dad, on the off chance he'd come home early. She wandered through the house, looking for signs of life. But his bed was still unmade and the same socks were strewn on the floor near his bureau. "Weird," she said, going into the master bathroom and finding his shaving kit missing. *Must be on a business trip and forgot to tell me.*

If true, she was disturbed at the thought. Her father came and went quite a lot, but since she'd moved back home, he'd never before neglected to tell her about an overnight trip. After Mom had passed away, he'd poured himself into his work more than ever, keeping constantly preoccupied—his way of dealing with grief. Most of the time, the approach seemed to work for him.

Going into the den now, she noticed his executive-style desk looked the same as it had the other day, when she'd come searching for the Lancaster County brochures and stopped to admire her mother's picture.

She felt uneasy not knowing her dad's whereabouts and then realized she'd intended to do the same thing, taking off for Pennsylvania without letting him know.

At least I planned to leave a note!

"Am I that disconnected from my own dad?" she whispered.

Moe and Igor came padding into the

room, both meowing. She reached down and picked Moe up, holding him in front of her face and looking into his copper-colored eyes. "Have you seen Dad lately?"

Moe stared back.

"Okay . . . don't tell me." She laughed softly, yet inwardly, she sensed something amiss. But she had little time to finish studying for her last exam tomorrow, although she felt confident she was ready.

If Dad didn't show up in the next couple of days, she would call him, find out where he was holed up. Or send a text message, even though he disliked the whole idea of "reverting" to what he said was an archaic shorthand—*"too slow,"* he often joked with her, insisting she stick with a phone call. *"So nineties,"* she'd reply. At this, he'd roll his eyes and she'd pretend to be appalled until he let loose his infectious laughter.

Slipping into her dad's desk chair, Heather leaned back as she swiveled around in a full circle. She touched his lamp and the light came on—simple . . . easy—just the way he liked things.

Mom's death had been much too complicated. It had really messed up everything about their lives.

But the final trip she and Mom had taken to Lancaster County had been effortless. Things had fallen into place so quickly, Mom had even remarked about it—how often did anyone acquire such perfect accommodations at the last minute? The day before they'd headed out by car, Mom had urged her to take along a nice dress and heels.

"We're going dancing?" Heather had joked, knowing better.

"We're going to celebrate us, and that's all I'll say." Her mother had been comically mysterious. Heather had played along, enjoying the fun.

Moe jumped up into her lap, interrupting her reminiscing. "Hey, you!" She stroked his neck and he stretched forward, leaning hard against her fingers. "I'll miss you . . . and Igor. You'll be good for the cat-sitter, right?"

Not responding with his usual meowsy reply, he snuggled close as she hugged him. She was glad she'd already made the call to the Lancaster naturopath. Getting in for an appointment would take nearly a full month, but she'd asked to be put on a waiting list. You never knew when someone might cancel.

———

After evening prayers, Grace caught Adam's sleeve before he headed to the stairs. "Let's go walkin' sometime tomorrow," she said.

"I'll have to see." He gave her a thoughtful smile. "You goin' to be all right?" he whispered.

She shrugged. "Honestly, I think someone should go and look for Mamma."

His eyes searched hers. "Remember what Dat said, though?"

"Jah." While she would indeed pray for Mamma's safety, she could hardly stand the thought of doing nothing else.

"Can we talk 'bout it tomorrow?" he asked.

"Sure . . . whenever you're free." She watched him hurry up the stairs, feeling renewed sadness at the thought of losing him to marriage. Not as depressing as losing Mamma's presence from home but a great loss all the same.

Yet tomorrow was a new day, as Mamma often said in an attempt to soften the blow of things gone awry.

Grace saw that Dat had gone outside instead of retiring for the night like the rest of the family. She could only imagine the pain of rejection *he* must be feeling.

After today, everyone will know Mamma's gone.

In time, no doubt, the bishop would come to speak privately with Dat. Deacon Amos, too—all the ministerial brethren would converge here, as was their way.

Missing Mamma, she went to her parents' bedroom yet again and slid open the drawer where her mother's hankies were kept. The slight scent of her sachets wafted upward. She'd looked for Mamma's things earlier today, but just now she wanted to breathe in the faint scent left over from the plump pillows of potpourri her mother was so fond of. All of them gone, just like Mamma's personal items.

Turning to look around the room, Grace cried for the loneliness her mother must have experienced. What was in Mamma's mind and heart that made her believe she had to go away? The question plagued her as she turned toward the bookcase—Mamma's pride and joy, she'd always said of it—hand-made by Dat not long after they'd become betrothed.

Bending down, she noticed a space where several books had stood. Mamma had often talked of her beloved poetry, though not recently. Grace could see that a few, perhaps two or three volumes, were missing.

She must've taken them along. Why? Were they more precious than her own children?

Grace dried her eyes and left for her room.

———

Unable to sleep, Adah sat up in bed, careful not to disturb Jakob. Dear man, he had not felt well all day. Truth be told, neither had she. The whole house seemed to resound with Lettie's absence.

She couldn't help but wonder where her willful daughter was sleeping this night. Any number of places, she assumed. Lettie had as many Plain relatives as the rest of them. Enough to form an entire church district if all of the aunts, uncles, and first cousins were to assemble in one place. And dozens of second cousins were scattered out all over the country—some in Holmes and Wayne counties in Ohio, and a good many in Indiana, too. She wished she'd kept in touch with some of her own first cousins who might have a clue as to Lettie's whereabouts—*if* Lettie had indeed gone to visit one of them. Adah was not at all eager to get the rumor mill churning. But heavens, would it be stirred up, beginning tomorrow, when Lettie's sisters Mary Beth and Lavina arrived to help wash down walls and whatnot to get Judah's side of the house ready for worship this coming Sunday.

Didn't Lettie consider this? Adah knew she mustn't permit herself to fall into the snare of aggravation, which led too quickly to anger. *Let not the sun go down upon your wrath,* from Ephesians, was one of the first verses her own mother, Esther Mae, had taught her so many years ago.

Adah refused to let her daughter's foolishness dictate her emotions, no matter that she wished to goodness she hadn't been so awful harsh with Lettie down through the years. Or so insistent, back when.

———

Nighttime had always been the pits during her mom's excruciating disease, especially the final weeks. Even now, as Heather brushed her teeth and prepared for bed, she had difficulty dismissing the memories of her own insomnia during that wretched time. Alarmed by her mom's steady decline, there were nights when Heather had wandered into the family room, only to find Mom reclining on the sectional, her legs stretched the full length of it, her head propped up. Always, she wore her pale pink fleece robe, even though the temperature in the house felt comfortable to everyone else. But Mom's circulation was poor, and she was continually chilly, particularly at night.

One evening, Heather had tucked her feet under her and sat up late, keeping her mother company long into the dark hours, trying not to think about the inevitable. In spite of her attempts to divert her mom's thoughts, somehow they managed to revisit the diagnosis—the ugly way it had slashed into their lives. *"My good life,"* Mom said, not in defiance but doing her best to embrace the reality of her cancer.

Heather had wanted to carry some of the suffering, thinking that if her mother's debilitating pain was so intense that it could seep over into her daughter's emotions, Heather just might be able to impart something positive in return. So she'd offered her optimism. They were like vessels spilling over onto each other—one draining herself of suffering, one filling the other's heart with hope. And so they'd passed those final fragile months.

Heather had memorized the words her mother had written in a "just be-cause" card some weeks before her passing: *I've always felt so well loved by you, Heather. What a beautiful mother-daughter bond we've had. In so many ways, you've taught me how to love more fully . . . as a parent and as a friend. With love, Mom.*

Presently Heather pulled up the blan-ket, encouraging both Moe and Igor to hop onto it. She smiled at them as their glowing eyes stared her down. "You guys are the best little pals ever," she said, turning out the light.

Tomorrow she hoped to hear again from Devon's buddy Don, anxious for an update. *Surely if he was worse, I would have heard.*

When she dreamed, both Devon and her mom were talking together, and she woke with a start, afraid the dream had some predictive meaning.

No . . . She groaned and reached to move Moe closer, until once again she fell asleep.

———

Lettie felt the sway of the train, the near-mesmerizing rhythm of the *clackety-clack* of wheels on the rails. She'd endured the stares of Englischers and the strong smell of cigarette smoke in Pittsburg upon disembarking. Thankfully, she had little trouble locating her second train. The connection in Pittsburg had been more nerve-racking than her boarding in Lancaster—so many more passengers. She'd found herself breathing a prayer when her fear began to rise, and somehow, she'd kept her wits.

Settling deeper into her coach seat, she exhaled, glad for the empty spot beside her on the train to Alliance, Ohio. Her head bobbed repeatedly until she eventually yielded to the sandpaper feel beneath her eyelids and fell asleep at last.

While she slept, she dreamed happily of bygone days—of gripping the softball bat in her youthful hands . . . swinging it hard and hearing the *crack* as the ball connected with the wood. That ball had sailed high over the girls' outhouse, sending the boys jumping the fence.

They were late for the clanging bell at the end of recess.

In her dream, she was a tomboy once again, just as she'd been right into her early teens. But that had changed after Samuel Graber's twinkling hazel eyes met hers during eighth grade, before graduation their final year at the Amish schoolhouse. Oh, how her heart had ached with longing when he looked her way and smiled across the one-room school. Samuel . . . her first true love.

When Lettie awakened, the train was pulling into the Alliance station, and she realized yet again just what she'd done to get this far. Looking at her watch, she saw that it was 1:30 AM. Most likely Judah would be up, spending time in the barn with his newborn lambs, a chore he hadn't asked her to share of late. She'd had her own responsibilities indoors.

Responsibilities I've left behind . . .

Her guilty conscience gnawed at her as she reached for her book and woolen shawl, gathering up the things she'd brought on board. All too soon, a time of reckoning would come.

chapter

seventeen

"Mamma won't be back anytime soon," Dat kept saying in the dream. Over and over the phrase was repeated till Grace awakened with a start. It was well after midnight, and she rose and reached for her robe at the foot of her bed.

Creeping down the steps and into the kitchen, she noticed the door was ajar, and peering out, she saw that the barn door was open, as well. Still feeling drowsy, she decided to take a look. In the past, they'd had lambs stolen—not by anyone among the People, she was sure, but newborn lambs had gone missing all the same.

Moving slowly across the backyard, she took in the night sky. Was Mamma looking at the moon and the sweep of stars tonight, too? Somewhere . . . wherever she'd run off to?

More than likely at this hour, her mother was fast asleep, and Grace wished she, too, might fall into a peaceful slumber. But a bitter root had taken hold in her, planted when Mamma did not turn to acknowledge her out on the road. She knew enough not to nurture it, to allow the memory to entangle her heart. Even so, the knowing and the doing were two different things.

Surprised to hear her father's voice, tentative and low, coming from the barn, she went in search of him and caught her breath when she spotted his dim silhouette, there in the faint light of the moon. He stood near Willow, his hand stroking her long neck. "Things are in a terrible mess, old girl," he confessed. " 'Tis my fault . . . and there's no goin' back."

Grace had never known her father to express himself so openly to anyone. Yet there he was near beautiful Willow, pouring out his regret.

She stepped back against the gate. Would there be no end to her family's pain?

———

Hours later, Grace awakened in her bed, still mulling over what she'd witnessed in the barn. She wished the dawn away as she lay stretching in her bed—she possessed little courage for what was sure to be a difficult day ahead, what with two of Mamma's older sisters coming. Lavina and younger sister Mary Beth were expected to arrive after breakfast. They would surely wonder why everyone in the house looked to be in mourning. She was fearful, too, of their reaction—what would they think? Would Mamma be harshly judged?

In her mistiness, Grace dozed off again. When the alarm awakened her, she sat up and reached for the Good Book, turning to the Psalms. Mamma had always loved reading them. *"Scripture set to poetry,"* she liked to say.

Grace finished and marked her place, pondering her upcoming talk with Adam. She wondered what he would advise about her engagement to Henry during such a time as this. Of course, by tomorrow the grapevine might already be rippling with the news of Mamma . . . so it wouldn't surprise her if it was Henry who decided to postpone their wedding, or even cut off their engagement. She truly hoped he would see fit to stand by her for as long as it took.

She leaned up on her elbows and peered into the dresser mirror. With Mamma gone, it somehow seemed all right to sit and stare at herself. So much had altered so quickly. She thought again of Dat speaking to Willow, of all peculiar things.

When Willow dies, many secrets will go with her, she thought as she got out of bed to brush her hair. She moved to the window, brush in hand, and raised up the blind. Looking out, she remembered the thrill of seeing Henry's light swirling on the windowpane just the night before last. Setting her brush on the windowsill, she leaned down and opened the window, then knelt there. Deeply, she breathed in the clean morning air. The faint scent of fresh beeswax wafted downwind from their beekeeping neighbors across the road.

She stayed on her knees till they ached. What had kept Mamma from saying she was leaving that night, here in the room where Grace had been so eager to listen? Instead, Mamma had written a puzzling letter . . . one that revealed so little.

She picked up her brush and finished counting the strokes, watching for a glimpse of a hummingbird just outside the window.

Judah moved slowly among his grazing sheep and the older lambs. Voices came from the road, and he looked to see two of Lettie's sisters—Mary Beth and Lavina—coming this way from the Riehls' place. He surmised their driver had dropped them off after picking up Andy, who'd planned to visit an ailing brother at Lancaster General Hospital.

Hearing the women's animated chatter, Judah was certain they knew nothing of Lettie's sudden and mysterious departure. He could only imagine how quickly their lightheartedness might turn to shock, and he wished he might soften the wallop they were soon to receive. It made not a lick of sense, Lettie's going away. Especially not with all the new lambs coming on.

Lettie's sisters continued their prattle as they made the turn toward the driveway. They waved to Adam and Joe, hauling feed, and his sons waved back, glancing at each other as if concerned for what their mother's sisters were about to discover.

Watching the women make their way toward the house, Judah pushed his hands into his pockets. Steeling his resolve, he hurried across the pasture to the side yard.

From the kitchen window, Grace saw her aunts headed toward the door. She had been watching for them and was surprised to see Dat running across the walk, calling to her aunts. She heard him ask if he might speak with them "before you's head inside."

She was tempted to stay right there, but she went upstairs to overhear her father's explanation through the open hallway window.

Dat's tone was ever so solemn as he relayed the news, sparing them all but the most pertinent details. "I'm sorry to have to be the one to tell ya," he said finally.

"Well, what the world's wrong with Lettie?" *Aendi* Lavina whimpered softly.

"Is she just wore out, maybe?" asked Mary Beth.

"You'll go and find her, won't ya, Judah?" Lavina asked, sounding all out of sorts.

Grace had wondered that, too, and waited for Dat to continue, but it was Mary Beth who spoke next. "Our Lettie's just upset, ain't so? What else could it be?"

"Hard to know," Dat replied, ending the conversation with an awkward thanks for their help today. He turned and headed for the barn, leaving Mamma's sisters to stand on the stoop, blowing their noses and drying their eyes.

They were whispering to each other now. "You don't think Lettie's first beau has surfaced, do ya?" Lavina said—at least that's what Grace thought she heard.

What a wretched thing to say! She refused to think less than respectfully of Mamma. Surely no one threatened her devotion to Dat!

When she heard the kitchen door open, Grace hurried downstairs to meet them, plastering on a smile.

Aunt Mary Beth had on her rattiest old brown dress and apron, but her hair looked nice and clean, pulled back in the usual tight hair bun, her Kapp strings tied loosely in back. Aunt Lavina's dark brown hair was already coming free of its bun, stray strands falling on the sides as though she'd been in a hurry to put it up. She wore a maroon dress and faded black apron, her smile too broad for the news she'd just received.

"Denki for comin' to help redd up," Grace said, suddenly conscious of the lump that threatened her voice.

"Oh, we're mighty glad to . . . 'specially now." Mary Beth's eyes locked with Grace's. "Let's get started upstairs."

Grace nodded. "Mammi Adah will be over in short order; she'll lend a hand. So will Mandy."

"Jah, *gut* . . . the more, the merrier," said Lavina. She caught herself and said, "Ach, sorry."

Struggling to remain composed, Grace called for Mandy, who promptly came over from the other side of the house. "Time to fill the buckets with lots of warm, soapy water. We've got plenty of scrubbin' to do," she said as the aunts hugged and kissed Mandy more fondly than Grace had ever remembered.

Mandy's chin quivered when Mary Beth put her arm around her. "Now, honey-girl, you just remember how much your mamma loves you. Always has."

"And always will," added Lavina.

Mandy nodded tearfully. But her eyes asked the question they all were thinking: *Then why would she leave?*

Lavina took some old rags out of the cupboard. "We've got work to do."

Grace reached a hand to Mandy. "Mamma always said to work hard when things are troubling, ain't so?"

Mandy nodded and followed dutifully, dabbing at her nose with a hankie. And at that moment, Grace felt as if she'd wholly taken over her mother's place, uncomfortable though it was.

————

Around ten-thirty, Grace and the other women stopped washing and sweeping and began cooking the noon meal. Earlier, Grace had laid out three pounds of lean ground beef to thaw—meat they'd purchased from the Stoltzfus cousins. She planned to make porcupine meatballs using Mamma's pressure cooker. Mandy set to peeling potatoes, and Mary Beth and Lavina brought up canned vegetables—asparagus, corn, and beets—from the cold cellar.

Gut, thought Grace, wanting to provide a delicious dinner for her father and brothers. "Be sure and invite Dawdi and Mammi over to eat with us, too," Grace told Mandy. She'd kept a watchful eye on her sister all morning.

It helps to have Mamma's sisters here, she thought.

"We'll have us a feast," Mandy said, offering a brief smile at Grace, who began to shape the meatballs.

A dinner without our mother . . .

She wondered if Mamma was safe and sound. Everything felt so strange and out of whack without her. Grace supposed they'd feel this way for as long as Mamma was gone from them, however long that might be.

chapter

---

eighteen

Every decorative plate and each of Mamma's teacups and saucers had been washed and dried and put back in their exact locations on the sideboard and china hutch. The furniture was polished to a sheen, and overall the house was spotless . . . gleaming from the rafters down to the smallest corner. Their abode was well prepared to become the temporary house of worship on Sunday. Now all Grace needed were cold cuts and freshly baked bread to serve two hundred souls—that and the benches and the old hymnals the bench wagon would bring tomorrow evening.

Grace had been particularly grateful for the extra cleaning help earlier, and although presently it was a bit chilly outdoors, she pulled on a sweater and went to sit on the front porch swing.

There, sitting where Mamma had sat three evenings ago, she waited for Adam to finish up his after-supper chores.

She could easily have gone to see Becky, but she wanted to talk with her brother first. Mandy was much too upset to attempt any sort of meaningful communication, on the verge of tears much of the time. Grace had offered understanding to her sensitive sister—all of them had. It was hard to see Mandy cry.

All day Lavina and Mary Beth had carried their dread and disbelief in their eyes, the color nearly all washed out. Yet they'd worked as hard as they had every other time before Preaching service here. By now they would have surely whispered their worries to their husbands at home and possibly their older children, who, in turn, would tell others. Soon, all of Bird-in-Hand would hear of Lettie Byler's departure. And there was very little, if anything, Grace could do about it.

"Hullo there, sis."

She jumped, startled out of her

reverie, and turned to see Adam draping his long arms over the porch railing.

"Ach, you must be ready, then?" She felt relieved to see him, knowing she could fully share her heart.

He nodded. "We'd better get goin' before I'm too tired to put one foot in front of the other. These nights of lambin' are catching up with me."

She rose and hurried down the porch steps to the lawn. "Where should we walk?"

He paused to deliberate, then suggested, "Let's take Sassy instead and go for a root beer."

"Sure, I'll forfeit the walk—for soda pop!"

Sassy was already hitched to the enclosed family buggy. Grace was glad Adam had thought to take that instead of his open courting buggy. She felt self-conscious just thinking about being seen out riding when the Amish grapevine might already be whispering about Mamma.

"So your hard work's finished, ain't?" he asked, referring to the thorough housecleaning.

"Sure feels *gut,* I'll say."

"And dinner was mighty tasty at noon, too." He let the reins lie loose on his knees. "You're nearly as *gut* a cook as—"

"Adam, don't say that," she broke in.

He frowned, shaking his head. "Honestly, I almost forgot Mamma was gone."

Naturally he would say that. He and Dat and Joe worked long hours outdoors this time of year, so Mamma's not being around wouldn't affect them as much as it did her and Mandy.

And Mammi Adah.

"Any idea where she might be?" Adam turned toward her, his straw hat tipped back.

"No." Grace shook her head. "This sort of thing doesn't happen amongst the People."

"And a mighty *gut* thing, too."

She wasn't about to divulge what Aunt Lavina had said to her sister. No point in that. Besides, it couldn't possibly be true—Mamma interested in an old beau?

"Dat's more than ferhoodled." Adam

removed his hat and set it on his leg. "I've never seen him so confused." He explained that he'd had to rewrite some of the feeding charts today, erasing many of Dat's entries. "Ain't at all himself."

"I can't imagine what he's feelin'."

Adam shook his head. "Me neither."

The horse pulled the buggy into the drive-through at the fast food place, where they stopped and placed their order for a single root beer. "You want one straw?" Adam asked.

"I'd like my own, please," she said, smiling. Her brother must've momentarily thought they were going to share, like he probably did with Priscilla. Like Grace did sometimes with Henry. "You're as ferhoodled as Dat."

He laughed, a light glinting in his blue eyes. "Fact is, we're all a mess, jah?"

She couldn't agree more.

When he handed her the frosty root beer, she took a long, slow drink. As they headed back, she soon began to shiver from the cold beverage. "I do hope *you'll* be happy when you're married, Adam," she said softly.

Happier than Mamma . . .

"And you, too." He smiled. "I'd best be fessin' up, Grace."

"Oh?"

"Well, your Henry told me he was comin' to visit the other night. He swore me to secrecy a few days before."

She listened, not sure what to say. Was Henry's and her courtship becoming common knowledge?

"So did he ask you?"

She nodded. "Jah, he did."

Adam stared at her. "And . . . ?"

She laughed at his eagerness. "I accepted, but now . . . with Mamma gone away and all, I wonder if we shouldn't hold off for a while."

"Aw, don't be takin' back your word, Gracie. What sort of girl does that?"

Sighing, she realized he hadn't understood. "I didn't say I was breakin' it off with him. Just that things are up in the air now."

"Jah, but do you think Mamma will be gone that long?"

"From what little he's said, Dat seems to think so."

Adam grimaced. "Still, I think you'll be

all right with Henry," he said, his tone confident. "Let Dat and Mamma's problems stay put with them. You . . . me, we have our whole lives ahead of us, Gracie. And just think—our children will be closer than your average cousins. I mean, with you marrying Priscilla's brother and all. It'll be fun raisin' them together. Nearly like siblings, don't ya think?"

For once, he hadn't heard her heart. She wasn't talking about breaking her engagement, rather simply waiting till she was sure Mamma'd be there for the wedding. All Adam seemed to care about was their marrying siblings—and this fall, too—so that Adam's children with Priscilla would be close cousins to Henry's and her own.

Grace sighed inwardly. *I should've kept my thoughts to myself.*

———

Distracted during evening prayers later, Grace pondered her conversation with Adam. Because of his failure to understand her, she thought it best not to tell of her new idea brewing. Her mind was already in a whirl, flying back to the day of the barn raising—the day that had brought on so many changes.

Dat seemed lost in a haze, too busy with daily chores to actively search for their mother. Worse, he seemed re-signed to her absence, hoping for the best but braced for the worst.

Hoping was far better, and in addition to her rote prayer, Grace whispered, *Please help us know what to do, Lord. Amen.*

Her idea came back to her: What if she could actually find Mamma—talk to her and convince her to return home?

At first the notion had struck her as silly. Other than horse and buggy—or calling for a hired driver—she had no access to transportation. Her ongoing domestic responsibilities, indoors and out, presented another problem—it wouldn't be fair to leave when Dat was so shorthanded with the lambing.

Even so, Grace felt she ought to do something, small though it might be.

With how close Mamma and Aunt Naomi always were, I wonder if Uncle Ike knows anything. Or maybe I should start by finding out who Mamma went walking with that day of the barn raising.

Despite her sadness, Grace found a sense of anticipation, even hope in this. The woe-is-me pit of misery Mandy and Dat had fallen into was not for her. She would rise to the occasion and find their mother, bringing her home where she belonged. Thinking back to Aunt Lavina's comment, Grace decided to talk first with Mammi Adah. She had a feeling her grandmother knew more than she was saying.

Possibly a lot more.

———

Saturday morning Grace and Mandy, along with Mammi Adah, baked oodles of loaves of bread for the common meal tomorrow, to be served following Preaching. All the while, Grace did her best to be attentive to Mandy. Before she left, Mamma had suggested that Mandy would need extra prodding, but Grace couldn't see doing that now. Grace fully understood her sister's sorrow but didn't dare let their loss freeze up her own ability to think and feel. Especially not with so much to be done before the Lord's Day. They were also hosting the bi-monthly Singing tomorrow evening, which meant Dat and her brothers would sweep out the whole second level of the barn this afternoon.

Along with putting in her hours at Eli's store, Grace would now have to juggle doing all that Mamma had done, too. Monday's day of washing and ironing would be followed by Tuesday's mending and darning of socks, as well as finishing up any stray ironing. Dat and her brothers would need socks without holes in them for the upcoming sheep-shearing day next week. The sheep's heavy coats required cutting before the summer, when they would shed much of the valuable wool. The sheep would also have their hooves clipped at the time of that all-day affair.

As for herself, the early morning hours next Wednesday would be spent weeding the family and charity vegetable gardens, as well as the long rows of berry bushes all along the rock wall out back. Thursday was the only weekday Grace might squeeze in time to go down to

Bart, assuming her talk with Mammi didn't turn up enough to go on. She shuddered at the thought of asking questions about her mother, yet she would not shirk from it.

Has the grapevine found its way that far south?

Prior to making that trip, though, she first wanted to visit Uncle Ike Peachey. After all, Mamma had gone through all of Naomi's books and personal things, carrying home several poetry books, some of which were now missing. Grace had read from some of them, but she couldn't see why they were so highly cherished by her mother.

Do they have something to do with a first beau? She hated to even think the thought.

Perhaps now, since four years had passed since Aunt Naomi's death, her husband might be willing to give Grace something more to go on.

She sighed. Truly the biggest hurdle in all this was her daily chores. Next Friday she and Mandy would clean this big old house once again, and Saturday was another baking day. And next Sunday, although not a Preaching day, was a time set aside to rest, read, write letters, and go visiting relatives and friends— the latter something they usually did as a family.

Presently, Grace turned her attention to starting the noon meal while the many loaves of bread cooled. Mandy would have to wash and dry dishes on her own, since Grace was scheduled to work at Eli's this afternoon. How strange it would be to venture away from the house alone for the first time since rushing up the road after Mamma.

She glanced at Mandy, glad her sister would be sheltered here at home from the endless stream of questions. *For the time being.*

chapter

nineteen

The parking area at Eli's was filled with cars and Amish carriages alike. Suddenly wary, Grace smoothed her skirt and sat for a few seconds after they arrived, not budging.

Adam glanced at her kindly. "No matter what, Gracie, don't let the rumors sting you." He leaned forward, one hand holding both the driving lines connected to Sassy. "Mamma has a mind of her own—and what she's done, well, it's not what we'd do . . . not Dat, either." He looked away, glancing across the road to the east, then back. "So don't let the gossip hurt you is all I'm sayin'." He smiled, which gave her courage.

In the store, she signed in and set to work right away, holding her breath when Nancy and Sylvia Fisher—two Amish girls from her church district—

looked her way. She responded in kind when Ruthie Weaver waved and smiled across the store at her.

Remember what Adam said, she reminded herself. His words had the power to both sting and cheer her. He hadn't bothered to listen to her heart yesterday when they'd talked, but she wouldn't hold that against him, and she certainly didn't want to borrow trouble. They had more than enough of that already.

———

Grace was thankful Ruthie did not show her face that afternoon in the small room set aside for coffee breaks. She pressed the button on the water cooler, waiting while the paper cup filled. She then moved to the doorway to look out at the expanse of the store while she drank her water, its coldness seeping down inside her. She slipped away from the room while the other breaking employees talked a blue streak.

Strolling the back aisle of the store, she looked over the selection of herbs she'd recently inventoried. She knew which ones were reported to elevate the mood and was picking up a bottle of va-lerian root and a box of passion flower herb, thinking of her despairing sister, when Nancy Fisher slowly approached her.

Ach no . . . Grace groaned inwardly.

———

Adah turned her teacup around slowly, disturbed by the bewildering news Marian Riehl had shared. "It's be-yond me, what you're sayin'," she told her neighbor.

"Jah, 'tis hard to believe." Marian stirred more sugar into her tea. "I'd like to think there's no truth in it, but . . ."

"Martin Puckett, you say?" Adah frowned, stunned. "Seems like an hon-orable man . . . and a driver lots of folk hire."

"We've called him, too."

Adah stared at her. "You say he took Lettie to the train station in the wee hours?"

"That's what I heard."

"And he sat right with her, waiting for her train for how long?"

"Hours, was what was said. And the man's been gone ever since, too."

Adah shook her head. "Puh! Doesn't sound right to me."

The sun broke through the clouds and shone through the kitchen window, glinting off the edge of the gas range. Marian turned and looked outside, so dramatic was the change in the room's light. "But Lettie *was* known to—"

"No, now, you listen here," Adah said. "Lettie's married to Judah and has been for a good, long time. *Married,* I say."

"Then why on earth would she leave him?" Marian's words hung in the air.

Why, indeed? Adah pursed her lips.

Their time of tea and cookies was cut short when Jakob wandered in, looking bright-eyed from his afternoon nap. Adah was so relieved she let out an immense sigh, which Marian must have noticed, because she quickly pushed back her chair and excused herself for home.

———

"Frankly, I hate to even whisper what I heard," Nancy Fisher was saying.

"Well then, you best not," Grace replied, the bottle of valerian root still gripped in her hand.

Nancy's round face drooped, her frown creasing her brow. "All I'm askin' is, can any of this be true?" She continued recounting the rumors.

Martin Puckett held my mother's hand at the train station?

"Oh, this is ever so awkward," Nancy said.

Grace could hold back her frustration no longer. "Awkward for you, Nancy? I have no idea where you heard any of this nonsense, but if I were you, I'd be careful 'bout repeating things that are false."

"Well, is your mamma at home or not?" Nancy paused. "Priscilla Stahl says she's left. And Martin Puckett's nowhere to be found!"

Adam's fiancée's talking like that about her future mother-in-law?

Without a further word, Grace headed for the front door. She needed some air, lest she become as dizzy as Mammi

Adah had been earlier this week. The last thing she wanted was to be carried back to the coffee break room and stretched out on the small sofa, being fussed over.

———

"What on earth?" Jakob asked Adah while she carried the teacups and saucers to the sink. "Marian looked mighty befuddled."

"Well, I guess some folk have little to do but flap their tongues." She would not repeat what Marian had said she'd heard from Sadie Zook, whose Englischer cousin, Pete Bernhardt, had supposedly witnessed the distasteful scene.

Why was Lettie at the train station? Where'd she go, for pity's sake?

"Ain't becoming of Marian a'tall," he said, indicating he'd overheard at least part of their neighbor's accusation.

Adah nodded. The gossip their neighbor had relayed was downright malicious. The way Adah saw it, it was wise of her to come over and get things straight from the horse's mouth, so such talk could be brought to a standstill. Except that Jakob had interrupted them before she'd had a chance to set Marian straight.

Lettie is quite respectable, she thought defiantly. *At least now she is!*

Even these many years past, Adah remembered all too clearly how Lettie's behavior as a youth had felt like a smack in the face—*her* face. How many times had she caught her daughter in the haymow with that one fellow? Sure, they'd merely sat out there talking and reading poetry to each other, of all strange things. But they couldn't seem to stay apart for more than a day or so, and he'd be right back with his books. Word had it Samuel Graber was already on his way out of the church even then. He'd ended up renouncing Amish ways soon after, when his family had pulled up roots and left for another state. Even so, while they were courting, Lettie had never smiled so much in her life.

Oh, but Adah was delighted when the whole lot of them moved away. The thought of Lettie's first beau made her blood pressure rise. Adah was better off not contemplating the no-good boy. She reached for the dish towel, the cloth loose in her hand as she stared out the window to the west, spotting Judah out there carrying one of his baby lambs. A right good man, tending his sheep with such care. She'd never regretted Lettie's marrying him. Jakob, too, had observed all those years ago how conscientious and steady Judah Byler was. *Still is.* The fact that he said very little didn't bother them much—not compared to Samuel, who was yakking nearly all the time.

Thinking again of the outlandish rumors, Adah felt disgusted at the grapevine's speed and influence. *I'll march right over to Marian's tomorrow, after Preaching,* she decided. Someone had to put out the brush fire before it got to the ministers' ears.

But as she washed her delicate teacup, Adah couldn't help worrying that Lettie's reckless youth had caught up with her at last.

———

The pretty boardinghouse was set back from the road in a small hollow.

Lettie made herself read in her comfortable room, looking up to take in the view of towering maple trees that grew in a haphazard zigzag behind the three-story house. The sky was the color of the sea.

She set the book aside and went to sit at the small writing desk and picked up the pen, feeling its smoothness between her fingers. With everything in her, she wished she could simply call Judah and let him know she was all right.

Still weary from her travels, Lettie was glad she wasn't in the habit of making such journeys. What a long trip she'd taken, arriving in the middle of the night in Alliance, Ohio. And she'd sat and waited a good while for the driver the innkeepers had arranged at her request. It was another nearly hour-long car ride before she'd observed yesterday morning's sunrise in the picturesque town of Kidron, where she had made a reservation at this charming inn.

She tore out a single page from her writing tablet and pressed her pen to the page. *My dear family,* she wrote.

Would they believe she truly thought of them as dear and always had? It pained her to consider what they must be feeling and thinking now. They all would know of her disappearance, even her parents. She especially hated what it might do to them, frail as her father was. Even Mamm wasn't so strong now.

And Judah?

A large fist seemed to grip her heart. She could not write what she ought, no more than she had been able to say it to his face. Oh, she'd tried, but she hadn't the grit . . . nor, in the end, had he. Had it been better to spare him?

To think they'd bickered the night before her leaving. And what would it possibly accomplish now for Judah to read her explanation on a page? Wasn't the damage done?

She hadn't been able to open her heart to him, because any sharing felt like tossing words at a windmill. And, early on, given her despair over losing Samuel, she'd felt it best for Judah to be kept in the dark about her deep love for her first beau . . . and his for her. But being so detached from her own husband over the years had caused permanent harm to their marriage.

She crumpled up the stationery. This was not at all the right way to do things. She must simply wait and tell Judah to his face.

When I can help him fully understand, I will.

———

Needing something to quench his thirst, Judah walked toward the house early Saturday evening. He was halfway across the backyard when he saw the bench wagon coming. Deacon Amos rode high at the reins but did not remove his hat, nor did he wave, as was his usual way. Today his face was austere as he climbed down and tied up his horse.

Judah reached back and massaged his neck, the burning pain growing more intense each hour. Seeing Amos's grandsons jump down and start the process of unloading the benches, he pushed down his hat and strode forward.

The deacon's bringing the bench

wagon was no doubt intentional. *We'll have us a very different Lord's Day,* Judah thought, picking up one end of a long bench, which would also serve tomorrow as a tabletop. Adah, Grace, and Mandy had the food all lined up, Grace had told him, thanks to some help from Marian Riehl. He'd seen their kindly neighbor arrive earlier to visit with Adah and Jakob. *Could be she's gotten word about Lettie.*

Just now the air was stiff with undeclared inquiry. He was relieved when Adam and Joe came running out of the barn and pitched in to help. Soon, Grace and Mandy stepped outside, as well, wiping their hands on their aprons, having just finished up in the kitchen.

No one had yet spoken to him directly about the calamity that had befallen his household, but he sensed it coming now as Deacon Amos caught his eye, a severe frown on his sunburned face.

"After a bit, it'd be best if we moseyed out behind the barn," Amos said in a low voice.

He nodded. His wife had brought disgrace to the Byler name, and he'd have no choice but to own up to his own grim part in the quarrel. Surely that's all her departure was—Lettie's response to their unfinished argument. So many years of unspoken tension. She had done strange things before—hiding letters that came for her alone, for one.

She had behaved curiously about attending the barn raising, too, he recalled. Someone—he didn't know who—had put a bug in her ear about taking food down there. That much he knew. When she'd first talked about wanting to go, she hadn't included Grace in the plans. It had been Judah who had insisted if she was going that far, she ought not be alone with Martin Puckett. It just didn't look right. Not that he didn't trust Lettie—of course he did. It was the appearance of evil that weighed on him . . . so he'd sent Grace out the door with her.

Now, though, it was clear Lettie shouldn't have gone at all. She'd returned moody and agitated, unable to lie still for a moment's rest. Unable, it seemed, to even remain at home. *Where she belongs.*

He set down his end of the heavy bench in the front room and followed meekly as Amos made his way out the door and down the front porch steps. Amos walked briskly around the side yard, then waited for him to catch up as they neared the barn.

"Do you know where Lettie is?" Amos had never been one to hem or haw. His eyes held Judah's, unrelenting.

"No."

"She's run off, then?"

"Might be."

"And you have no idea where to?"

Judah shook his head.

"All right, then . . . I must bring up the rumors that're flyin'."

Puzzled, he braced himself.

"One of the local drivers, Martin Puckett, was last seen in Lancaster with your missus in the early mornin' hours this past Thursday. He also seems to have disappeared."

This was the first Judah had heard such a thing.

"Why do ya think Martin would accompany your wife somewhere, Judah?" Amos's slightly sunken gray eyes looked increasingly weary as he spoke, as if he hadn't slept much.

Truth was, Martin was one of the men Lettie felt most comfortable with driving her—Judah felt the same way. In his opinion, Martin was a fine man. And his Lettie had never given him any reason to doubt her fidelity.

"You'd have to ask Martin 'bout this," Judah replied.

Amos glared. "You ain't much help."

"Well, I know nothing 'bout it."

"Surely you realize that Lettie's rebellion is an outward show of disobedience to you, her husband, as well as to her parents, who raised her to be a God-fearing woman. We'll investigate this further." Amos turned away.

Judah matched the deacon's pace. He noticed Andy Riehl's horses out grazing, several of them standing head to tail.

"The ministerial brethren will be lookin' to me for a report of our discussion," Amos added.

"Do as you must," Judah said, uncertain why Amos seemed bent on trying to put the fear of God in him.

"Preacher Smucker will seek you out tomorrow, followin' the common meal."

Nodding, Judah said that was just fine. In all truth, he'd much prefer talking things over with Josiah, the younger of their two preachers, if he was to own up to his fault in the matter. No sense putting off that confession. Some ministers in other districts could be downright domineering, even specifying how often the marital bed was to be used for the purpose of procreation—but neither of their preachers was that outspoken. Still, Judah knew he had some personal fessing up to do.

chapter

twenty

Grace stood beside her grandparents' front room window, watching two squirrels give chase. They pattered across the front walk, up the steps, and over to the porch swing. Anymore, each time she looked at the swing, she thought of Mamma.

"What's on your mind?" her grandmother asked from her chair behind Grace.

Turning, she went to sit next to Mammi Adah, watching the tatting hook fairly fly across the border of a pretty yellow hankie. Her own birthday handkerchief had not been used at all since the wonderful supper Mamma had cooked. Grace had nearly forgotten about it and her other gifts. Nearly everything had stopped when her mother had gone away.

"I heard some awful things today," Grace whispered.

A softness came over her grandmother's wrinkled face. "I think I might've heard some of that, too."

"Well, it ain't true . . . is it? Mamma'd never do such a thing." Something powerful rose up in Grace. "I'm goin' to go and talk to Dat's cousins, the Stoltzfuses, down south."

"Ach, why?"

"Because surely one of them knows who all was there for the March barn raising."

Mammi's face fell.

"There was a woman I'd never seen before."

"Why, sure . . . a *gut* many folk, I 'spect." Mammi's voice sounded strained.

"Jah, but this woman seemed to know Mamma. She went off walkin' with her."

Mammi's tatting hook hung loose in her hand as she took that in for a moment. Then she asked, "Do ya recall what she looked like?"

"Not sure I can describe her, really.

Her Kapp was altogether different from any around here, so I figured she was from elsewhere, but I don't know for sure." She sighed. "Frankly, I don't know at all."

"And that's why you want to see your father's cousins?"

Grace wondered why Mammi Adah was so full of questions. "Ach, you should've seen Mamma jump up during the noon meal to go to her."

"So ya think there might be a connection 'tween that day—and the strange woman—and your mother's leaving?"

"Sure seems like it." She hadn't meant to sound wavering, but she hadn't expected her grandmother to take such a disbelieving tone.

"Oh, Grace, I hate to dampen your spirits, but I just don't see how that can be."

"Well, I want to find Mamma."

"Why, of course you do . . . we *all* do."

Her grandmother's petite features and light hair made her look nearly angelic. Or at least like some of the delicate pictures of angels Grace had seen in one of the poetry books Mamma had brought home from Aunt Naomi's bookshelf. One of the missing books, in fact.

Grace scratched her head through her Kapp. "You must not think it's a *gut* idea, then?"

"I'm saying we ought to leave your Mamma be" came the surprising response.

"Maybe she just needs rest, jah?" Grace suggested. After all, Mammi Adah should know Mamma best . . . aside from Dat.

"Well, she doesn't need you or anyone beggin' her to come home, I daresay."

Grace was astonished. "So ya think she'll return on her own?"

"Perhaps . . . when she's ready."

Fear pricked her chest, making it suddenly tight . . . so tight Grace thought she might not be able to draw her next breath.

What exactly does Mammi Adah know?

Once Grace left, Adah went straight to the kitchen. She stood at the sink and ran cold water over her wrists, hoping to slow her pulse. Why should Grace, or anyone, go looking for Lettie? Wasn't there too much to be done here? And wouldn't Grace risk losing her job at Eli's?

The coolness soothed her as she leaned against the sink, staring out at the two-story barn beyond the yard. Ever so slowly, she began to feel calmer. No, all the work here was not the biggest argument against Grace's searching for Lettie. Not at all.

She wiped her hands on a small towel, then patted her face, as well. Calling for Jakob, she made her way upstairs to find her husband reading the Sugarcreek-based paper, *The Budget.* "We might have us a problem," she said, recounting Grace's earlier announcement.

"Well, she's Lettie's daughter, so there's no stoppin' her." Jakob looked up with worried eyes.

She sat in the chair next to him, wishing Lettie had just stayed put. This was more than a mere complication. "We need to discourage Grace somehow."

"Jah." He closed the paper and

folded it in half. "No tellin' what poor Gracie might discover out there."

She gasped. "So you must think Lettie's gone back to Ohio?"

"We live life as though it matters, jah?" he said mildly. "And since we believe it does matter . . . then in Lettie's mind *all* of it must count for something."

She understood perfectly. And it was precisely what she feared . . . that Lettie was suddenly determined to undo her past. "Do ya think she's goin' to make things right, once and for all?"

"What other explanation is there?" he asked, his chest rising and falling rapidly.

She hadn't known until now how much she looked to Jakob for his opinion. How much she depended on his levelheaded point of view . . . his cautious yet deliberate manner. If only she'd paid more attention to his advice on handling Lettie's teenage whims.

Given the chance, Adah realized she'd go back and do everything differently. Just as she feared Lettie had now decided to do.

Lord, help her!

Grace headed outside to see how many more dozens of hymnals were yet to be unloaded. Deep in thought, she inadvertently brushed against Mandy, not seeing her.

"Ach, Gracie?"

She turned.

"You ain't ignorin' me, are ya?" Mandy's face scrunched up.

"Sorry, sister." She touched Mandy's arm. "You all right?"

"Truthfully, I've never . . ."

"Aw, Mandy." She led her around to the front porch. "Let's sit awhile."

Mandy chose Mamma's spot on the porch swing, and Grace sat across from her in the wicker chair, Mammi Adah's favorite. "Now, tell me, what's a-matter?"

"What *isn't*?" Mandy muttered, not looking at her. "Things are even worse than I feared. It's all over the place that Mamma has run off with another man."

Grace folded her arms tightly. "You can't believe everything you hear," she said. "We have to cling to what we know, Mandy. Remember that."

"But nearly everyone's sayin' it."

"Well, *we* aren't. . . . We know it has to be a lie."

"Then where is she?"

"Time will tell that." Grace shifted her position, not wanting to reveal her desire to find Mamma and bring her home. "Meanwhile, we've a lot to do round here. Adam and Joe could use some help deworming the sheep next week, for one."

"I hate helpin' with that." Mandy got up and sat on the railing. "And the sheep hate it, too."

Grace subdued a smile. She had seen Dat and Adam—Joe, too—firmly holding the sheep as they fought having the syringe stuck in their mouths. The sheep bore no love for shearing, either. Some of them nearly fainted during the process, and Dat kept water in a bucket close by to revive them if they did.

Always before, Mamma had assisted with the lambing. Every year, as far back as she could remember, Mamma had taken her turn at night, checking to make sure the wee ones were nursing frequently. Despite some rough patches, she and Dat had always made an attempt to demonstrate their silent unity in that and other things—at least up until last month.

It seemed her sister needed continual reminders that life must move ahead with or without Mamma, for as long as that might be.

"There's lots more work . . . with Mamma absent," Mandy said glumly.

"Well, and we all have to pull our share," Grace replied.

"Sure doesn't seem fair, does it?"

"Sometimes life just isn't."

"You'd think Mamma would send word. Tell us she's all right." Mandy's voice was muffled.

"We'll just keep praying for her safety. Something's troubling her, that's certain."

The floodgates opened, and Mandy bowed low into her hands, sobbing like her heart had broken into more pieces than could ever be mended.

Grace rushed to her side and rubbed her back like Mamma would have. And Mandy reached for Grace's hand and held on for dear life.

When Becky came over to lend a hand with the setup for Preaching, Grace suddenly felt tense, worried she'd come to discuss Mamma's absence. But her friend surprised her by simply carrying in hymnals from the bench wagon. She also brought word that her mother was getting some additional help with baking pies for the common meal tomorrow.

"This'll be *gut,*" she told Becky as they placed the hymnals on the end of the wooden benches, along the center aisle.

"Well, we want to help." Becky's eyes were moist. "Trust me, we do."

Grace gave her friend a quick hug and whispered, "Denki . . . ever so much."

———

"Pocketful of Sunshine" began playing on her iPhone, and Heather reached to see who'd sent her an email. "Don!" she shouted.

Unsure what to think, she opened the update from halfway around the world.

It looked from Don's email like Devon was back on his feet and should be returning to the base soon. *I'm sure he'll be in touch,* he concluded.

"And Dad thinks this is all so primitive," she scoffed, wondering again where her father was.

Her thumbs flew over the surface of the digital keypad as she typed back a swift response. *Thanks. Great to hear it!*

The phone beeped and it was her dad. "Where've you been?" she answered.

He was laughing . . . really laughing, like she hadn't heard for a while. "You'll never believe this," he said.

"Um . . . what?"

"I just bought some land in the middle of Amish country. How weird is that?"

She nearly shrieked. "You what?!"

"You heard me." He was still laughing, and it made her smile.

"Well, where?" There were numerous Plain communities around the country.

"Just north of Bird-in-Hand. You must see it sometime," he said. "I'm in Lancaster County now—remember all the summers here?"

"Hey, cool, Dad." This was just too coincidental. She couldn't believe it. "So you bought land for what?"

"I don't know—I'll have a hobby farm or plant vegetables."

"Dad . . ."

"I'm serious."

"So, you're moving there?"

"First I have to put a house on it." He mentioned using some of the proceeds from Mom's life insurance policy. "Of course, I could sign the land over to you, Heather . . . for your wedding dowry." He chuckled into the phone. "Like the Amish."

She laughed at the thought. *Dad and his crazy ideas . . .*

"I'll be home in a few days."

And I'll be leaving. . . .

She was still surprised he was calling from Pennsylvania. "Uh, Dad?" Should she tell him she was heading there, too?

"Look, honey, I've got to run. We'll talk again soon."

"Okay. See ya." She found this all so amazing. *Wow, to think we're on the same wavelength for the first time. How weird is this?*

Wondering if Don was still at his computer, she sent him another message: *So terrific hearing from you! You guys be safe.*

Hoping for more, she carried her phone around for the rest of the evening. But she heard nothing further as she added another few pages to her thesis.

———

Judah spent a good part of Saturday night looking in on his lambs. He'd given Adam and Joe the night off—they needed to catch up on sleep. And it wasn't fair to ask Grace and Mandy to help outside, since they'd done so much to get the house and barn ready for tomorrow's Preaching.

It was his responsibility to make sure this brand-new set of twins survived and were not rejected by their mother— although he was seeing signs of that already. At least one of the newborns might have to be adopted by another ewe, which meant even more hands-on work. He was willing and able to do it, but the prospect of the continuing lack of sleep was daunting right now.

Recalling Lettie's restlessness, he wondered if her exhaustion had been part of the reason for her depression. Judah let out his air in one long breath. It was impossible to know what had been on her mind. He rubbed his sore neck, thinking back to the evening before his wife had left.

"I want you to hear this from me," she'd said, eyes intent on him.

Hear what? That she loved someone else?

Impossible, he thought. A desperate lump of regret churned in his gut, devouring him.

"Was it 'cause she didn't think you'd listen?" Adam had boldly asked at the table, in the hearing of his brother and sisters. And none of them, not even Grace or Mandy, had defended their father.

What if he *had* stayed to hear her out? Would Lettie still be here? He shook his head. *I can't change the past.* The thought gave him no consolation, and he was consumed with worry for his

troubled wife, out there alone somewhere in the modern and wicked world.

He hoped, if nothing else, she was
getting some rest at last. Sleep, and the
Lord's watch care, might just work
wonders.

Long after the newborn lambs had
finished nursing, Judah remained there
in the hay, soon limp with sleep.

———

Andy Riehl's rooster crowed and
awakened Judah with a start. It was the
Lord's Day, and he rose, shaking the
straw off, aware again of the shooting
pain in his upper back and neck. But he
couldn't let it slow him down; he must
begin a flurry of chores, just as on a
weekday.

He made haste to the house and got
Adam and Joe up and going. He didn't
need to prompt Grace, who would be
rising soon to start breakfast, rousing
Mandy once the meal was underway.
His younger daughter wasn't much for
rising early. He remembered once smiling with Lettie about that.

He wondered if his wife was up and

dressing for Preaching, wherever she was staying. He opened the pasture gate and let the sheep out to graze, watching the mighty frisky baby lambs bob after their mothers. The smallest ones worried him most. Keeping them alive was sometimes a chore and a half.

Adam and Joe came downstairs quickly, no dillydallying. The Lord had given him some mighty fine sons and daughters. A good thing, too, because there was much work to be done. He expected a good forty or so lambs this spring, assuming they all survived.

He glanced at Adam and Joe as they headed to the sheep barn. They'd need to freshen the straw for the new mothers-to-be. He hoped none of the ewes would go into labor today, with church being held here.

There was the not-so-small matter of Preacher Josiah Smucker, too. Anticipating the coming confrontation drained him, and he hoped whatever Josiah had to say wouldn't take up too much time. Truth was, Judah had neither knowledge nor time to spare. He thought of calling Martin Puckett tomorrow to see if he'd drive him over to the blacksmith shop first thing—although word had it Martin had disappeared the same day Lettie had. All that hearsay seemed out-and-out strange. Martin and Lettie?

He would not allow the ridiculous murmurings to cloud his judgment. Lettie—and Martin, too—were surely innocent of any wrongdoing. Might be a good thing to let the unsuspecting fellow know what was being said about him.

Reaching for his hayfork, Judah shook his head. *Des hot ken Verschtand!—This is absurd!* He wondered if Lettie had any idea what a hornet's nest her departure had stirred.

chapter

....

twenty-one

Sometimes innocent things done in a spirit of kindness—even out of intended care—came back to bite you. Martin pondered this on the drive to the church where he and Janet had attended all their married life. He'd gone to this church even longer, having joined at seventeen. *Nearly an eon ago.*

Keeping his hands at ten and two o'clock on the steering wheel, he wondered if something was up with his Amish regulars. Despite his having been out of town for several days, he had returned to find not a single message requesting transportation from any of the Bird-in-Hand folk. Even those who called from farther to the west—Intercourse—and to the north, from Stumptown, had not contacted him since last Thursday.

He thought again of Lettie Byler . . . and of Pete Bernhardt's standoffishness at Penn Station. Had Pete anything to do with the major drop-off in business? Martin certainly hoped not.

Pulling into the church parking lot, he spotted Victor Murray, one of their long-time ushers, and waved. He got out and hurried around to open Janet's car door.

If Martin didn't hear something soon from either Andy Riehl or Judah Byler himself, he'd have to wander over there and make small talk. The silence was not only disconcerting but utterly deafening.

———

Judah hung back a ways from the house, fanning himself with his straw hat. From the backyard, he observed Adam and Joe, along with their boy cousins, greeting the People as they pulled into the driveway in their buggies. Adam had designated certain lads to help unhitch horses and lead them to the barn for water.

Judah was mighty pleased at the efficient assembly line before him, considering what his sons were going through. Folk looked right through to your heart at a time like this, and Judah himself was ready to have the day over and done with. He reached back to rub his neck; the pain was nearly unbearable now.

Here came Josiah, waving him down. "Mind if we have a word, Judah?" The preacher had caught him off guard in the yard where the menfolk lined up to file into the house for the Lord's Day gathering.

"Jah, fine." He followed the younger man out to the barn. It was important to demonstrate a willing spirit, even though he was already becoming weary of the questions. No matter how many were asked, none could bring Lettie back.

They walked to the sheep side of the barn and Preacher Josiah asked to see the newest set of twin lambs. A Scripture verse came to mind, one Judah had read so many times he'd committed it to memory without even trying. *They that wait upon the Lord shall renew their strength . . . they shall run, and not be weary.*

Judah felt tense as the preacher made small talk about the weather for longer than necessary. Unlike the deacon, Josiah had never been one to leap into a particular topic but rather preferred to wander around to it. So, biding his time, Judah remained patient as they walked toward the pasture.

Judah noticed the last few horses were being unhitched, back in the driveway. Most of the membership had arrived, and he wondered if the preacher might be setting him up as an example. *Hard to imagine that of Preacher Josiah, though.*

He kept up with the preacher's long stride, and finally Josiah got to the point. "Your wife's been absent from Preaching off and on since March," he began.

"Jah, twice."

"For health reasons, would ya say?"

The hair on Judah's arms prickled. "She never said."

The morning sun cast a wan light over the grazing sheep. Kindly, the minister placed a hand on Judah's shoulder. "I take it Lettie didn't say she was leavin'?"

Judah shook his head.

Preacher Smucker looked down at his feet, shifted them, and removed his straw hat. "Well, I don't mean to put you on the spot. You've heard the rumors 'bout Lettie and another man." His voice was quiet. "Would you know of any reason for your wife to go away?"

Judah resisted the question. Up until now, he'd refused to consider the possibility. But what if the rumors were true?

He recalled how affectionate he had been with Lettie early on in their marriage, like any young couple. Those days of passion had produced four healthy children.

He glanced toward the house, bustling with activity as the crowd swelled. Drawing a long breath, he removed his hat, holding it in front of him. "I've been remiss as to my wife," he confessed. "Not as attentive as I should be . . . confidentially speaking."

A slow frown gathered on Preacher's brow. "Husbands are not to deprive their wives, and vice versa—except, as the Scripture says, to 'give yourselves to fasting and prayer.' "

Judah bristled. In his defense, he might have mentioned that raising sheep took every ounce of his energy— had for years. He was no longer a young buck. Sure, he could offer any number of legitimate excuses, but none would hold up in Josiah's eyes.

Nor the Lord's.

"I can assure you, Lettie's not the sort to stray" was all he could manage to say.

"I see." The preacher straightened. "If what you say is true, then surely she'll return. And we'll discuss this further at that time, if need be."

Josiah extended his hand and Judah shook it.

Preacher raised his hat to his head and set it down on his thinning hair. "I won't be speakin' with the brethren on this," he said, his gaze fixed on Judah.

Judah's throat felt as dry as dust, his mouth too parched to speak. He nodded his appreciation, then watched the kindly minister hurry back toward the house.

Running his fingers over the edge of his hat, he felt the relief of having come clean, his transgression laid bare before the man of God.

Judah put on his hat and headed to the barn to check on his expectant ewes once more before the start of Preaching.

Grace saw her father walking back from the barn, his shoulders visibly slumped. She'd noticed Preacher Smucker strolling with him earlier, though the man had returned to the other ministerial brethren some minutes ago, ready to get church underway.

He's heard about Mamma. She swallowed hard. *Has everyone?*

She saw Henry arriving with his family, and when he looked her way, he smiled faintly and gave a quick, discreet nod of the head. There was no way to tell from his cautious gestures if he was upset at the news swirling about Mamma's disappearance, since Henry had always been prudent in his greeting at Preaching services. Even at Singings, he was subdued.

Will he want to marry into the Byler family now?

It would certainly make an upstanding young man think twice, she guessed. She had better dismiss the niggling thought, or her ability to pay close attention today would be out the window.

Glancing over her shoulder, Grace saw Henry line up to enter, his face hidden from view.

———

Heather spent Sunday morning sleeping in, vaguely aware of her dad's arrival sometime after midnight. The garage door's rumble had awakened her momentarily, but she'd fallen back into slumber.

She dreamed of a long weekend with her mother in Amish country, and in the dream Mom, completely well again, was pointing out some beautiful blossoming pink and yellow plants. There was the sound of water trickling, lending a peace to their surroundings. All was well . . . Heather and her mother were relaxed and happy, together once again.

When she awakened, Heather wondered if the dream was confirmation she was doing the right thing by returning to Pennsylvania to get well.

Later, at breakfast, which was late enough to be brunch, she sat with her dad, watching him eat his usual sugar-laden cereal, with a small dish of apple-sauce—cinnamon sprinkled on top. "The works," he said, wearing navy sweats, his dark hair rumpled. He took a sip of his coffee and set it down next to his OJ. "Feels great to be home."

"I was beginning to think you'd gone on a never-ending trip." She leaned forward, blowing on her coffee. "Sounds like you succumbed to an impulse purchase."

His sleepy eyes shone as he described the parcel of land, which the former owners had reluctantly carved from their larger acreage. "They were in need of emergency cash, and they sold as little as they could—only four acres. I guess back there, that's really too small for a farmer to do much with."

"So what are *you* going to do with it?" She ran her fingers through her hair, still damp from her shower. "Are you serious about a hobby farm?"

He smiled, radiating confidence. "I'm leaning more toward growing potatoes. You might be surprised at how much fun it could be. I think you'd like it, too."

"I have a phobia about dirt under my fingernails and multi-legged creatures that fly, don't forget."

"Well, *I'm* ready for the next chapter in my life. I've had it with the corporate fast track, for one, and besides . . ." Here, he paused for so long she wondered if he'd forgotten what was on his mind. "Your mother was crazy about that area. She told me countless times she wanted to retire there someday."

She agreed. "Obsessed with the place, yeah . . ."

"I'll start building a house in a while." His face was alight with the possibility. "Will you help come up with a plan for a small, old-style farmhouse? The kind of house unique to the back roads?" He paused, a faraway look in his eyes. "Doesn't make sense to build something contemporary in Amish country, does it?"

"Sure, I'll help you design it." Heather got up for more coffee. If she stayed sitting, she might easily cry. That would never do, not today. Nope, for the first time since Mom's passing, Dad's sights were set on the future, and no way would she interfere with that.

———

Grace appreciated all the help from the womenfolk during and after the common meal. Marian Riehl, along with Aunts Lavina and Mary Beth, acted as self-appointed shadows.

Opening the side door to the kitchen, Grace propped it wide with the doorstop. Several blossoming lilac bushes she and Mamma had planted years before gave the air a delightful sweetness.

She glanced down at the springhouse and saw Yonnie Bontrager talking with Becky. It was a little odd to see them together in such seclusion, but who could resist Yonnie's contagious laughter and merry spirit?

Looking away to give them privacy, she noticed Henry out near the wood-shed with several other young fellows. And surely plenty of gossip was spreading now that everyone had seen for themselves that Mamma was nowhere around.

There was much left to do to clean up after the big meal, what with a record attendance this Lord's Day. Uncanny, really. The sadness—even disbelief—of nearly every woman present had been overwhelmingly apparent.

Returning to the kitchen to help wipe down the tabletops, each comprised of several benches, Grace was relieved to see Mammi Adah talking with Deacon Amos's mother. She and Dawdi Jakob both seemed quieter than usual, sitting at the table with the eldest of the group, finishing up their slices of snitz. Becky, her mother, and many of their extended family had baked many pies for the oc-casion, and Grace went over to offer her thanks.

One of the kindest neighbors ever.

She finished drying off the tables, except where the older folk still lingered, and was just returning to the sink when Becky came up behind her, face beaming.

Becky tugged on her sleeve gently. "Come! I must talk to ya." Her friend led her outside and down the driveway a bit, past the front porch and the mailbox. Grace would check it again tomorrow for word from Mamma.

"Ach, can ya keep a secret?" Becky's big eyes twinkled her joy.

"Well, don't you look awful pleased this Lord's Day," Grace said.

Becky gripped her hand, pulling her closer. "Yonnie's close to decidin' who he'll court."

"He told you this outright?" Grace thought it presumptuous.

Becky laughed and shook her head. "That's just his way. Truth is, I have a feelin' I just might be one of the girls he's considerin'. Oh, Gracie—can it be?"

"Well, you know what I think already."

"But not what *Yonnie* thinks."

Grace laughed. "I say you'll be surprised when he makes his choice. You wait and see if I'm not right."

"You're a peach." Becky kissed her cheek. Then quickly her expression changed to concern. "Ach, I shouldn't be goin' on so . . . not with you—"

"Now, don't even mention it. I'm awful happy for ya, honest."

"You goin' to be all right?" Becky asked, her eyes solemn.

"Why, sure." Grace remembered something. "Becky, can you come up to my room real quick?" They hurried back to the house and up the stairs to Grace's room. She showed her the case of colored pencils. "Remember these?"

"Jah. And goodness, they're just beautiful. . . ." Becky lifted out the pale blue pencil and held it in her hand.

"I want you to have them."

"Oh, Gracie—are ya sure? They were *your* birthday gift, after all."

Nodding, Grace gave her the case. "Make more pictures of hummingbirds, if you want to. I'd love that."

Becky smiled, eyes blinking. "I can hardly believe this. Denki!" She gave Grace a quick hug.

"Might be best not to tell the Spangler girls, ya know."

"I'll keep mum, not to worry." Becky eyed her. "You *sure* you'll be all right?"

"I live each day as it comes." Grace wanted to be strong. "But it's just like you to be so caring."

An hour later, after Becky had run off to find her family and head home, Grace realized she'd forgotten to tell her friend her own good news.

She smiled at Yonnie's unique—even peculiar—approach to finding a life mate. Curious as it seemed to some, there was something to be said for taking one's time in the matter. *For sure and for certain, he'll make Becky mighty happy.*

———

Heather leaned close to the laptop screen, trying to make sense of what she was reading. She gathered her hair in a high ponytail and sighed. "So Devon *wasn't* really sick."

She should've suspected something like this. Deep in her psyche, hadn't she feared this very thing? She read the email again, shaking her head repeatedly.

How could I have been such an idiot?

Reliving even their slightest disagreements now, she could not come up with a single issue that would have pointed to this. Why had she been so naïve, trusting him with her feelings? How could she have so completely missed who Devon Powers was?

Obviously, he wasn't the man of her dreams after all. In the blink of an eye, he'd found someone new—*someone from my unit. We didn't plan this—it just happened. It's unbelievable how much we have in common,* he wrote.

"Yeah, I'll bet!" She wanted to throw something. "So now I'm chopped sushi?"

She wanted to leap through the computer screen. "This is what I get for being loyal?"

I really hate to hit you with this, but face it, Heather . . . I'm halfway around the world, and we haven't seen each other in months. It's not like your life will change. He signed off with nothing more than his name.

She closed her laptop. "You can have your soldier girl," she whispered.

She'd heard enough sob stories from her sorority sisters to know this was how things went for some people—a never-ending rotation of new relationships and breakups. For some, it was actually the thrill of starting up a relationship that did it for them.

But *she'd* wanted a long and committed love. None of the casual boy-meets-girl stuff of the campus scene.

And here I thought I'd found it. . . .

She clicked on her phone, needing a tune. The louder and more teeth rattling the better—anything to get through the first night. She marched through the house, a fitting angry-girls-who-hate-guys band cranked up.

She forced a laugh. Devon was a total jerk.

"I messed up," she whispered through tears, realizing there wasn't a single shoulder to cry on. No one she felt like telling. Devon had been her best friend, her first and only true boyfriend.

That kind of relationship was hard to come by, at least for her.

It was definitely time to get away.

Great timing, Devon, Heather thought angrily. *If only you knew . . .*

chapter

twenty-two

Despite her heart-to-heart talk with Adam over root beer, Grace could not shake off her inner concerns about a fall wedding. Watching her father slowly unravel over Mamma's absence fed her worries. Was it just the timing of her engagement to Henry, or was it the idea of marriage itself that made her shiver?

She pondered this all through the fast songs at Singing as she sat among the girls on one side of the long stretch of tables. Nearly as many fellows mirrored them on the opposite side.

Henry sat directly across from her, as if sending an uncharacteristically bold signal to the other fellows that he'd made his choice. Interestingly, Adam never once sat near Priscilla at Singings . . . and wasn't tonight, either. Rather, her brother had planted himself across from Mandy and was making faces at her, no doubt trying to cheer her up.

Maybe that's *why.*

Priscilla Stahl was seated farther down, surrounded by her close-in-age sisters and girl cousins. Becky Riehl sat next to Grace, leaning near every so often, as if to show her care. Grace treasured Becky's devoted presence.

Yonnie Bontrager kept to himself at the far right end of the boys' side of the table, sporting a broad smile at no one in particular. She hoped Becky wouldn't be hurt by this young man and his unusual ways.

She glanced at her friend, not surprised at all that Yonnie, or any boy, would like her. Becky was, after all, a spontaneous and fun-loving young woman.

Turning, she saw Henry staring at her. She felt surprised by his noticeable attention and quickly looked away.

What must be going through his mind?

While her courting-age grandchildren sang in unison with the other youth in

the old bank barn, Adah sat on the front
porch with Jakob and Judah, enjoying
the voices drifting their way. Adah recalled having gone down to talk straight
to Marian Riehl this afternoon, once the
house cleared out from Preaching.
She'd felt the need to speak her mind
about Lettie to her neighbor, dear as any
friend she'd ever had. Not surprisingly,
Marian had looked askance, but not for
long. And Adah had made her attempt
to put a stop to the senseless rumor.

At least that one, she thought now.

Jakob's head bobbed to the melody,
and his upper torso swayed now and
then as he obviously enjoyed the sound
of music coming from the upper level of
the barn built into the side of a hill.

"Sounds right *gut,*" Jakob com-
mented, looking at Judah, who nodded.

"First time we've had us a Singing in
a while," Adah mentioned, hoping to get
her son-in-law talking.

"Do ya think young Joe's out there,
too, even though he ain't courting age
just yet?" Jakob ran his long fingers
through his graying hair.

Adah waited to see if Judah might bite.

"Wouldn't be surprised if Joe's hidin' away somewheres, observing high in the haymow." She paused—goodness' sakes, Judah was quieter than usual. *To be expected, I guess.* "Joe idolizes Adam, ya know."

Jakob nodded several times, as though deep in thought. "Both fine boys, I'll say."

Sighing, Adah felt the familiar frustration of trying to carry on a conversation with Judah—one reason for Lettie's own frequent irritation. "Grace has a mind to go lookin' for Lettie," she said. "What do you think of that, Judah?"

He planted his elbows on his knees and bowed his head. "All this talk about Lettie has me ill," he said. "That's what I think."

She folded her arms, peering over her glasses at him.

And there you have it.

Truth was, all their finagling to get Lettie and Judah together—mostly Jakob's doing—had returned to haunt them.

Judah excused himself and headed into the house, going directly to the hall-

way stairs. Adam would see to extin-
guishing all the lanterns and latching the
barn door once Singing ended. Judah
feebly made his way to his bedroom,
still exhausted from the previous night.

The day had been a long one—too
long. The endless stares, the worried
looks on the faces of so many womenfolk.

Out of the blue, he remembered an
especially carefree moment when his
wife's eyes had lit up with delight as
they rode home from visiting one Sunday afternoon not long ago. Lettie had
spotted their Englischer neighbors, the
Spanglers, outdoors with two of their
toddler-age nephews, all of them laughing and playing fetch with their golden
Labrador retriever.

*Are her eyes filled with sadness or joy
right now?* he wondered.

He recalled the lovely way Lettie's un-
pinned hair fell around her shoulders in
blond waves after being done up all day
in the unyielding bun. He'd never felt the
need to say much with his wife. Her
presence in the house was nearly

enough to bring him contentment. *Not so for her, it seems. . . .*

He looked out the window, still able to make out the tall, pointed shadows of the windbreak of trees. Shaking his head, he found it annoying how Lettie's mother had pried shamelessly on the porch tonight, trying every which way to snoop enough to get him talking. He hadn't refused out of stubbornness, though it may have seemed that way. Honestly, he had felt he might keel over from the aching in his head and neck. It had been weeks since he'd slept through a single night. The way he saw it, rest was a gift from God's own hand, just as the Psalms stated: *He giveth his beloved sleep.*

Quickly closing the door, Judah went to the dresser and pulled out his pajamas. Once changed, he drew back the covers and slipped in. He stared at Lettie's pillow, then reached for it to clench it to his chest, the sound of youthful singing still wending its way from the barn to his open window.

———

After Singing, Grace accepted Henry's invitation to go riding in his fine black buggy. The old stone wall and the fields across the road were still visible in the fading light. As the crescent moon rose on the thin horizon line to the far east, its light cast an eerie stream across the now-silvery fields.

She got into the open carriage and sat to his left. She'd worn her best maroon dress, nearly violet in color, with Mammi Adah's birthday hankie tucked into the pocket. So far the night was only slightly chilly, but she'd brought along her woolen shawl, just in case.

Henry's flashlight lay on the seat between them, the very light that had brought their relationship to this point. How swiftly she'd forgotten the excitement of seeing him standing outside last Wednesday night.

Four long days ago!

Henry reached for her hand as soon as they were on their way. Since they rarely made more than a little small talk, enjoying the quiet of each other's company instead, this night was much the same as all the others.

The moon had moved above the row of pin oaks on the east side of the road, near where the Amish schoolhouse sat silhouetted on Gibbons Road.

Out of the blue, Henry steered the horse onto the shoulder of the road and parked in front of the schoolyard where they'd both attended all eight grades. Was he feeling sentimental, even romantic? She found it hard to believe this of Henry. Maybe he *did* have an impractical side.

He helped her down, and they walked toward the little one-room school together, side by side. All around the perimeter, they strolled in silence.

After a time, they made their way to the area where they'd played baseball as children, though, not being much of a tomboy, Grace had preferred to jump rope or, when she was younger, play with her faceless cloth doll.

When it seemed as if Henry had in mind only to walk in a pleasant setting, she could hold back no longer. "You must've heard 'bout my mother," she ventured to say.

"I did."

"Then you understand why things are so *verkehrt* these days. For me . . . for my family?"

He barely nodded.

"It's downright upsetting." She sighed, frustrated. "Everything's all jumbled up."

He looked at her. "But life keeps on going, jah?"

She shivered. Was that all he could say?

"You're shearin' sheep, birthing lambs, ain't?" he said unexpectedly.

"Keepin' mighty busy, jah."

They walked over near the swings. "No word from her?" he asked.

"Not yet, but I'm sure we'll hear soon." She moved to sit on one of the swings, and Henry did the same. "I don't know how you feel 'bout this," she said, "but I wonder if we shouldn't postpone things. For now."

"Why?"

"Till all this is past," she explained.

"Ain't necessary, is it?" Henry's quick reply surprised her. "Surely your mother will return in time for the wedding. November is seven months away yet."

So he doesn't think ill of me. . . . The thought brought her a measure of reassurance as she pulled her shawl around her, then clutched the chains of the swing. "All right, then, we'll leave things be."

He paused, turning in the swing next to her, his expression hard to make out in the dimness. "Remember, you're not like your mother, Grace."

She let out a little gasp, not knowing what to think. If he'd meant to compliment her, he was certainly going about it all wrong.

Perhaps sensing something was amiss, Henry quickly rose and went to her, reaching for her hand to help her from the swing. "We should head home," he said. And that was that.

———

Grace noticed a light still burning in her grandparents' front room after Henry dropped her off. She longed to visit with Mammi Adah, wanted to curl up in her loving arms and be rocked to sleep like a young child.

But she was a grown woman, and she

must weather this storm. Even so, she might glean some wisdom—perhaps even some comfort—from Mammi Adah tonight.

If she's the one up.

Surely her always-sympathetic grandmother would understand her unease over what to do about her engagement. Grace had welcomed Dawdi and Mammi's presence since they'd moved into her father's three-story farmhouse several years ago. And even though Mamma and Mammi Adah were apparently on edge much of the time, Grace's seventy-year-old grandmother was ever ready to help. Mostly, though, she stayed busy taking care of Dawdi Jakob, who'd slowed down considerably in recent years. Rarely did they share meals with the rest of the family, other than birthdays and holidays, and the arrangement seemed to suit Dat and Mamma just fine.

Grace moved silently through the lawn and up the few steps to Dawdi's back door, letting herself in. She saw that while a gas lamp remained lit, no one was nearby in either the kitchen or the wide front room, where Dawdi and Mammi liked to sit and talk and read after supper.

She noticed her grandfather's big German Biewel on the sofa, as well as Mammi Adah's tatting hook and a handkerchief in the process of being finished. Calling softly, she assumed Mammi had failed to outen the light, and she was moving to do so when a letter sticking out of the Bible caught her eye. She glanced at it and saw it was addressed to Mrs. Adah Esh and Miss Lettie Esh, at a street somewhere in Kidron, Ohio.

Opening the Bible, she peered more closely at the envelope, recognizing now that it was a steadier version of her grandfather's writing. The return address was her grandparents' former home on Weavertown Road, where they'd resided prior to moving here.

Curious, she tried to see the postmark but could not make it out. Hearing someone on the steps, she quickly pushed the letter back inside the Bible and closed it, then hurried out to the hall.

"Well, Grace . . . it's you. I thought I

heard someone." Mammi Adah looked tired, her hair flowing like silk all around her, clear to her knees. "You're gettin' in a bit early from a date, jah?" Mammi glanced at her.

Grace nodded. "I ought to just head off to bed."

"But you're here now. . . ." Mammi said. "Care to sit awhile?"

"Well, it *is* late . . . 'specially for you."

Mammi shook her head, eyes softening. "Never too late for my Gracie."

She could not resist, so she sat in Dawdi's upholstered chair while Mammi got settled on the small sofa, next to the Bible with its odd letter. She glanced at the Good Book, wishing she could get up the nerve to ask Mammi Adah about the letter inside. The strange Ohio address had filled her with questions, yet the peculiar way Mammi had acted about Grace's idea to search for her mother made her hesitant to ask. Besides, she had a more pressing matter on her mind tonight.

"Have you ever done something you wished you hadn't?" Grace asked.

Her grandmother's smile faded and

she picked up her tatting. "I daresay we all do such things—ofttimes when we're young—and even after we're all grown up, too."

"Things that might hurt another, even though we don't mean to?"

Mammi nodded. "Why do you ask?"

Grace truly wanted to preserve something of Henry's and her privacy, but she also was anxious for Mammi Adah's advice. "Can you keep a secret?"

Mammi nodded. "You have my word, dear."

"Well, even though my beau doesn't agree, I wonder if we're doin' the right thing by goin' ahead with our wedding this fall."

Mammi smiled. "So this must be the news you wanted to share with your Mamma."

"Jah, 'cept now . . . well, bein' engaged doesn't feel quite right . . . with Mamma gone."

"I see why you might feel thataway."

After a moment, Grace said quietly, "I'm not all that sure 'bout things in general, truth be told."

"About marriage?"

Nodding, Grace recalled how she'd felt when Henry had offered his hand tonight, when she was sitting on the swing in their old school yard. There were times when she believed she had done the right thing by saying yes to his proposal. But lately so many doubts had begun to surface—beginning the night of Mamma's talk with her about Henry's reserved nature.

The night of my birthday . . . before Henry came to propose.

"Well, I'll be the first to say 'tis a challenge," Mammi said. "There's nothin' easy 'bout puttin' two people under one roof as husband and wife, tryin' to make heads 'n' tails out of living together and raising a family."

Grace considered the blunt words and wondered about her grandparents' courtship. "Dawdi must've loved *you* an awful lot."

"Why, sure. But love's altogether different when you first meet and court and all. It changes and deepens into something that can withstand the storms, ya know—something worth fighting for as you grow older." She paused to look up from her tatting. "Or it doesn't grow at all."

She understands, for sure and for certain.

Mammi continued. "Course, some folk might begin to appreciate each other again, but it takes time." She kept tatting, more slowly now. "But some marriages are merely tolerated," Mammi Adah ended in a whisper.

Grace stared at the afghan lying on the ottoman, the one Mammi had made specifically to keep Dawdi's unsteady legs warm. "Did you know for sure . . . I mean, when Dawdi asked you to marry him, did you know . . . ?"

"That he was the right one?"

"Jah." Grace blinked away her tears.

"Honestly, Jakob couldn't keep his eyes off me—wanted to come and tell me things first before anyone else. And we always enjoyed each other's company. There were lots of strong signs such as that."

"Tell me things first . . ."

Henry was not the first person Grace longed to share with, she suddenly realized. In fact, she scarcely ever thought to confide in him. And since he rarely spoke his mind to her, evidently she was not his first choice, either.

Like Mamma and Dat, she thought sadly.

Grace ran her fingers over the hem of her apron, deep in thought. "I'm glad you left your gas lamp on, Mammi."

"Well, bless your heart . . . so am I." With that, her grandmother rose, smiling. "I'll leave ya be for now."

"See you in the mornin'." Grace remained seated.

"Jah . . . and sleep well, dear."

If I can. She glanced at the Bible, still curious about what lay tucked between its pages.

chapter

....

twenty-three

On washday morning, Grace took time to shake each wet garment carefully before pressing the shoulder seam or waistline to the clothesline. She secured each item with wooden clothespins, using only two of the several lines today. Mamma's clothes were distinctly missing.

When she'd finished, Grace hurried down the road to the shanty phone and dialed the number she'd memorized. Martin Puckett answered on the second ring.

"Hullo. It's Grace Byler."

"Why, yes." He sounded exceptionally pleased. "How can I help you?"

"I need a ride to Orchard Road."

"What time would you like to be picked up and where?"

"Out at the end of the driveway is just

fine," she told him. "And as soon as possible."

"Is twenty minutes from now soon enough?"

"That'll be *gut.* Denki."

"All right, I'll be there."

She said good-bye and hung up, hoping she wouldn't soon become the topic of a new wave of gossip by being seen alone with her mother's early morning driver.

Frowning at her own cynicism, she scurried back to the house to give Mandy instructions for dinner at noon, in case Grace wasn't able to return in time. But when she arrived, Mandy was nowhere to be found. She wrote her a note instead, then dashed out to the barn, where it turned out Mandy was helping with a difficult delivery—triplet lambs.

Reassured that all was in order, Grace stepped inside to the main hall to get her shawl and once again left the house. Walking along the roadside, she discovered she'd picked up her mother's wrap by mistake, but she kept going, not wanting to keep Martin Puckett waiting.

"If only wearing it could help me understand what Mamma's been thinkin',"
she whispered.

She dug into her shoulder purse, glad
she'd remembered to bring the payment
for the driver. It wasn't a long ride over
to Uncle Ike's place, and he would probably be surprised to see her. She could
only hope she'd find him home, so as
not to waste her hard-earned money. It
wasn't like her to make a trip with a single stop.

When she spied Martin's van, she felt
sure this had not been the vehicle she'd
seen when Mamma left. If he had indeed driven her mother, why had he
chosen to take a car?

"Good morning." She waited for him
to slide open the passenger door.

"Such a nice day." He stepped aside
as she got in.

She nodded, wanting so badly to ask
if he'd taken Mamma to the train station,
as the rumors had it. But she spared him
the embarrassment of facing up to the
gossip. No matter the usual poison of
the grapevine, it was beyond her how all
this had gotten started.

"Where would you like to go today?" asked Martin. She gave him the address. "Ah, to your mother's kin." He nodded. "I recall the place."

"If you can return for me, I'd be grateful," she added quickly. "I'll be there only about an hour or so."

He glanced in the rearview mirror, his eyes kind. "Very well."

She tried to ignore her unasked question by taking in the sights of fertile fields and babbling creeks as she rode. Spotting a robin landing on a neighbor's birdbath and shaking its wings, she thought again of Mamma.

They rode for a ways without more conversation, until Grace could hold it in no longer. She simply had to know. "Ach, Martin, I hate bringin' this up, but there's word you drove my mother to the train station last Thursday," she said. "Do you happen to know where she might've been headed so early in the mornin'?"

Their eyes met in the rearview mirror again. "Your mother was quite upset." He looked back at the road. "I tried to talk her into staying, but she was insistent about going. I've no idea where she was headed."

He turned slightly to look over his shoulder, as if uncomfortable about divulging more. "She asked me not to say anything." He paused. "So then, she hasn't returned?"

"Not yet . . . and none of us have heard from her, either." Grace sighed, feeling too tenderhearted to mention the rumors flying about Martin and Mamma. *No need,* she thought. It was quite clear from what he'd said that Martin hadn't gone anywhere with her mother, though Grace didn't understand why she'd wanted him to conceal her trip.

"I hope she's all right." His voice was thick with concern. "Frankly, I worried about her traveling alone like that."

"Well, I pray the Lord's watchin' over her." Looking out her window again, she tried to appreciate all the beauty around her—the morning skies were clear, promising sunshine. Yet the world seemed cold and bleak.

Thinking now of Uncle Ike, she hoped that he might know something to lead her to Mamma. "I mean to find my mother and bring her home," she stated suddenly.

Martin's head bobbed. "For your sake and your family's, I hope you will."

Ike Peachy's farmhouse was coming into view, and even before Martin got out of the van, he promised to return as she'd requested. Grace waited for him to come around and push open the heavy door before she stepped out. "Denki, ever so much," she said.

Ain't a speck wrong with Martin Puckett, she decided.

Martin backed up and turned around before pulling onto the road, relieved that Grace Byler had been so sympathetic toward him. Lettie's disappearance had evidently caused her daughter great confusion and grief—her bloodshot eyes gave that away. He wished he might somehow alleviate the family's pain.

I should've tried harder to keep Lettie from going. . . .

He drove to Ronks, south of Route 340, to pick up several Amish ladies who wanted to go to Belmont Fabrics in

Paradise. Grace's request for him to come back for her in an hour or so made for perfect timing. He was definitely using plenty of gas by juggling customers, but he was glad to be busy today after a weekend without any calls—at least none that had reached his voice mail. And since Grace had phoned him and spoken directly about last Thursday, Martin began to feel less concerned that the weekend's quiet had anything to do with Lettie Byler.

———

Judah could bear it no longer. Dejected, he left the birthing stall. He pushed open the barn door and walked across the yard, toward the road. He and Adam had done everything in their power to save the third lamb. *Triplets . . . ach, think of it.* But the more he pondered whatever had gone wrong, the more miserable he felt.

Not caring where he walked, he muttered to himself, "If Lettie had been here, things might've turned out better." From the early days of their marriage, she'd always been so gentle and caring with the ewes. She'd spent hours with him in the barn, or checked on the newborns herself to spell him.

What happened in March that changed her so much? He shook his head, not wanting to entertain irritating thoughts about his wife, the beautiful bride of his youth. Lettie had not always been a worry to him. No, there had been many pleasant days.

How long had she been gone? Seemed awful long already. He felt as helpless now as he had watching the smallest lamb struggle for air, the will to live so strong in the poor, tiny thing.

"Mornin', Judah!"

He looked up to see Andy Riehl and two of his older sons out planting corn. Judah waved and spotted Andy's nephews in the field to the east of their house, spreading manure. Looking toward the Riehls' house, he realized he'd turned left on the road and come this way in the midst of his daze. Marian and Becky were hanging out the last few trousers on the clothesline.

Washday, he thought. *Where's Grace?*

The sun felt warm on his aching neck and shoulders as he walked past the Riehls'. If anything, the pain was increasing, rather than diminishing as he'd hoped. He ought to return to the barn and help Adam dispose of the dead lamb, yet he was not up to taking on that chore just now. His children needed at least one confident parent around these days. Perhaps he would return stronger for the walking.

Suddenly he understood something of Lettie's need to walk at night: It was so she could manage to keep her chin up all day long. *Helped her hide whatever was troubling her.*

He began to run, swinging his arms, work boots pounding against the road . . . his breath coming faster. All the way to Preacher Smucker's house he went—a good half mile or so. Buggies clattered up and down the road, some folk waving and calling to him, some rattling past.

Let them think what they will.

Judah wasn't sure if the moistness in his eyes was perspiration or tears, but he kept up his pace, unable to stop.

Grace could hear voices inside Uncle Ike's house, so she didn't bother to knock but rather made her way in through the summer porch, where she noticed thick cobwebs in one corner. *Aunt Naomi would never have allowed that.* She turned toward the kitchen, and there she found Uncle Ike having a breakfast of fried scrapple, eggs, and toast. Two of Grace's elderly great-aunts sat at the table with him.

Lest she startle them, she coughed softly. All three turned to look her way. "Well, lookee there . . . it's Judah's Gracie." Ike half rose out of his chair, then just as quickly sat down. "Come . . . come and eat with us."

The older women smiled and nodded before returning their attention to breakfast. "What brings ya?" asked the older one, her fork midway between her plate and mouth.

"Just wanted to talk with Uncle Ike a bit." She sat where Aunt Naomi had always sat, the seat still vacant after her passing. "Would ya mind?" she asked.

"Not if you don't sit and stare at me all through my breakfast." His eyes twinkled mischievously, and he reached for his coffee. "What would ya like to eat?"

Since she'd already eaten, she wasn't much hungry. But she supposed if she was to get any information, she was going to have to politely settle in with a plate of food and visit first. *Unless . . .* "My driver's comin' back for me in an hour," Grace said, hoping that might hurry things along.

Ike glanced at the window. "Wasn't that Martin Puckett I saw bringin' you?"

She straightened. "Was indeed."

"Well, why would ya want to—"

"Ain't a thing wrong with Mamma callin' on Martin to take her to catch a train, is there?"

"Well, it was wrong of her to leave town, ain't so?" Ike said, wiping his plate clean with a crust of toast. He took a final swallow of his coffee and stiffly rose out of his chair, motioning Grace into the front room to sit down.

Grace quickly changed the subject. "I know you're busy, but I thought you might be able to fill in some pieces of a very big puzzle for me," she told him.

"Which puzzle's that?" Like so many farmers, his cheeks were ruddy from many years of working in the sun. His puffy lids nearly covered his eyes; his age showed since Naomi's death.

"Well, the puzzle of Mamma's earlier years." Grace explained that she felt sure her mother had cherished the poetry books Aunt Naomi had once kept. "Did Aunt Naomi ever tell you where the books came from?"

The whites of his eyes glistened suddenly. "I wish I could help ya, Grace, but I'm afraid I have nothing to tell. Naomi never did say why she had those books, and I never thought to ask." He paused, his eyes searching hers. "Do you really think some old poetry books are important?"

Grace hesitated to tell her uncle her suspicions, fearing it might open her mother up to further criticism. "I just can't see why Mamma would have bothered to bring them home if they didn't have some special meaning for her."

Uncle Ike sighed. "I'm sorry ya had to come over here for nothin'. S'pose you found it hard to get away with so much to keep you busy these days."

Grace gave a small nod, her thoughts still on Mamma as her uncle began to speak of spring planting and whatnot.

———

Set back from the road and nestled in its private grove, the boardinghouse looked surprisingly the same as it had years ago. Even the paint on the outside was exactly the same color, Lettie recalled, although the front porch had been extended.

Nowadays a much younger couple, Carl and Tracie Gordon, ran the quaint inn. Lettie was thankful for that, as well as for having gotten an upstairs room, so she wouldn't have to hear latecomers tramping overhead.

Four days since the train left Lancaster, she thought, both dread and anticipation filling her. It had taken this long to discover Samuel's exact home address from a handful of leads, beginning with someone her cousin Hallie had

recently mentioned in a letter. Aside
from the innkeeper's phone number and
the driver they'd recommended, the list
of telephone numbers she'd brought
along had proved little help. Although
the innkeeper's wife had gently suggested that if Lettie had attempted to
access a computer, she might have
found Samuel's address more quickly.

In such a small town, she'd expected
her search to be far easier. But Samuel
hadn't belonged to an Amish group for
years—not since his family had left Bird-
in-Hand so long ago.

She was astonished at how many list-
ings for Samuel Grabers there were in
the area. By the time she'd worked her
way down the directory, calling one
number after another using the Gordons' telephone, she was discouraged.

*To think I had such high hopes of
walking right up to his door and ringing
the bell!*

But today she had a new lead and
new hope that she might finally see her
former beau, a recent widower after
twenty years of marriage.

The bishop's long-ago words to her

rang in her ears: *"Do you accept this man as your husband, and do you promise not to leave him until death separates you?"*

Lettie pushed away the remembrance and straightened the bed. She was glad for a bright corner room. Not so different from the one she'd stayed in before in this historic inn. She and her mother had come at the recommendation of dear friends, Mamma had explained to her that bitter winter's day. And they'd stayed only a short time, if her memory served her now.

She looked about. The pale green-striped wallpaper was attractive, although some of it was peeling off near the wide doorframe. Surely she would have recognized the color if this were the same room.

She went to the door and glanced back at the small dresser, where she'd stowed away her personal things— plenty of space for the time being.

"What God hath joined together, let not man put asunder. . . ."

Sighing, Lettie sat next to the window, there in her private haven. She reached for her beloved poetry book and leisurely read the last few pages. Then, clutching the slip of paper, she stared longingly at the address. "My last hope."

chapter
twenty-four

Heather brushed away tears as she backed out of the curved driveway, casting a pensive look at her family's red-brick colonial house.

I'm doing this for you, too, Dad. She stared up at her window over the garage—that sweet and cozy spot she and her father had created just for her.

She'd hardly taken any time at all to pack, piling a bunch of clothes and personal stuff into the trunk of the car and the backseat before heading off in search of a stress-free summer. As she saw it, serenity was the first ingredient necessary to health. Lancaster County, the Garden Spot of the World, would perfectly fill the bill. For her, gardens equaled tranquillity . . . and tranquillity, wholeness. Not that she was going to start espousing that Mother Earth mumbo jumbo, but nature was natural, after all.

Glad for the GPS mapping system on her iPhone, she'd have no trouble navigating her way to Pennsylvania. The map routed her up to Interstate 95 through Baltimore and then she would take Interstate 83 into Pennsylvania.

Listening to one song after another, Heather already felt herself relaxing. She was eager to meet Marian Riehl, who had been so accommodating by phone, even to the point of suggesting Heather pay by the week. *"We'll give you a nice discount as a long-term guest . . . and remember, we don't charge on the Lord's Day."*

She'd never heard anyone refer to Sundays like that and found it charming, even intriguing.

———

Hours later, as she took the exit off of Highway 30 and turned onto 340, Heather wondered if her dad had spotted her note by now. Glancing at the digital clock, she realized he wouldn't have seen it propped up on his desk as of yet.

Four o'clock. He's still at work. . . .

He really didn't need to know the hard facts about her leaving, except that she was on a self-imposed getaway. She'd made it clear she would keep in touch and had decided at the last minute to take her phone along. She couldn't imagine living without Twitter or instant messaging or email.

She had been quick to delete a former draft of an email she'd written to Devon last week, telling him she would be tied up for a while—*going to hang out in an exotic community for the summer.* Now that he'd dropped his bombshell, her only love would never know of her plans—or of her disease.

Suddenly she noticed a real live horse pulling a quaint gray buggy in front of her car. She let out a gasp and remembered how remarkable this old-fashioned sight had been the very first time she'd visited here with her family, as a girl. Seeing the Amish mode of transportation so very close brought it all

back . . . the reason they'd kept returning here.

Gone now were Heather's health concerns . . . gone her perplexity over Devon's choosing someone else over her.
At this moment she was zeroed in on
the incredible sight before her eyes. She
never got past the awe no matter how
many times she'd come here. This was,
after all, the twenty-first century, even
though she felt like she'd fallen through
a time warp somewhere between Virginia and here.

Heather stared at the red triangle on
the back of the buggy and noticed the
thin, wobbling carriage wheels on either
side. *No chance of surviving against a
speeding car.* Cringing, she crept along
at less than ten miles per hour behind
the boxlike carriage, traveling that way
all the way to Bird-in-Hand. Nervous for
the family inside, she could see several
towheaded children peeking out from
the back. She checked her rearview mirror, aware of the lineup of cars behind
her.

*They're content to go at a snail's
pace,* she thought.

The GPS indicated how many feet she had to travel before turning. She marveled at this cool technology while her car followed the horse and buggy. "Okay, now for the turnoff."

Almost there . . .

Once more a small face turned to look at her through the rear buggy opening. She got a glimpse of corn-silk hair and wide eyes, and a sudden knife of pain sliced at her heart. Dr. O'Connor had said she might never have a child of her own now.

A wall of fear rose up and towered over her. Had she done the right thing in refusing conventional medical treatment?

But no, she wanted to at least try to conquer the disease her way. She wouldn't second-guess her decision. She mustn't.

This trip was all about her . . . and about the path her mom wished she'd chosen. Heather could nearly pinpoint the moment when she'd turned so inward, or whatever it was referred to by more charitable people. After all, someone had to look out for her now. If Heather didn't, then who would?

Again she considered Devon's blunt email. If she didn't view prayer as an overall waste of time, she would send one up for his new girlfriend, asking God to protect her from Devon the Terrible, who broke female hearts at will.

It wasn't as if she didn't know first-hand about faith. Her greatest hope had been dashed when God ignored her pleas to spare Mom's life. He must've been too caught up in other more important things, too busy to heal Mom through the treatments the doctors had claimed were essential.

In the end, the treatments had been stronger than her mother. *Yeah, they worked all right. Like killing a fly on the wall with a shotgun.*

Making the turn north onto Beechdale Road, she felt conflicted. Sure, she had run away, but she hoped to recapture some semblance of peace here. She hoped, too, that the naturopath—Dr. Marshall—might be optimistic about her chances for recovery.

She spotted the old stone farmhouse,

described to a tee by Marian. Vines clung to the exterior all across the expanse of the front porch, with its white railing. Heather noted several smaller houses adjoined the main one, something she'd seen before in this area. A long clothesline stretched across the side yard, much like her grandparents' place years ago.

A plump chicken crossed the driveway and two chubby girls with pigtails wrapped around their heads went chasing after it.

This could be fun. She opened the car door and breathed in the fresh smells of the farm, replete with cow manure. And she laughed.

———

Ever so glad for the referral for a driver, Lettie was headed to Fredericksburg, just south of Kidron, the location of the Gordons' inn. She was on her way at last.

She felt a pang of guilt for leaving Judah on such shaky ground.

Will he ever forgive me?

Recalling the strain between them,

she regretted their final disappointing conversation. How much better would it have been if she'd simply kept quiet? Absolutely nothing had been accomplished this past month by her repeated attempts to talk to her husband.

And what of Grace and Mandy? She'd thought so many times of the cooking duties and other chores thrust suddenly upon her girls, and Grace having to squeeze in her hours at Eli's, too.

My family must think little of me now. . . .

———

Willing herself to breathe more slowly, Lettie double-checked the numbers on the mailbox in front of the bungalow-style house—Samuel's house, supposedly. The front door stood open, the screen door dimming her view inside as she walked up the porch steps.

Two clay pots filled with red Dragon Wing Begonias bloomed profusely on either side of the doorway. *Samuel always loved bright colors,* she recalled, a wind chime dinging softly on its hook in the corner of the porch.

She straightened to her full height, inhaled deeply, and reached for the doorbell—then hesitated. She could not bear to hear a loud ring today. Gently she rapped instead on the unlatched screen door, which bounced a bit. She heard a woman's voice calling, "Just a minute . . . my hands are full."

Samuel's twin—Sarah? She couldn't be sure, and the woman was not visible.

Patiently waiting, Lettie wondered if the woman might've mistakenly gone around to the back door.

"Hello there," a blond English woman said as she rushed to the door. "Sorry to keep you . . . just here watering plants."

"Oh, not to worry." Lettie stepped back as the young woman opened the door. "Is this Samuel Graber's house?" Her voice was a mere breath.

The woman smiled. "He's out of town—left just yesterday. Helping redo a friend's roof."

Lettie nodded, disappointment washing through her. She'd come all this way. . . .

"Is there something I can do for you?"

"Do you happen to know when he'll return?"

"Sometime this weekend. Would you like to leave a message?"

"No . . . no," Lettie said, putting on a smile. "I'll return another time. Denki— er, thank you."

The day suddenly seemed very long. She trudged back down the newly painted porch steps, wanting to glance back and take in the full effect of the pretty sitting area on Samuel's porch.

Will we sit together there when we talk . . . at long last?

Lettie had rehearsed such a private meeting dozens of times in her mind. But now she was forced to wait longer to tell him what she yearned to say—if she did not lose heart by then.

chapter
twenty-five

"Come in . . . come in. *Willkumm* to our home, Heather." The lady of the house, Marian Riehl, was well into middle age, Heather guessed, yet she insisted on carrying in two pieces of luggage at once. Heather protested repeatedly, but Marian appeared determined to roll out the carpet of hospitality.

Heather paused to take in the vast reach of sky and land—lush green fields and majestic silver silos marked the iconic landscape. The setting was something out of a movie—a windmill, woodshed, milk house, and even a hand pump to the well, not far from the back door. "Beyond amazing," she told Marian as she followed her into the house. If the place had been advertised online, she'd never have gotten a room—the Riehls would be booked up for years.

"Would ya care for some warm chocolate chip cookies and fresh lemonade?" Marian asked, showing Heather into the spacious kitchen.

"I really shouldn't, but . . . well, okay!" She laughed and accepted a glass of lemonade, as well as a cookie from the plate of homemade treats. The table, adorned with a red- and white-checked oilcloth, stretched for yards in the center of the large room, and a gas lamp dangled over its middle.

"Just make yourself at home," Marian said. "For as long as you're here, our home is your home, too."

Heather realized again how completely removed from the real world she felt. Modern society as she'd known it had vanished, replaced by old-time surroundings and a pleasing level of hospitality. As many visits as she'd made to Lancaster County through the years, she had never actually stayed with an Amish family.

"Have you ever heard of a Dr. Marshall?" she asked as she appraised Marian's attire—her bare feet poked out from beneath the long green dress and full apron.

"We certainly have. Miss Marshall's treating our minister's wife." Marian's eyes brightened as she found a tablet and pencil in a drawer. She began to sketch a map without Heather's asking, finishing quickly. "You shouldn't have a speck of trouble findin' her office— smack-dab in downtown Lancaster."

Heather smiled her thanks, hoping she hadn't grinned too broadly. With Marian's quaint speech, twinkling blue eyes, and the rosiest cheeks on record, the woman was as delightful as a story-book character.

"I'll take you to your room," Marian said after greeting two other guests that came into the kitchen, her face alight. "If you're ready."

Heather followed, making note of the lack of wall pictures and not a single electric light fixture. A tall corner cup-board stood in a smaller room off the kitchen, and she wondered if this was the dining room, minus the table, or sim-ply a place to display more teacups and saucers than she'd ever seen. Decorative plates stood on edge on a wooden ledge that ran all across the wall.

Strange as it seemed, Heather already felt completely at home here, in this place she'd never before stepped foot in.

Maybe this wasn't such a crazy idea, after all!

———

Adah loved everything about the way sticky buns smelled—and oh, the texture, too. She removed a large baking pan from the gas-fired oven, smiling at the remarkable convenience of it all as the yeasty-sweet fragrance permeated the room. She had half a mind to call Jakob and give him a taste, but he'd already exceeded his daily sugar limit, what with his penchant for dunking a pastry into his coffee first thing of a morning.

But Marian Riehl . . . now *there* was a woman who could use a few extra pounds, wiry as she was. Besides, Adah was itching to get outdoors, such a pretty day it was. So once the buns had cooled slightly, she would go and surprise their neighbor, who was expecting their new guest sometime this afternoon.

Imagine always havin' strangers for company. . . .

Adah went to the front room window, which faced east, and looked down toward the Riehls' treed lane. Sure enough, a navy blue car was parked there.

Not wanting to admit that it was more out of curiosity than benevolence, Adah gathered up enough sticky buns to feed all of Marian's big family, as well as their several overnight patrons.

When she arrived at the Riehls' back door, she called to Marian, who came rushing to open it. "Hullo. Wie geht's, Adah . . . come in and sit awhile."

"How've you been?" She set the basket of warm breakfast rolls on the table.

"Just fine," Marian said, eyeing the delicious goodies and grinning. "You shouldn't have, ya know . . . but smells mighty *gut*."

Adah nodded and uncovered the basket, and Marian bent low to breathe in the delicious aroma. "You won't have to bake so much for tomorrow, jah?"

Marian replaced the basket lid. "Ach, I don't mind bakin'. But this here's ever so nice of you." She motioned for Adah to sit down. "I'll pour ya some tea, how 'bout?"

"Sounds fine."

"I'd like you to meet our newest guest. The one I mentioned last week . . . remember?"

Adah didn't admit to being eager to meet the young woman with the shiny blue car. She merely nodded.

"Well, round the time you and I are finished havin' our tea—you watch—she'll be back downstairs." Marian's eyes glinted with delight. "I can tell she likes it here already, and she's only just come."

"Why, sure she does. Just as all of your guests enjoy your warm hospitality." Smiling, Adah smoothed her dress, daintily crossing her bare feet beneath the table.

They talked all around Lettie—in circles, really—and Adah found it silly. Marian asked about Judah, Adam, Grace, and the rest . . . even Jakob, but never a peep about the *missing one.*

Adah was stirring sugar and several

droplets of cream into her hot tea when in came the tallest young woman she'd ever seen. Why, the girl had to be nearly six feet in height, with golden-brown hair and a smile that undoubtedly would stop a young man in his tracks.

Quickly Marian introduced her. "This is Heather Nelson, from Virginia."

"Very nice to meet you, Heather," said Adah, enjoying this.

"And, Heather, I'd like you to meet my longtime friend, who also happens to be my neighbor . . . Adah Esh." Marian motioned for Heather to join them. "Care for some tea?"

"Thanks." The young woman nodded and smiled. Adah and Marian were both wearing dark green cape dresses with an apron to match, and Heather appeared to be taking it all in. "Your kitchen smells fabulous," Heather said, sitting at the table.

"Guess we should offer Heather some of your delicious pastries," Marian said, opening the basket. "After all, they won't be this warm tomorrow . . . or near as fresh."

Heather laughed softly—like she was

singing—before reaching in to pull out a great big bun, oozing sugar.

"Nobody can eat just one," Adah said right quick, glancing at Marian.

Heather bit into the bun and her eyes grew as wide as quarters. She nodded her head again and again, apparently unable to speak. When she was finally able, she said, "Wow. A person could get addicted to this rich stuff."

"Ain't that the truth," said Adah.

"None of us should eat so much fat . . . or sugar," Marian added.

"What we *should* do and what we do are often very different," Adah put in. Goodness, but she'd surprised herself by saying right out what was in the depths of her heart. *Oh, Lettie . . .* She realized anew how empty Judah's big house must seem to him and the children.

How very empty. And for a moment, she felt nearly afraid.

Heather found herself completely taken in by the backwoodsy talk at Marian Riehl's table. She loved the comical topsy-turvy idioms of the Amish. Things like, "throw the horse over the stall some hay," or "those naughty boys oughta get more birchings—switchings!" and "outen the light." To think she was going to spend her summer in the middle of all this charm!

Although Marian was a real sweetie, Adah Esh's spunk and folksy wit appealed more to her. The way the older woman paused before speaking, her lips parted, seemingly thinking how best to express herself, caught her attention. She could just imagine Adah's thoughts swirling . . . and what striking gray eyes!

"Your last name's Nelson?" Adah asked her during a lull.

"That's right."

Marian raised her cup to her lips. "We don't hear that name much round here."

"You know, I heard a man named Nelson bought a small piece of land up a ways." Adah tilted her head. "Could it be someone you know?"

The grandmotherly woman put things together faster than an e-book could download. "Might be my dad."

The Amishwomen looked at each other.

"Unless there's other land for sale nearby."

Marian shook her head. "Land's at a premium anymore—you just can't get your hands on it. I'd say your dad's mighty fortunate, if true."

"What's your father's name?" asked Adah.

"Roan Nelson," replied Heather. "He's talked of building an Amish-style farm-house on the four acres."

"Oh?" Marian's eyes brightened. "Will the house have electric?"

Heather laughed. "I sure hope so!"

"Will you raise a few head of cattle or have a dairy cow or two, then, also?" Adah asked.

"Neither one, I'd guess."

This brought a trill of laughter, and Heather could see they were equally as interested in her as she was in them—if not more so.

————

Grace's younger brother, Joe, came in for a drink of water, and she leaned against the counter, listening to him talk about the Riehls' latest boarder. "Mammi

Adah says she brought all kinds of stuff with her," Joe said, talking up a storm.

"What sorts of things?"

"Armloads of books, mainly, Mammi said." He scratched his head. "You must've heard 'bout this Virginia girl already, jah?"

"Mammi told me she was coming."

Joe gulped down a tall glass of water and went to the sink for more. "Mammi says she's come to stay put for a while. Has something called a thesis to write."

Grace hadn't heard this. "Must be highly schooled, then."

"It'll be interesting having another Englischer in the neighborhood, jah?"

Grace thought suddenly of Martin Puckett, certainly considered English, too. "Listen, Joe, I want you to help me stamp out the rumors 'bout Mamma and Martin Puckett. Okay?"

He nodded. "I was thinkin' the same thing at Preachin'. He's such a nice man . . . always so helpful to us."

"*Gut,* then. Tell everyone you know that Martin's at home and not off with Mamma. He never was, either." Just saying it made her feel queasy.

Joe frowned, rubbing his chin. "Well, that might quiet the tittle-tattle where Martin's concerned, but Mamma's still gone. That much ain't a rumor!"

"Gone, jah." *Though hopefully I can change that.*

chapter

twenty-six

The uncommon stillness awakened Heather the morning after her arrival. She lay in bed, pressing her fingers gently into her armpits to find the same tiny nodules—still no pain. She moved her hand along her rib cage, relieved there were no changes there, either. Her getting away might prove to be truly therapeutic. That, and being free from a deceitful toad of a fiancé!

She lay there relaxing, stretching, and pleasantly aware of the comfortable surroundings. She sighed, realizing she'd never again be held in Devon's strong arms.

Where did I go wrong with Devon?

But she couldn't let herself think of him anymore. He was out of her life through his own actions. Wasn't it better this way than finding out later, closer to the wedding . . . or worse yet, even after?

She rolled over, fighting back a jumble of emotions—anger and sadness and bewilderment—and reached for her phone.

Sitting up, she checked for any missed calls during the night, never having been one to sleep with her phone on—and without electricity here, she needed to conserve her battery. She was glad to have brought along several replacement batteries for her laptop, but the phone had little power left, thanks to using the GPS so much yesterday. She'd have to go out and charge it up at a coffee shop somewhere, maybe look into getting a charger to use in her car, too.

When I'm back in real time, she thought ironically, surprised at her own reluctance to venture away from the Riehls' insulated setting.

At that moment, her dad's cell number showed up and she listened to her voice mail. *"Why such a cryptic note, Heather? Where'd you go? Please call."*

Hearing his voice made her unexpectedly homesick. He was all she had now. But if he was true to form, he had a zillion office projects to see to—he wouldn't have been home much even if she'd stayed. And who knows? If she kept feeling this great, she'd keep her word and help him come up with a plan for his new house. *Right down the road . . .*

Perhaps one of the Riehls might direct her to Dad's land. Or better yet, take her there in a buggy.

Heather switched off her phone to preserve the power. Who could go for long disconnected from cyberspace? Could she live without all the bells and whistles of her modern life for several months?

Getting out of bed, she staggered to the window and immersed herself in the refreshing view. Yet in some inexplicable way, the loveliness of the landscape heightened the lingering hurt she felt at receiving Devon's jolting email.

She turned away from the window and from the splendor of farmland, sky, and trees. Returning to bed, she fell back onto the pillow. "I'm in the most peaceful place on the planet, and I really just need a shrink."

So is it God who lets this stuff happen? Losing Mom and then Devon? Not to mention some doctor says I'm going to die if I don't get treatment. Yet if I do get it, I could end up like Mom . . . sicker because of the things that are supposed to help me. And all this is okay with God?

Burying her face in the pillow, Heather managed to pull herself together. By the time she'd showered—in record time, since she had to share a bathroom with three other guests—she was pretty sure her eyes were no longer lobster red.

When she called her dad, she hoped her voice sounded less froggy, too. Her call went directly to his voice mail, so she left a quick message.

"Hey, Dad . . . I've escaped to another era." She laughed softly. "I needed a break after the last semester, like I said in my note. Maybe I can get out in a horse and buggy to search for the land you purchased. Well, my batteries are dying and electricity is forbidden here, so we'll have to catch up later. Bye!"

Downstairs, at breakfast, she was surprised at the spread of food—like the ultimate bed-and-breakfast experience, only better. A fluffy omelet with fresh steamed asparagus and topped with cream cheese, a platter heaped with sausages, three kinds of sweet breads, every imaginable jam and spread, and the same decadent sticky buns that Adah Esh had invited her to preview yesterday.

The other guests seemed equally astonished at the offerings as they talked and chewed and passed food. One guest—an attractive man in his thirties—singled her out with his gorgeous hazel eyes, even winking at one point when he thanked her for passing the cream for his coffee.

Real men don't use cream!

She enjoyed observing Becky and her mom . . . and the lineup of Becky's six siblings. Who had *this* many children in a single lifetime? She remembered reading the average Amish family had eight children, with some having fifteen and more.

Becky Riehl was as delightful as her

mother. After getting settled yesterday in her small, cozy room under the eaves—given the small amount of bureau space and zero closet space, that proved a challenge—Heather had accepted a buggy ride with Becky. They'd driven past the general store and the Bird-in-Hand farmers' market, as well as another place Becky thought might interest her, Eli's Natural Foods. *"You'll find plenty of health foods and supplements at Eli's,"* Becky had said with a Dutchy accent.

Now, taking her first bite of the delectable omelet, Heather was doubly glad her dad wanted to build a house nearby. Maybe Becky could teach her how to cook like this!

She cut into her sausage patty and thought how foolish she was to assume that Becky Riehl might view her as a good choice for a friend.

Not if she really knew me . . .

———

Dat began shearing the sheep right after breakfast. Grace and Mandy rushed out to help once the dishes were cleaned, dried, and put away. Grace had gotten up early to weed and hoe the vegetable garden, knowing the rest of the day would be taken up with helping to trim the sheep's hooves—Mandy's and Joe's and her chore today. Dat, Adam, and Uncle Ike were the brawny ones who could steady the sheep for the yearly shearing. It was important to shear in the springtime, once the weather was warm enough for the animals to do without their fleece, yet before the hot summer sun had a chance to burn the sheep's skin.

"Ten minutes per sheep," Mandy told her. "That's what Dat wants to try and get the time down to."

"Even so, it'll be a long day." Grace recalled how in previous years Mamma was always one of the first ones outdoors on such a day, murmuring softly to the young ewes while she worked.

"What do you think Mamma's doin' right now?" asked Mandy, as if sensing Grace's thoughts.

Grace kept her eyes on the sheep's feet. "Depends on where she is."

"Well, where do *you* think she went?"

"Far enough away to take a train," Grace answered.

That was all they said about it. Mandy worked her mouth, as if trying not to cry. Dwelling on the negative aspects of their lives was no help to either of them. And Grace needed to work fast today so she had time tomorrow to go to the town of Bart. Maybe there she would have more success than she'd had with Uncle Ike, who had shed no light on the significance of the poetry books or anything else related to Grace's search for Mamma.

Surely it's worth a try. . . .

Grace was relieved to see her grandmother come outside to stuff stray clumps of wool into bags. *Many hands make lighter work,* Mamma had always said. And Mammi Adah—and for a very short time, Dawdi Jakob, as well—helped in this way while the assembly line of sheep, clippers, and shearers streamed along.

Around half past eleven, Aunt Lavina brought over two large pans of Busy Day casserole, with cubed ham and diced vegetables, topped with biscuit dough and grated cheese. The work came to a swift halt as all of them headed indoors to wash up. Grace and Mandy set the table right quick, then put out two kinds of dinner rolls, along with butter, strawberry jam, and apple butter. There was also a large crock of coleslaw and some chowchow, too—a fine feast of a meal, thanks to Mamma's days of canning last summer . . . and her sister's thoughtfulness in bringing the main dish.

Later, when the men had resumed the shearing, and Lavina, Mandy, and Grace were cleaning up in the quiet of the kitchen, their aunt asked about Mamma. "Have you heard anything?"

"Not yet, if you must know." Mandy had never been so pointed with their aunt, nor had she looked so pale.

"Oh, sister," said Grace, chagrined.

"*Es dutt mir leed*—I'm sorry." Mandy looked first at Aunt Lavina, then at Grace. She sighed. "Guess I'm feelin' under the weather."

"Of course you are, dear." Aunt Lavina reached for a tea towel and began to dry the plates. "I shouldn't have asked."

"No . . . no, it's only natural you'd wonder," said Grace, putting her hands back in the dishwater.

"She's *your* family, too," Mandy added.

"If . . . or *when* we hear something, I'll tell you right away." Grace carefully placed each glass in the hot rinse water on the right side of the double sink.

Lavina's oval face broke into an encouraged smile. "I'll be holdin' my breath, then."

Nodding, Grace said she hoped they'd hear something soon. Anything to end the not knowing.

chapter
twenty-seven

Later that afternoon, Heather headed out to her car to explore the back roads. She glanced toward the little chicken house, her digital camera case slung over her shoulder. One of these days, she hoped to feed the hens with Becky.

The sights and smells of farm life captivated her as she looked toward the south, taking in the fields of newly planted corn. Birds twittered and called back and forth in the trees and beyond. This would be a great day to locate a coffee shop. After that, she wanted to drive the byways she and her parents had explored together in the past.

She was just getting into the car when Becky came running out, feet bare, skirts flying. "Wait . . . Heather!"

"Yes?"

"I . . . well, I just wondered if you'd

like to go on another ride, maybe."
Becky's eyes sparkled with excitement.
"I'd be ever so happy to take ya."

Heather hadn't expected this; she
could always drive to Lancaster later.
"Sure. That'd be super."

"Come, I'll show you how to hitch the
horse up to the buggy." Becky laughed.
"If you want to watch, that is."

"I never pass up a guided tour." She
closed the car door, not bothering to
lock it. She'd heard Marian tell the flirta-
tious man at breakfast this morning that
nobody locked anything here. *"Not even
your house?"* one of the other two
women guests had asked. Marian had
seemed nearly offended at the question,
which got the two women talking at
once. The room had seemed as chaotic
as a group of CNN pundits hashing out
the current political landscape.

Didn't outsiders pose a single threat?
The idea was nearly as startling as the
earthy smell rising from the nearby manure pit. But even the strange smells
added to her carefree feeling—she felt
alive, in spite of everything that was so
completely wrong with her life.

"Come, Heather!" Becky was calling for her.

"Jah, comin'," she whispered, smiling to herself.

———

Judah was happy to see his neighbor Andy Riehl walking across the pasture to help with the shearing. Having rushed back and forth between the newborn lambs, the pregnant ewes, and the shearing, he was nearly ready for another fine dinner—and a good long nap, too. Yet here it was only three o'clock, and three agitated ewes were complicating things by showing signs of early labor. They'd isolated themselves from the herd, refusing feed, Adam reported when checking on their latest arrivals.

A while later, when he and Andy were hand pumping well water for a drink, Andy himself brought up what had become the consensus among the community. Judah's ire rose quickly. "Listen here, Andy: I don't want ya speakin' so about my wife and Martin. Both of them are good folk. You must continue to call

Martin for transportation." He shook his head. "It just ain't right not to."

Andy removed his straw hat. "But—"

"No buts to it. I know my wife . . . and I know Martin. Just shut the People up 'bout this, ya hear?" Judah strode away, down toward the springhouse. "What's come over me?" he muttered.

He'd never spouted off to Andy like that . . . nor to anyone else.

Is this how I am without Lettie?

———

Heather was surprised at how quickly Becky Riehl located Dad's plot of land.

She reined the horse over to the side of the road so Heather could get a better view. "I wonder where we'll build." Heather surveyed the sweep of grassy field.

"Well, I see several choices, really." Becky pointed out the various locations. "It would be nice, though, to have the house shifted off to one side of the property—maybe over there by the trees. A *gut* windbreak, I daresay. And if you do plant anything, you should rotate crops so as not to wear out the soil."

Heather laughed and explained that her dad would need plenty of advice about such things. "You know . . . my mom would have liked this idea of his."

"Your mother's not living?"

Heather shook her head.

"Ach, so sorry."

"I am, too." *Every single day . . .*

"Was it recent?" Becky's face was somber.

"Still feels like it." Heather nodded. "She passed away eighteen months ago."

Becky appeared to take that in. "Grief's harder for some than others," she said thoughtfully. Then she asked if Heather had seen enough of her father's new place. "If you like, we can circle around Bird-in-Hand."

"Sure, I'd like that. And if it wouldn't be too much trouble, I need to find a spot to recharge my phone." She smiled a little, saying this to a conventional Amish girl.

"I know just the place." Becky picked up the reins and urged the horse into a trot.

Looking over her shoulder at the

piece of land, Heather could hardly believe Dad was embarking on this extraordinary adventure. She stared until her neck got a kink, then turned to face the road. "I feel like I've been missing out on something my whole life," she blurted, her emotions dictating her words. "Ever feel like that?"

Becky shrugged. "Around here, we just take things in stride." She glanced at Heather. "Maybe that's not what you meant."

"I'm the only child in my family. Maybe that's why."

A sympathetic look spread over Becky's face. "Aw . . . no wonder, then." She paused. "Maybe you know that Plain folk are surrounded by lots of siblings and family, grandparents included. And we look after each other."

Heather asked, "Is everything really family focused, then?"

"Pretty much." Becky smiled. "And I'd say we're more about the whole community, though families are mighty important. The ministerial brethren oversee each church district, and their word comes down to the family through the heads of each household. It's the men-folk who rule . . . some more kindly than others."

So much for freethinking women. Heather could not believe how similar this system was to the one she was addressing in her master's thesis, on the patriarchy of colonial days. For a moment, she wished there was time to change the topic to the role of the Amish patriarch, since she was here, living the research.

"The oldest men in the church district have the biggest say—'the most clout,' Mamma likes to say, always with a twinkle in her eye." Becky covered her mouth, stifling her laugh. "But 'tis ever so true."

"What about women—do they have any choice on personal preferences?"

This brought more laughter from Becky. "Such as what?"

"You know, things like fabric colors for dresses or quilts, or who to name their babies after."

Becky's eyes lit up. "To tell you the truth, Mamma's well known round here as good at namin' babies." She explained how her mother had once given some suggestions to their neighbor when her first daughter was born—"my *gut* friend, who lives in the first house to the west of us. Her name's Grace. She was the first of many children Mamma helped to name."

Heather had no idea what Becky meant. "So . . . do the People have some sort of old-time naming ritual?"

"Well, let me tell ya . . . Mamma holds the baby up and turns around three times. Then she closes her eyes real tight, says the alphabet backward and—" Becky's face burst into a grin. "No, I'm just pullin' your leg, Heather. All she does is look at a new infant to see if a particular name fits. That's all."

"But who would let someone else name their baby?" Heather asked, hoping she wasn't corrupting Becky with her modern mind.

"Oh, no one. People do ask her for ideas, though. Lettie Byler would never have come up with Grace on her own. Ain't such a common name amongst us." Becky glanced at her. "Sorry . . . we joke a lot round here."

They continued to ride through the farmland, abounding with willow trees and laced with a wide, flowing creek. They saw dozens and dozens of grazing cows as, at Heather's insistence, they kept discussing community versus the individual. She wished she had her laptop along to take notes when Becky made an interesting comment: "God put in the heart of His creation—in all of us—the need to belong. Husbands to wives, families to one another, and all of us to our heavenly Father." Becky said this with such wide-eyed conviction, Heather scarcely knew what to think.

Soon, they arrived at a small house set near the road, with a sign out front: *Emma's Cupboard.* "My mother's cousin has electric here," Becky said. "Emma's Mennonite. She'll be happy to let you charge up your phone or what-not all."

Heather was glad for this chance, but if asked she would have admitted to not missing her phone at all today. Quite satisfied with her decision to come to Amish country, she followed Becky into the adorable white clapboard shop with black shutters.

———

That evening Heather sat at the long kitchen table with Becky, who was drawing with colored pencils. Three hummingbirds in flight, each subsequently larger than the other.

Heather had decided to chronicle her trip longhand, with the plan to transcribe it to her journal file on her laptop later in her room. She continued writing about her day and the collision of emotions she'd experienced while sorting through her feelings about her illness and Devon in this almost magical setting.

It's the last day of April, and I've been in Lancaster County for only a little more than twenty-four hours. Mom loved coming here so much, yet I miss her less here than when I'm home.

Well, about my first day back in Plain country. I observed marked differences between Emma, a Men-

nonite shopkeeper who allowed me to recharge my phone, and Becky, with her Amish customs. Becky wouldn't think of owning or driving a car, or having anything run on electricity.

As much as I love my high-tech toys, there's an undeniable appeal to the simple life. That's saying a lot for moi!

I do think it's a good thing I was born modern, though. I couldn't tolerate living in this thoroughly male-dominated society, even with the trade-offs. Getting to run barefoot half the year sounds good to me!

Of course, I plan to indulge my modern side, too. The thirty-two shops at the Kitchen Kettle Village await. Looks like a hoppin' place!

I've already pinpointed three additional things I'd like to do—"must-sees," according to Marian and Becky. First are the back-roads tours offered by the Mennonite Information Center; the second, a visit to Central Market, on the square in downtown Lancaster.

And finally, the Landis Valley Museum looks fascinating. Mom and Dad took me there when I was nine, I think. I loved it then, and I'm sure I'll enjoy it even more now. This is definitely what the doctor ordered. (Well, not exactly!)

Heather glanced across the table at Becky, who had almost completed her drawing. Maybe this trip wasn't what the doctor had ordered, but for today, it was all the medicine she needed.

———

Judah stood at the footboard and stared at Lettie's side of the bed, his eyes lingering on her pillow. How long had it been since they'd held each other? Turning, he reached for the Good Book, bearing its weight to his chair near the bureau. He sat with a groan. Opening to the Proverbs, he read: *"A soft answer turneth away wrath: but grievous words stir up anger."* The lantern on the dresser shone brightly, yet in it he saw his future, which looked downright lonely. If Lettie did not return, she would eventually be cut off by the church—no matter that she was already estranged from him.

No wonder . . . the peculiar way we started out, he recalled. At the first Jakob Esh had been something of a go-between for Lettie and himself. Not that Judah hadn't laid eyes on her years before and decided she was something to behold—a real catch and a natural with a baseball bat. He would have pursued her then, except she was only fourteen. Her pretty face—*ach, her eyes*—he'd carried the memory into his dreams. He'd set his sights on her as the girl he wanted to wed and settle down with to have a family. But being two years older, he'd waited for her, without making his intentions known.

My first mistake, he'd thought many times since.

Lettie, it turned out, had a mind of her own when it came to boys. Judah hadn't foreseen that Samuel Graber, with all his fancy leanings, would beat him to the punch.

Little good it did him in the end, he thought.

Sitting in the stillness of his room now, Judah knew it wouldn't have mattered a whit back then had he realized how off-putting Lettie might become. He'd loved her in spite of her sullenness and determination to have her own way. Besides, now that they were married, what could he do about it? Under God, they were joined till death separated them.

He wiped his brow. It was one thing to speak downright pointedly to Andy Riehl, admonishing him not to put credence in gossip. It was quite another to chop off the grapevine at its root.

chapter
twenty-eight

Heather pulled on her jeans, peering down at the loose-fitting waistband. This pair had fit well the last time she'd worn them, so why were they getting baggy now, after all the rich Amish food she'd been eating since arriving two days ago? Saggy jeans annoyed her, and these certainly were getting there.

How had she managed to drop a few pounds—every girl's ambition—while pigging out on Marian's mouthwatering meals? Was this proof that a disease actually lurked within her body?

Once downstairs, she followed Becky out to the chicken house, where she watched her scatter chicken feed. Heather reached into her own bucket and mimicked Becky, enjoying the swarm of chickens near her feet, some flying with a great *swoosh* through the air. "Wow, are they starving or what?"

Becky laughed. "You'd think we never feed 'em." She explained that as a young girl she'd been afraid to carry them water or to throw feed from her apron. "The chickens would fly right at me," she said. "Nearly knocked me down."

These were definitely some ravenous critters. *Puck, puck,* they carried on, feisty in their frenzied pecking of feed.

"Come, let's water the horses next." Becky motioned to Heather and glanced at her tennies. "You might want to wear older shoes or my brother's boots, maybe?"

"Or run barefoot?" Heather couldn't help it; she giggled just like Becky. She tried to ignore the fears brought on by her weight loss—at least till her appointment with Dr. Marshall.

———

Thursday was typically market day, but Grace was scheduled to work at Eli's later this afternoon. Since she was needed at home to cook the noon meal, going straight to Bart after breakfast would work best.

On the way to the phone shanty, she was surprised to see Dat just hanging up the receiver. His hair was all clean and shiny, minus his straw hat. "You must be headin' somewhere, too," she said.

"Martin's comin' by in a few minutes," he replied.

"Oh, would ya mind if I share the ride?"

Dat shook his head. "Might as well kill two birds with one stone."

They turned back toward the house, walking along the left side of the road, as she'd always walked to school. Here lately, those days seemed like another lifetime ago.

Dat didn't mention where he was heading, so she decided not to mention her destination, either—not unless he asked outright. She wondered how he'd react if he knew. *Likely he won't say anything.*

Her father's lack of communication could be maddening at times—Mamma had all but admitted to feeling the same.

Like any married couple, she and Dat had experienced disagreements. Why was it, once two people tied the knot, their troubles seemed to surface?

Grace had secretly read a love poem in one of Mamma's books. According to that, marital happiness was simply a matter of being willing to give yourself fully to your beloved. Had Mamma read it, too?

Something akin to dying to one's self, as the Lord commands?

She walked silently with Dat, pondering these things and wondering if she might ever feel so terribly frustrated with Henry . . . years from now.

Enough to leave him?

Once again, Grace was amazed by how talkative Dat could be as he hashed over the planting season and the weather with Martin Puckett while they rode. Was he bending over backward to indulge their driver because of the appalling rumors?

It surprised her, as well, to see what a short distance Dat was going today by van. Normally he'd hitch up the horse and buggy to go to the bank, his first destination. He mentioned to Martin he needed to withdraw some cash to pay his bill at the harness shop, which was his next stop.

Martin pulled over and parked.

"Won't be but a minute," Dat said.

Even though she was anxious to get to Bart, Grace didn't mind sitting and waiting for her father. His errands wouldn't take long, and it would be no time before she and Martin were on their way south.

The banking line was longer than usual, and here Judah had been so sure he'd beat the morning crowd. He had filled out his withdrawal slip before ever leaving the house, and he noticed several other Plain folk ahead of him, mostly young mothers with children in tow.

Where are you today, Lettie? he wondered while watching two small girls play behind their mother's long skirt.

When he stepped up to the teller window, he handed the clerk his withdrawal slip with the requested amount and his

account number, along with his picture-
less ID—like a driver's license of sorts,
without the photograph. The English lo-
cals had made this provision for the
many Amish residents, and he was
mighty grateful not to have to squabble
over the church ordinance on yet another issue. Enough of that went on already.

"I'll need your code word, please, Mr.
Byler," the clerk said, sliding a small
blank piece of paper toward him.

Quickly he scribbled the name of
Grace's beloved horse, *Willow,* and returned it to the clerk. She counted out
the bills and handed him a receipt and a
printout of the balance of his account.

Looking at it, he realized there had
been a mistake. "Excuse me," he said.
"The balance is too low." He leaned forward, not wanting to make a scene.
"Much lower than I expected."

The clerk asked if he wanted to see a
list of his recent account activity, to
which he nodded. She ran it through the
printer, and he glanced over his shoulder to see Martin's van in the parking
lot. He almost wished he'd come by

horse and buggy instead, not wanting to keep Martin—and Grace—waiting. Of course, he couldn't have predicted the bank mix-up. The nagging pain in his neck worsened.

The clerk handed him the sheet and pointed to the transaction for Wednesday, April 23. Five thousand dollars had been withdrawn in the form of cash that day.

His breath caught in his throat, but he managed to thank the clerk and move away from the teller window.

Lettie?

Staring at the printout, he shuddered to think his wife had withdrawn money from their joint account without asking, or even mentioning it after the fact. Nearly the sum total of her earnings from last summer's market sales had vanished on the day of Grace's birthday.

So, Lettie must've planned her trip down to the penny, Judah thought. Truly, it appeared she was not coming home any time soon . . . if ever.

When Dat appeared at the bank entrance, looking ashen, Grace wondered if perhaps there had been a problem. But he quietly got in the front seat next to Martin without saying a peep about anything amiss.

Naturally, he wouldn't, she decided. Yet it seemed odd that he had ceased his previous chatter.

By the time they arrived at the harness shop, Grace wondered if her father might be feeling ill. As Martin turned into the parking area for the harness shop, Dat said, "Listen, Martin, I think I'll stay round here for a while."

"Fine by me," Martin replied.

"What do I owe ya for Gracie and me?"

Martin told him the amount, then added, "It'll be a while before I get back here to pick you up, if that suits you."

"Oh, I can easily hitchhike a buggy ride home." Dat glanced at Grace just then. "I'll see ya for dinner at noon, jah?"

That was all he said—no inquiry about where she might be going today. *Doesn't he care to know?*

She nodded and forced a smile. Mamma had always said Dat's appetite for food was one of his primary concerns. When he closed the door, she felt overwhelmed by sadness.

As they rode, Grace observed the familiar landmarks on South Ronks Road . . . then Fairview Road and eventually down to the main street in Strasburg. She looked longingly at the creamery on the northeast corner as they waited for the red light. Henry had taken her there late last summer, when they'd first started dating, coming all this way for ice cream on a Saturday night. He'd been so uncomfortable and shy, he'd said scarcely one word that evening, she recalled.

Sighing, she leaned her head against the window, not sure who baffled her more these days: her father or her fiancé.

———

Judah breathed in the rich, leathery scent of the harness shop. It was one of his favorite places for that reason alone. Intensely aware of his mounting neck pain, he wondered if he might be on the verge of a stroke. His great-aunt had suffered with such pain for months prior to the brainstem bleed that eventually took her life.

There were times when he could not make sense of what he truly felt about Lettie's departure. And now this—it was unthinkable for her to withdraw such a large sum without discussing it. Was her need for money the reason she'd struggled so to tell him? And why hadn't she contacted him or anyone else since leaving? Her exasperating silence struck him as uncaring and downright cold.

He reached in his pocket to fish for an aspirin and found none. If the excruciating pain didn't subside soon, he'd have to see a doctor. *Prob'ly should've before now,* he thought, waiting his turn for the smithy, who was finishing shoeing a horse.

Hurry up and wait today . . .

Hazily, he heard his name spoken behind him.

"Judah Byler! I was hopin' to see you this week."

Turning, Judah saw a tall blond man in his early twenties. He'd slipped in the door unnoticed till now.

"Yonnie Bontrager." The young fellow

offered an engaging smile and a solid handshake in return. "Will you spare me a minute, sir?" He explained that he'd planned to stop by the house. "But since you're here . . ."

Judah nodded, unsure what the boy could want.

"*Gut,* then." Yonnie's grin was infectious. "I'll wait out by my buggy."

When the smithy finished up with his other customer, he caught Judah's eye and hurried to the back room to get Judah's repaired harness. Soon he returned, hauling it out and laying it down on the long table. "You'll be glad to know the amount came to less than we'd agreed on. Don't hear that too often, jah?"

Judah nodded and pulled out his wallet. *Every little bit helps . . . 'specially now,* he thought. While tallying up the correct amount of cash, he recalled the bank clerk's hushed counting of these same bills. And his sinking feeling when he realized Lettie had taken so much for herself.

He slung the harness over his shoulder and headed outside. Yonnie stood near his horse and open carriage.

"Here, let me help." Yonnie took the harness and carried it to his own buggy, lugging it inside. "Looks like you could use a ride home." Going around to the driver's side, he hopped into the courting buggy. "That is, if you don't mind ridin' in my new wheels."

One ride's as good as another, Judah decided and got in.

Yonnie's eyes grew serious now as he reached for the reins. "If it's not too forward, I'd like to ask you something."

"Speak your mind," Judah said absently.

Yonnie pulled out onto the road, letting the horse trot a ways before speaking again. "Would it be too much to ask . . . well, to give your blessing for me to court your daughter Grace?"

Judah had never heard of such a request. Certainly, among some of the more conservative Mennonites—even the Brethren folk—the potential groom was expected to ask the girl's father for her hand in marriage but not prior to merely courting. "I believe Grace is spoken for," said Judah, looking at Yonnie.

"Puh! I'm too late, then?"

"You'd know better 'bout who's pairing up at Singings and whatnot."

Yonnie raised his eyebrows. "Glory be, if Grace's spoken for, she doesn't look too happy 'bout it."

Judah flinched. Grace *was* carrying the weight of the world on her shoulders, but not for the reason Yonnie now assumed. "Tell you what: I won't stand in your way if Grace wants ya. How's that?"

Yonnie patted his hat and gave a whoop. He clucked his tongue and the horse moved from a trot to a near gallop.

Now, here's a boy in love, thought Judah, thinking back to his own courting days.

There had been a mighty stir among the area youth when Samuel Graber started showing up at Singings before the appointed time. He was only fifteen, if that, when he first came and sat high on the bales of hay, just watching the youth sing. Nearly staring them down, some said. Gawking, said others.

Then, when some of the couples started pairing up, Samuel wandered around the barn, always with a book tucked under his arm and a pencil stuck atop his ear. Some of the girls thought he was getting ideas for poetry, but Judah didn't know what to make of that. Sometimes he struck up a conversation with a couple, or several girls, and other times he simply strolled along the perimeter of the social gathering. Then, after a time, he went and sat again, making drawings of faces and profiles in his notebook, or writing snippets of rhyme.

There was enough hearsay to know this Samuel was mighty strange. And Samuel seemed to know, somehow, that he wasn't truly accepted by the other youth, but that didn't seem to discourage him one iota. He continued to overstep his bounds by attending all the youth-related events.

Then, along about the time Lettie Esh started attending the get-togethers, Samuel suddenly quit coming. Later, word had it he was seeing Lettie on the sly at her house—according to two of her sisters, anyway. Samuel was known to go over there several times a week, which was considered giving a girl the rush—nobody did anything like that. Not that Judah had heard of, anyway. Still, none of that seemed to matter to Lettie, and the two of them were frequently seen after the common meal on Sundays, their heads nearly touching as she sat behind the barn with him, watching him write in his so-called poetry book.

Meanwhile, Judah realized he'd dallied and hadn't acted quickly enough. More of an observer than a go-getter, he'd lost his chance with Lettie—and to Samuel, of all fellows. Samuel, who wasn't too keen on following the Lord in holy baptism, or taking the required instruction to join church. Some said he was working on getting Lettie to "see the light, too" and making other disturbing remarks against the church.

Judah figured if that was the kind of fellow he was, then Lettie must be on the fringes, too, or heading there. So Judah began seeing other girls, hoping to find a devout, hard-working wife from among the remaining group of eligible young women.

Months passed, and by the time he heard that Lettie Esh and her mother had gone to assist an ailing aunt out in Ohio for a time, Samuel Graber and his poetry books were long gone.

Meanwhile, Judah was dating a new girl, though not one nearly as pretty as Lettie. It was much later that Jakob Esh came knocking one morning, and they went talking, man to man. Although he'd thought at the time how unusual it was for a father to play such a role, Judah was still plenty interested in having a chance to court Lettie—willing and ready, in fact, having never forgotten her. And while he was nothing like Samuel, he hoped she might come to love him. Judah's talent was laboring with his hands and by the sweat of his brow—he had never read a poem to a girl or even to himself, let alone written one. At only eighteen, he worked the soil hard and tended to sheep.

Once he started seriously courting

seventeen-year-old Lettie, he gave her the courtesy of not speaking about Samuel. For her part, she, too, never uttered his name. At least, not intentionally.

There were times, though, when Lettie sometimes whispered Samuel's name while she lay sleeping. Judah had refused to let it bother him. He knew as well as the next fellow that plenty of young folk didn't end up hitched to the first girl or fellow they took a shine to.

Most important, Lettie had agreed to marry *him.* And nearly ten months later, she bore him a fine and healthy son. The Lord had been good, seeing fit to give them four wonderful children and twenty-three years of marriage.

Till now . . .

———

Grace was greeted warmly at the back door of the Stoltzfus home. Cousin Rose actually threw her arms around her. "Oh, it's so nice to see ya!"

"And you, too." She was glad when Rose suggested they go walking on the road, which was rather unlike their own busy street. The unpaved road more resembled a private lane, and Grace began to relax, the warmth of the sun on her face as Cousin Rose chattered away. Grace was surprised—and pleased— when she realized the grapevine had not wended its way this far concerning Mamma. It made things much easier all around.

At last Grace hesitantly asked Rose about Mamma's friend at the barn raising. "Do you remember the woman? She wasn't from around here, I don't think."

"Goodness, I believe I *do* know who you mean," said Rose. "That was Sarah Graber, visiting from Ohio, though I can't be sure of the exact city. Might be in Wayne County." Rose fanned herself with a hankie. "She lives *somewhere* out there, anyway."

"Is she related to you . . . or to Mamma?"

"Not to me, no. She was in town to see her grand-niece's baby, is what I heard." A sudden frown appeared on Rose's plump face. "Ach . . . I 'spect you might not know who Sarah's twin is, then."

"No."

"Well, that would be your mother's first beau, Samuel Graber. He was already on his way out of the church right around the time he and your mother started courtin'." Rose paused and drew in a slow breath. "Seems from what was said back then, he had a real hankering for fancy, modern books— poetry and whatnot. Even wrote some himself. I believe I've got that right . . . so long ago now."

That explained the books Mamma had retrieved from Uncle Ike's; they must've come from Samuel. *But how odd that Mamma wanted to keep them.* Grace blinked her eyes, trying to absorb the news. "Why didn't they marry?"

"Well, like I said, Samuel wasn't much interested in joinin' church. And your mother surely was."

Mamma certainly had married someone devoted to God and the church. "She's been a stickler for goin' to Preaching all my life." *Just not so much recently,* thought Grace, not knowing what to make of all this. She'd never heard Mamma breathe a word about her first beau, yet she'd chosen to keep the poetry books ... even taking some away with her. *Of all things!*

Rose asked in a roundabout way about Grace's relationship with her parents, and Grace saw through it. No doubt Rose wondered why Grace had come all this way to ask something her own mother could have answered.

"Your Mamma was better off without Samuel, I'll say," Rose added. "Some called him a troublemaker."

Grace knew she ought to be heading home right quick. "Denki ever so much, Cousin Rose, but it's 'bout time for me to start back—I have dinner to make."

Now Rose was frowning to beat the band, staring over her glasses at her. "Is your mamma too sick to cook today? You can certainly stay and eat with us ... that'd be just right fine."

She had slipped up but good. "Another time, maybe," Grace said quickly. "My driver will be returning soon. It's kind of you to visit with me. Thank you again ever so much."

"Anytime, Grace ... just anytime at all." Rose took off her glasses and cleaned them with her hankie. "Tell your family hullo from all of us down here. We sure miss the Sunday visits."

Nodding, Grace told how busy they were now, what with lambing. She hoped Rose wouldn't ask specifically again about Mamma and open up that can of worms.

Very soon, Martin Puckett's van came inching along the narrow lane. *Just in time, too.*

———

All the way home, Grace could not begin to understand what her mother and the twin sister of Mamma's first beau could have had to talk about on their long walk. It seemed very awkward.

Has Mamma kept in touch with Sarah through the years? Could that be?

If so, she felt it was a prickly thing—nearly inappropriate.

She stared out at the sky, glad to be sitting behind Martin as he drove. That way he wouldn't feel at liberty to talk as they traveled, nor to make eye contact in his rearview mirror. There was so much to ponder now, her head all filled up with strange names and odd circumstances. Hearing about Samuel was jarring, especially since Joe said Mamma had been hovering near the mailbox all those days before she escaped.

Who was she expecting to hear from . . . and was it related to her leaving?

Aunt Lavina's vague comment about Mamma's first beau rang in Grace's memory. Oh, but she did not want Martin Puckett to glimpse her face now. She was afraid that the confusion all tangled up in her heart would surely be registered there.

chapter

twenty-nine

Martin's wife called him on his cell phone, asking if he would like to come home for lunch. "I've made a nice batch of chicken salad," she said, enticing him with one of his very favorites.

He agreed to head right there. And while doing so, he considered Judah Byler's upbeat attitude earlier today and, in contrast, his daughter Grace's sullenness. He couldn't get over why she'd wanted to travel so far for such a short visit, but that was neither here nor there. He was just pleased for the opportunity to be working again, because the calls from the Amish—especially those in Bird-in-Hand—were still far fewer than usual.

Janet had the round table in the dining cove set and ready when he arrived.

He kissed her and went to wash his hands at the sink.

"Business picking up?" she asked.

"Only two passengers so far." He reached for the towel and dried his hands.

"Might be the last two," she said softly, "from what I heard at the spa." Janet had gone for a facial and overheard two women talking about a silly rumor that had turned into a mountain of a story.

"Well, for goodness' sake!" His heart sank as he pulled out his chair and sat down.

"Seems more like the doings of small-town busybodies than a typical Amish community." Janet reached for her napkin and placed it on her lap.

"Plenty of gossip everywhere, I suppose."

Janet was staring at him now. "It's tantalizing to pass along something seen at a train station, I guess."

He squeezed his lips together. So she'd heard what *must* have originated with Pete Bernhardt that day. "Well, not *all* of it is fact."

She leaned over the table, reaching for his hand. "You didn't run off with an Amishwoman, did you?"

He laughed. "Not unless *you're* Amish."

She leaned back and sighed. "Considering we left for our long weekend that day, I'd already figured *that*."

"Evidently someone needs more than a little amusement." He shook his head. "At my expense."

"And Lettie Byler's. How must her husband feel?"

No way did Martin think Judah Byler believed any of those rumors. Not as friendly as he'd been on the way to the bank today.

"The whole thing will die down," Martin said. "Except for the fact that I did drive Lettie Byler to Lancaster, as you know." He explained that Lettie had left a slip of paper with several phone numbers on it, so he'd gone in to return it to her. He leaned over and kissed Janet's cheek. "You have nothing to worry about, love."

She smiled back. "What can we do to put a stop to all this?"

"Live our lives honestly, just as we do."

She reached for the salt and pepper. "Have you thought of addressing the rumors with her husband?"

He considered it, but Judah wasn't one to make a to-do over something. And Judah trusted Martin with Grace, so why not with Lettie? No, it seemed clear Judah Byler did not believe the rumors. *He's too sensible to believe hearsay.* "If he brings it up, I'll tell Judah my side of things. How's that?"

Janet didn't question his response, and they continued the lunch by talking about their married son's plans to visit next week. Later, Janet's face glowed as she shared a description of her hour-long facial. "I wouldn't mind going every few months," she added. "If it doesn't tax our budget."

Martin nodded, trying to think of ways to woo back his Amish customers. *Janet's spa habit will keep me working!*

———

Grace had left lean ground beef to thaw on the counter while she was in

Bart. When she returned to the kitchen, she was happy to see Mandy already assembling the ingredients for the meatloaf. She stood in the doorway between their large sitting room and the kitchen, watching her sister stir together the eggs, oatmeal, mustard, onions, ketchup, and tomato juice to add to the meat, then prepare to shape the finished mixture into a mound.

"Ach, you're doin' such a nice job," she said, finally moving into the kitchen.

Mandy looked up, smiling. "You were planning on having meatloaf today, weren't you?"

"That'll be fine," Grace said, going to get some pinto beans out of the pantry. She enjoyed working side by side with her sister. Grace put the beans in a pot with some smoked meat, brown sugar, mustard, onions, catsup, vinegar, and other seasonings to make the baked bean side dish.

The way Mamma always makes them.

When she'd put the beans in the oven, she headed up the stairs to change into an older gray choring dress. She would simply change back into the better blue one as the time came closer to heading for work.

In her room she sat on the settee near the window and reread Mamma's letter. The thought nagged at her that she ought to share at least some of what Mamma had written with poor Mandy. Yet she feared doing so would stir up more sadness in her sister, just as it would in any of them.

"Did it in Dat?" she whispered, gazing out the window.

It was nearly impossible to understand how her father could talk so animatedly with Martin Puckett so soon after practically ignoring his own daughter on their walk back from the phone shanty. She would almost prefer him moping around the way Mandy did, carrying such pain in her eyes. Truth be told, that was the way she felt, too, though she kept her saddest emotions hidden for the sake of her family.

Returning the letter to its hiding place, she decided to seek wise counsel from her grandmother. Mammi Adah would know best.

And, too, Grace hadn't forgotten about the old letter stuck in Dawdi's Bible. Why on earth had Dawdi and Mammi saved it?

Back downstairs, Grace began to peel, then boil a heap of potatoes for mashing. Next she finished making the brown gravy. Hurrying to the cold cellar below, she chose a canning jar of chow-chow and one of red beets to round out their meal.

Close to noon, she noticed Dat and her brothers emerging from the barn. They stood outside talking—what about, she couldn't guess. "Remember to put on the bread and butter," she told Mandy, placing the hot dishes on the table.

"Dat likes his apple butter, ain't?" Mandy asked.

"He plain loves to eat." Grace returned to the sink area and gave her sister a sideways glance. "What would ya say 'bout takin' turns cooking?"

"Actually, today in the barn Dat suggested I help you more. Did you say somethin', maybe?"

Grace shook her head. "Nary a word." She was frankly surprised their father had noticed her plight.

"Well, I'm sure willing to pitch in more." Mandy began slicing a loaf of bread on the large cutting board. "Just wish there was more I could do to help Dat. 'Tween you and me, I think he's ever so miserable."

"No doubt."

Mandy continued. "I was really tuckered out myself for a few days there, Gracie. I felt I couldn't keep goin', sad as I was." Mandy stacked the slices of bread on a plate. "But you know what? I've decided not to be so glum anymore," she said. "I don't understand why Mamma left, and I don't like it one bit. But if she doesn't want us to know where she's gone—or why—then she must have a *gut* reason."

Grace looked at her sister. Hers was an interesting view. As for herself, she couldn't simply dismiss Mamma's strange behavior—or the tragedy of her abandoning them. "It's hard to know what Mamma's thinkin'," she said.

"Jah, but if we ponder it too hard, it'll just drive us all mad, ain't?"

Grace had fought through anguished moments in the night when she thought she might awaken the house if she gave in to sobbing. "Think I'll go over to see if Dawdi and Mammi want to join us for dinner today," she said.

"Jah. They ought to join us every day," Mandy agreed. "Seems odd for them to live under the same roof but only eat with us once in a blue moon."

Mamma's doing, thought Grace, though to her sister she said, "That's a wonderful-*gut* idea, Mandy." With that she hurried through the sitting room and across the hallway to their grandparents' side.

During the tasty meatloaf dinner, Grace noticed Mandy seemed more like her old self. No doubt she had happily noticed all the lip-smacking at the table.

Later Grace helped Dawdi Jakob back across the house to his favorite chair in the sitting room. Once he was settled, Mammi motioned her into the kitchen so she could look at a new cookie recipe.

"I received it in a circle letter from one of my cousin's friends," Mammi Adah told her.

Grace looked at the recipe and smiled. "A healthy cookie?" She'd seen them at Eli's, all packaged up in cellophane near the cashier. She'd even tasted one.

Mammi Adah asked what she thought of substituting agave nectar for sugar, as called for in the cookie recipe. "You would need less of it, for one thing . . . and for another, the texture would be more cake-like," Grace told her.

But as interesting as the recipe was, Grace was anxious to discuss other things. And the minute Mammi put the recipe on the kitchen counter, Grace said, "I've been holdin' on to Mamma's note to me, not sure what to do." She explained her uncertainty, how she feared it might especially affect sensitive Mandy. "Dat's read it, though."

Mammi frowned. "Does it explain why

your father thinks Lettie's not comin' back?" Her voice was flat.

"Might be. But it's hard to say, really."

Mammi Adah's eyes were somber. "Would ya mind if I read it?"

"Well, only if it won't make you feel awful blue. I'd hate to—"

"No . . . don't think that." Mammi reached out a hand. "You're a gracious soul, dear."

She felt embarrassed but squeezed Mammi's hand. "There's something else on my mind, Mammi."

"Jah?"

Slowly, choosing her words carefully, she began to share what she'd learned from Dat's cousin Rose about Mamma and her long-ago beau. "Now that I know who Sarah Graber is, I'm still befuddled as to Mamma's excitement at seeing her down at the barn raising."

Her grandmother sighed softly, and pretty soon big tears slipped down her wrinkled cheeks.

Grace felt the tight, prickly feeling in her stomach again. "So, dare I ask you . . . why would Mamma be so thrilled to see Samuel Graber's sister?"

Adah had to be careful what she revealed to Grace about her mother and Samuel. The last thing she wanted was to influence her granddaughter in any negative way. No, Grace mustn't think any less of her Mamma for her youthful interest in worldly young Samuel.

Grace's blue eyes were wide as she waited for an answer. She crossed her legs and leaned forward intently, a bare foot sticking out from beneath the hem of her choring dress.

"My dear girl, I have no idea why your mother was so happy to see Samuel's sister." Adah was conscious of the beating of her own heart.

"Ever so peculiar, ain't so?"

Adah straightened her apron and willed herself to remain calm. "I wish I could tell you that your mother fell first for a devout boy, heading toward church baptism. But, alas, Samuel would have taken her away from the church." She patted her face with her hankie. "It was providential that one of

Dawdi Jakob's elderly relatives—your mother's great-aunt—needed some live-in care in Ohio. Your Mamma and I went there to assist her for a few months . . . till she died."

"But was it also to get my mother away from Samuel?"

"Well, by the time we returned home, Samuel and his family had surprisingly moved away. Your mother was heartbroken beyond belief, but your Dawdi and I were relieved." Adah brushed away her tears. "Not a soul approved of Samuel courtin' our Lettie, including Dawdi and me."

"So the People knew of their courtship, then? It wasn't a secret, like we keep it nowadays?"

"Oh, it was meant to be secret, all right, but the few who knew how much time Samuel was spending with your mother each week were concerned."

Grace looked surprised. "Who else knew?"

"The ministerial brethren had gotten word, for one."

"Did Dawdi Jakob tell them?"

Adah bowed her head. That had been

her doing, as she recalled—such a painful position to be in. "I daresay we've talked enough 'bout the past, dear one."

Grace rose and walked the length of the kitchen with a determined look and glanced toward the sitting room.

Adah assumed she was looking to see if Jakob had nodded off to sleep in his chair. "Ach, Gracie, you mustn't let this trouble you so."

"I must confess somethin'," Grace said suddenly.

Adah jerked her head fully upright. "Oh?"

"I saw an envelope sticking out of Dawdi's Bible the night I came in to see you, all discouraged after a date. Remember?"

"Jah." Adah's heart was pounding faster now.

"I don't want to snoop, Mammi, so I'm askin' for permission to read the letter Dawdi Jakob sent to you and my mother in Kidron." Grace blinked her eyes too quickly. "All right?"

"Why, dear?"

Grace shrugged. "There must be a reason you or Dawdi saved it, jah?"

Adah sighed. "Best not, Gracie." She tried to keep her emotions steady, but Grace was pushing much too hard for her own good.

chapter

thirty

Judah awakened from a fitful sleep, glad his inner clock hadn't failed him. His turn to check on the lambs. *Can't afford to lose another one,* he thought, fumbling for his robe in the darkness.

He staggered down the stairs to the hallway and sat on the deacon's bench to pull on his work boots over bare feet. Although still in something of a stupor, he managed to get to the barn, where he made his way to the lambing pen. There he monitored the two-day-old twins, born Wednesday afternoon while he and Andy Riehl sheared the rest of the sheep. Thankfully, Adam and Joe had kept watch over the laboring ewe, and there had been no complications.

Unable now to repress his feelings of anxiety, Judah knelt in the hay. The pain in his neck had developed into a constant torment, a continual reminder of his loss. Blame saddled him down with a weight he felt powerless to escape.

What Judah wouldn't do for some rest . . . deep, restorative sleep to submerge the memories and ease the enduring pain.

Let us lay aside every weight, and the sin which doth so easily beset us . . .

He mustered up the energy to inspect the two remaining triplet lambs, as well—one of which needed frequent bottle-feeding. That done, he slid open the barn door, closed it again, and slogged back to the house. He kicked off his dirty boots, then gripping the banister, he pulled himself back up the stairs to his room.

Almost too tired to move, Judah fell into bed with his robe still tied at the waist. His feet hung off Lettie's side of the bed.

Dear wife of mine . . .

———

The sun peeked over the distant green hills, and Heather was awake enough to turn on her phone to check her email. Several college acquaintances had sent updates in an attempt to get her to return for some summer fun.

Fleetingly, she wished she had a sister. It would be a relief to have someone to confide in, whether about Devon or about her diagnosis and the upcoming appointment with the naturopath. It wasn't that she questioned her decisions; she just felt so alone in the world.

When she heard a knock on her door, she set aside her phone. She really needed to work on her thesis today, once she got her inbox down to zero.

She opened the door and there stood Becky, dressed for the day in a dark green dress with an apron to match. "Would ya want to come help make chocolate waffles, Heather?" she asked, eyes shining.

Heather had indicated an interest yesterday, but this minute? She craved some time alone. She had enjoyed Becky's company, but as was her usual way with potential friendships, she felt herself backing away, even though her initial connection with Becky Riehl had been so strong.

"Heather?" Becky repeated.

"Maybe another time?"

Becky's smile faded.

Heather felt bad—she hadn't wanted to hurt the younger girl's feelings. "I just need to keep working, that's all." The explanation sounded lame even to her ears.

"I'll call ya when breakfast is ready, then."

"Thanks. I appreciate it." Heather closed the door.

She shook her head. *Why do I always do that?*

Heather crawled back onto the bed with what looked to be her best friend in the world right now—her phone.

———

Surprised to see Dat's door wide open, Grace looked in on her father, who was still sleeping. She'd come up to check on him after Adam and Joe asked why he hadn't gone directly to the barn after dawn, their usual habit.

She didn't have the heart to waken

him as he slept crisscross on the bed. *Must have checked on the lambs earlier.* Thinking it best to leave him be, as weary as he'd been for the past week, she softly closed the door and tiptoed downstairs to put breakfast on the table.

Dawdi and Mammi came over without being asked today . . . quite cheerfully, too. Evidently they were all for Mandy's suggestion they take meals together as one big family.

"Dat's under the weather," Grace said as they sat. Then they bowed their heads, ready for Dawdi Jakob's blessing.

Grace placed her left hand on Mamma's vacant chair and asked the Lord to look after her while offering her own silent thanks. Dat had instructed them to remember Mamma and her safety in their prayers. She was tempted to pray for a safe and quick return, too.

After the blessing, Mammi Adah looked at Dat's empty chair before mentioning the coming no-Preaching Sunday. Dawdi Jakob also entered into the discussion. "Any suggestions who we should go visit?" he asked. "Has your Dat talked of anyone?"

Both Adam and Joe shook their heads.

"Well, we can't all fit in one carriage," Mammi said, "but Adam could take his courtin' buggy and put the girls in it."

"That'd be fun," Mandy piped up, her fork resting between her fingers.

"It's been the longest time since we've seen Dat's cousins in Bart," suggested Joe.

Grace sucked in a breath. "But . . . without Mamma?"

Adam locked his gaze on Grace's. "Jah . . . those cousins probably aren't the best choice this time."

"Might just get things stirred up worse than they are," Dawdi agreed, wiping crumbs from his gray beard.

"What about Dat's parents, then?" Joe asked. "We could go down near Ronks to see them . . . then come back and visit the Bontragers, maybe."

"Two families in one afternoon." Mandy smiled and looked back and forth between Grace and Joe.

Grace studied her younger brother.

What was he up to? Was he sweet on Yonnie's younger sister Mary Liz, just maybe?

Adam suggested they wait to see what Dat wanted to do. "He's not sick, is he, Grace?" he asked, frowning.

"Considering everything, I'd say he's all tuckered out," she replied.

At that, everyone nodded, seemingly in unison. Truth was, and she could see it in their eyes, they were all worried Dat was pining hard for Mamma.

———

Jessica and Brittany Spangler stopped by with three loaves of banana nut bread midmorning. Such kind and caring neighbors, as always. "Thought you maybe could use an extra bit of baking," Brittany said, looking much too serious.

Grace assumed they'd heard by now of Mamma's leaving. How could they not? Even though nothing was said about it, she'd have to be blind not to see the knowing glint in their made-up eyes. "Come see us, Grace!" they urged before saying good-bye.

So the news had traveled even farther

than the People. Surely the most remarkable tittle-tattle to hit the area in recent years.

Grace ambled through the kitchen
and across the hall, heading upstairs to
Mammi Adah's sewing room. Earlier,
Mammi had asked Grace to help cut
yard lengths of thread for quilting, and
Grace had agreed. She greeted her
grandmother and settled in across the
worktable from her, all the while knowing it was time to come clean. "I hope
you know I didn't just let Mamma go
that night," she finally said. "Not without
calling to her. Well, pleading . . . truly."

"Of course you tried to stop her."
Mammi sighed, her bosom rising slowly.
"I'm sure you did, dear, just as I
would've."

"There's something else," Grace said,
nearly in a whisper.

Mammi looked up, scissors and
thread in hand.

"I went looking for your letter in the
night," Grace said, swallowing hard. "It
was wrong of me. . . . I'm sorry."

Mammi's eyes grew wide.

"I can't stop thinking 'bout Mamma. If

the letter Dawdi wrote to you and
Mamma might help . . . well, why not let
me read it?" Grace began to cry. "Oh,
Mammi . . . I just thought, maybe . . .
Ach, I'm ever so sorry."

"There, there, honey-girl." Mammi
Adah reached across the table and
touched her hand.

She wept softly, wishing she could
get ahold of herself. After a time, when
she'd wiped her eyes and blown her
nose, Grace caught her breath. "Could
the address on the envelope be the
same as Mamma's present location?"

Mammi Adah nodded slowly. "I can't
tell ya how many times I've wondered
that myself since she left." She fidgeted.

"If so, Dat could just go and bring
Mamma home."

"Well, if your mother's gone there, I
can tell you she would not want any of
us followin' her." Mammi's breathing
was audible as she resumed her measuring and cutting. "It's best we leave
things with the Lord."

Grace pondered this and stretched
the measuring tape along the thread.
She wasn't content to do as Mammi

suggested. What if Dat did travel out to Ohio, only to be rebuffed as Grace had been the day Mamma left?

Suddenly, Dawdi Jakob called up the stairs, "Ach, the brethren have come to see Judah!" and Mammi excused herself right quick, looking quite distressed.

Grace's heart beat hard, yet she made herself stay sitting quietly in the tranquil room where her mother had sometimes come to work. Mammi's old treadle sewing machine stood silently in the corner like an old friend.

The psalm she'd read early this morning came to mind: *Trust in him at all times . . . pour out your heart before him.*

She bowed her head to pray.

Judah had awakened with a jolt, flabbergasted to find himself still in bed at this late hour. He'd quickly gone downstairs to shower and dress and was just coming out of the washroom when Adah motioned him to the back door. "The ministers are here to see you, Judah." She stepped aside and swiftly left the kitchen.

If it's not one thing . . .

He inhaled deeply, uncertain what was ahead. He went to the door and took the steps slowly, not trusting his legs. In spite of his unintentional long rest, they were as unreliable as rubber.

"Mornin', Judah," Preacher Smucker said, the first to greet him.

Judah gave a nod but made no effort to speak, preserving his energy for whatever was to be addressed. And surely there was trouble ahead, with all four ministers in his yard—the bishop, two preachers, and Deacon Amos.

The bishop took the lead. "We've come to offer our help," he said, glancing toward the barn. "If you want to try to locate your wife."

She doesn't want to be found, he thought bitterly.

Judah spied part of Joe's face peeking out from behind the barn door. He frowned at his son, who immediately disappeared inside.

"I have many new lambs. . . ." Surely the brethren realized that to go now would put his very livelihood at stake.

"Even so, perhaps you could be doing more to find her," Deacon Amos suggested.

The intimation seemed harsh to Judah's ears, and it was all he could do to stand upright.

"Preacher Smucker says you have no clear understanding as to where she's gone. Is that it?" The bishop looked at him, his brow pinched into a frown. The oldest man of the group, his beard was long and wispy and as white as washed wool.

Breaking into a cold sweat now, Judah mumbled that he knew nothing of Lettie's whereabouts or motives. And the deacon's remark caused him further embarrassment—was Amos questioning the quality of his marriage? Were all of them?

He'd kept secrets from them, from his family, too. Yet was it anyone's business that Lettie had taken money from their account? As far as he could tell from that, she had no intention of returning home, even if found.

"Judah?" The bishop was awaiting a response.

Judah opened his mouth, and the backyard whirled as if he alone were caught on a windmill.

He gasped and reached out a hand to Amos to steady himself. But he missed, and his legs were suddenly too weak to hold him. "Oh . . ." He stumbled backward and fell to the ground, the sky a spinning bluish gray. The sum total of four beards, four faces, and four straw hats hovered over him, all part of the churning background.

"Judah, what's happening?" asked Preacher Josiah Smucker.

"Ain't rightly sure. . . ." He uttered words that made no sense, as though someone else were speaking for him.

Great drops fell from his eyes, down his face, and into the thickness of his beard. He crossed his arms over his chest while his sorrow and confusion poured forth.

"I cannot go on. . . ." His breath no

longer supported his words. And he was sobbing.

"He needs rest" came the kindly voice of Preacher Josiah—Judah knew that much. But he did not comprehend much else as the men linked arms, raising him up to carry him into his house.

chapter

thirty-one

From the sewing room window, Grace could see her father encircled by the brethren, though it appeared that only the bishop and the deacon were doing the talking. Unexpectedly Dat teetered to the left, clutching for Amos before stumbling back and falling to the grass.

"Oh . . . Dat, no!" she cried, horrified.

Quickly, the ministerial brethren surrounded him. Then, with great care, they lifted him into their arms and collectively carried Dat toward the door.

Grace flew down the stairs, meeting them as they brought Dat, pale and trembling, into the front room. They laid him out on the only sofa in the room, his feet hanging off the end.

Preacher Josiah rushed off to alert their neighbor Mrs. Spangler, a registered nurse. After he'd gone, Deacon

Amos suggested calling an ambulance, but the bishop said to wait for the nurse's opinion on that, not wanting to get more Englischers involved "unless necessary."

Grace knelt and touched her father's forehead. "I'm right here, Dat," she whispered, leaning near to his face. "It's Grace . . . I'm here with you."

When she realized she was alone with her father—no doubt the others were waiting outdoors for Preacher Josiah to return with Mrs. Spangler—Grace raised the hem of her apron and gently dabbed his dear face, spotty with perspiration. Her poor, grief-stricken father had silently borne his anguish, and now . . . "Sleep," she said, caressing his cheek with the back of her hand. "Just sleep."

His eyes fluttered but did not open. He raised one hand momentarily, and she clasped it in both of her own. "Grace . . . denki," he managed to say.

She covered her mouth with her hand, not wanting to cry again. Broken in mind and spirit, Dat had asked them to pray for Mamma's safety, and oh, she had. But now someone must carry her father's great need to the Almighty.

O Lord, look down on Dat here . . . and grant him health and peace.

Rising quietly to avoid distressing him further, she backed out of the room and dashed off to find Adam and the others.

———

For several hours, Dat slept under Grace's watchful eye. Mrs. Spangler had taken his vitals and determined that he most likely was suffering from sheer exhaustion and dire stress—the latter she confided softly to Grace alone.

Mammi Adah assigned Mandy to help her prepare the meals, for the time being. And Adam and Joe solicited help with the lambing and the barn chores from the ministers and other Amish neighbors.

Word of their father's collapse spread swiftly. To prevent unnecessary disturbances, Mandy posted signs on the main door and side kitchen door, alerting would-be visitors or well-wishers not to knock or raise their voices. And come they did, bearing hot casseroles,

canned fruits, meats, and even mone-
tary gifts. Preacher Smucker stopped
by, as well, speaking quietly to Grace,
expressing both his concern for her father and his hope that he might be able
to speak with him again soon.

When Dat awakened for the first time,
he asked to be helped upstairs to bed,
and his sons supported him on either
side. Grace held her breath the whole
way, following close behind.

Ach, Mamma, if you only knew . . .

Adam helped him undress as Grace
and Joe waited in the hallway, exchang-
ing anxious glances. Then, when Adam
emerged with concern etched on his
face, Grace asked if he thought she
should go inside.

"Just see what else he might need."
Adam worked his jaw, fighting back
tears.

She touched his arm and thanked
him, even though it seemed odd for her
to do so. After all, she was as appre-
hensive as he. Now, however, she was
determined to oversee Dat's recovery,
not allowing a single hitch in his getting
the restful, healing sleep he required.

Pulling a chair next to his bed, she asked what he wanted to drink. "You'll need something sooner or later." He had not eaten since breakfast.

"Just water . . ." He struggled to keep his eyes open, then his hand went limp, and she realized he'd already given in to slumber once again.

Finding a quilted coverlet in Mamma's blanket chest, Grace spread it gently over her father. She moved silently to the door and, with one more glance, slipped out of the room.

———

The late afternoon sun spread a golden light over Dat's grazing land, where a half dozen new lambs romped about, trailing their mothers. Needing some time outside, Grace watched the younger, more playful lambs bounding over the dark green meadow, soon to be teeming with a sea of golden dandelions.

To her, spring had always signaled the advent of new life. And it was nearly impossible to contemplate the rolling landscape before her without realizing anew how it altered so completely with the movement of the seasons.

Time and nature were tied together somehow. She'd once read about the change from winter to spring . . . that the shift had the power to jumble up people's emotions. She wondered if it affected the sheep Dat raised in the same way.

She was amused by the animals' hesitancy around strangers. They backed away quickly, only one of the older rams brave enough to inch forward at the sight of someone new.

Looking toward the road, she spotted a young woman—an Englischer—coming up from the Riehls' place. She was sniffling and wiping her eyes with her fingers. Grace wondered if this was the young woman staying at the Riehls' for the summer.

The woman began to run hard, like a runner in a race, and Grace could hear her sobs. She appeared to catch herself and slowed again to a walk, wrapping her arms around her middle. She reached up a hand to brush back more tears, her shoulders rising and falling.

Grace's heart went out to the jean-clad girl. And she wished she could help somehow.

———

Judah rolled over in the big bed to reach for Lettie's pillow, scarcely conscious of the hour before again falling quickly into the enticing comfort of sleep. He was only faintly mindful of Grace when she appeared now and then with cold water in a glass or to check his pulse. Did she think he'd expired?

It was the Lord's Day, the second morning following his collapse, and Judah crept his way downstairs to bathe and shave. But not to dress.

Grace was in the kitchen with Mandy and came out to assure him he need not check on the animals. "We've ample help." No mention was made of their visiting relatives or friends this particular Sunday, and he felt sorry for putting a damper on the family day.

He took the stairs carefully again, without help, pleased at this small feat. Strength was slow in coming, yet returning all the same. He savored the smallest progress as he sat in his chair near the window, sunshine pouring in.

He opened the Good Book and found his place. *I was dumb with silence, I held my peace, even from good; and my sorrow was stirred.* The relevance of what he read struck him, and Judah was moved to pray, grateful to God and his family for their tenderness toward him.

Grace brought his dinner up soon after and placed the tray by his side. He thought of telling her how much her care meant to him, but the words were lost somewhere inside him.

———

Judah slept again, waking up just as night began to fall, surprised at the stillness in his usually bustling house. What had his children done to create such tranquillity?

For the first time since his collapse, he thought of Lettie's parents. Was Grace looking after them, too?

Getting up, he moved gingerly to the edge of his bed. He had a hankering to slip into his trousers, to know how good it might feel to be fully dressed again. "Tomorrow," he promised himself.

He rose to walk the length of the hallway and did not see a soul. Then footsteps broke the quiet.

"Oh, Dat, so good to see you up again and walkin'," Grace said as she came to check on him. A full smile lit her dear face.

"My legs are finally cooperating." He was surprised when she linked her arm through his and walked back with him. "Guess I just needed some rest."

"That and some tender loving care." She looked away, but he'd seen her tears. "You had us awful scared, Dat."

He sighed, winded, and sat down on his chair. "Shouldn't it be mornin' instead of dusk?" He stared out at the darkening sky and stretched his legs before him.

"Hungry?"

He nodded up at her as his daughter moved to the doorway. *Ach, she radiates goodness.* "You're a fine nurse, Gracie."

She smiled again; he had used Lettie's nickname for her, and she'd noticed. "Do you want pie or cookies and ice cream for dessert?"

"I'll eat whatever you bring." He turned back to the window. The birdbath Lettie had chosen for the side yard was nearly invisible in the graying twilight.

Leaning closer to the window, he saw his own reflection on the pane, faint yet recognizable. And he felt a sudden wave of relief come over him. He was going to be all right.

———

As she began to take down her hair, Lettie was struck by the thought that she simply could not wait any longer. She'd napped soundly that afternoon, falling into a sleep fraught with dreams. So many dreams of her family, especially her children. An urgency stirred within her as she'd awakened—she must get word to them that she was safe.

Quickly winding her hair back into a makeshift bun, she pinned it up and hurried downstairs to the common area, where a telephone was available for the guests. She'd brought along a card with prepaid minutes and had used it only once since leaving home.

Martin Puckett urged me to call for any reason, Lettie remembered, not wanting to contact Marian Riehl on her barn phone . . . afraid her neighbor friend might take the opportunity to scold her. She couldn't bear that now.

Going to the chair near the fireplace, she reached for the receiver.

Martin heard the phone ring and was glad Janet answered, leaving him to watch his news show. His feet propped up on the ottoman, he leaned back in his lounge chair and enjoyed a bowl of popcorn Janet had made the old-fashioned way—in a pan, on the stove.

"Martin," she called, her voice strained. "It's Lettie Byler. Sounds like she's crying."

"Well, good night . . . What's this?" He reached for the portable phone on the lamp table. "Hello?"

"Ach, Martin, I hate to call you so late and all. I'm truly sorry."

"This is fine . . . just fine." He paused, not wanting to sound too relieved to hear from her. "Are you all right?"

"I . . . just . . ." She sniffled, then spoke again. "Would it be too much trouble to ask you to get a message to my family—'specially to Judah?"

"No trouble, Lettie. What would you like me to say?"

Janet had come into the TV room and stood in the doorway, facing him with a quizzical expression.

"Could ya just tell him I'm safe?" Lettie asked.

"Anything else?" Martin asked. She sounded as tense now as she had at the train station, and he waited for more. Something solid to go on—where she was staying, perhaps . . . when she planned to return.

"Tell my husband I'll be in contact later."

He was baffled by her still-distant tone. "I'll deliver your message first thing tomorrow."

"Denki, Martin. Again, I hope I didn't disturb your evening."

"You take care now."

She said good-bye and hung up.

He switched off the phone. "She's all right."

"Sure didn't sound like it." Janet frowned. "Why would she call here?"

"Her family has no house phone, you must remember."

His wife nodded as if it hadn't occurred to her.

"When I took her to the train station, I suggested she call here if she needed help." He added, "It seemed like the right thing to do."

"Well, of course." Janet sat on the ottoman and touched his knee. "You're a good man, Martin."

He reached for the remote. "She must be visiting someone."

"She didn't say?"

"Well, when she left she had a list of phone numbers and said someone was meeting her." He was glad to see the assurance return to Janet's eyes. She'd had no reason to ever be uneasy.

Tomorrow he must deliver Lettie's

message to Judah—and explain why she'd contacted him instead of any of her people.

———

Grace had seen Martin Puckett pull into the drive numerous times before, so she didn't think anything of it when he arrived after she'd finished hanging out the Monday washing. She assumed Adam needed transportation, because she had not phoned Martin, and Dat was in no shape to go anywhere.

Martin got out of the van and came around to the side door.

"Goodness, this is service," she said, welcoming him inside.

"I won't stay but a minute." He stepped into the kitchen but glanced back at the door. "I see your sign. Is someone ill?"

She explained that Dat had been sick but was improving. "He's still not takin' visitors, though . . . and he'll be sorry to miss you."

Martin's concerned look caused her to offer him a seat at the table and some cookies, which he declined. "I came to bring you news from your mother," he said, continuing on without waiting for a response. "She wants your father to know she's all right."

Grace tried but could not speak.

"Will you relay the message?" She nodded and he explained that he and his wife had received a call last night. "I don't know where she was calling from—the number was blocked."

Grace managed to thank him. "I'll tell Dat you dropped by."

Mamma says she's all right. But where?

Irritation grew within her—why hadn't her mother said where she was? Did she always have to be so mysterious?

Grace could think of only one way to quell her intense anger. Only one.

———

While her hearty vegetable soup simmered on low, Grace saw her chance to leave for a walk. The morning was warming up—already the fifth day of May. A light breeze swayed the tops of trees, and the windmills in the distance moved steadily. She was glad for the

fresh air on her face after rushing
around to get breakfast and then assist-
ing Mammi Adah with some piecework
for a quilt after cleaning her father's
bedroom and doing laundry.

Dat had declared he was strong
enough to wander out to the barn, with
Adam and Joe keeping close watch. It
did her good to see the color returning
to his cheeks. They'd all had a bad
scare.

One Mamma might never know about,
she thought, resentment rising.

The road was as empty now as at that
dark hour when she'd run after
Mamma . . . ignored, despite her pleas.
Grace looked all around her, assuming
she'd found the very spot.

Then, folding her hands, she bowed
her head and voiced the prayer she'd
contemplated since seeing Dat fall at
the feet of the brethren, shattered by his
own grief.

"I'm here, Lord, because I'm weary of
my bitterness. And I want to ask forgiveness." She paused. "No, that ain't
quite right. . . ."

She struggled against every bit of

frustration pent up inside her. "I want to forgive my Mamma," she said, lifting her eyes. In her mind, she saw again her mother hustling away from her with the bulky suitcase, filled with nearly every bit of clothing she owned. "I'm askin' you to carry away my anger, Lord. And the resentment I feel every time I think of that awful moment."

She was weeping now, unable to stop. "I'm sorry for the ugly feelings I've kept inside me, nurturin' them." Stopping her prayer, she went to lean against the sheep fence. "Oh, Mamma, I don't understand why you had to go. But with God's help, I won't tend this bitter root in me any longer."

She wiped her wet face on the handkerchief she'd tucked into the sleeve of her dress and sighed as she glanced back at Dat's big house in the distance.

She was surprised, but she already felt ever so much lighter.

Forgiven.

She thought of the hummingbird drawing Becky had slipped beneath the side door yesterday. A thoughtful thing for her friend to do, knowing Grace was

sitting nearly round the clock at Dat's
bedside. Mandy had brought the drawing upstairs to her, not speaking, only
pointing to Becky's lovely handiwork.
Made just for her with those pretty birthday pencils Grace had given her friend.

*No wonder Mamma loves humming-
birds. They're unfettered and free.*

She thought again of her own strug-
gles. Only through daily and deliberate
forgiveness could she, too, find freedom. *Just as Mamma taught me . . .*

She turned toward home. As much as
she understood about forgiveness,
Grace knew it would take time for healing to come.

She was nearing the turnoff into the
driveway when she noticed Henry and
his sister Priscilla riding together in the
market wagon. The minute Priscilla
spotted her, she began waving excit-
edly. Grace waved back, pleased to see
them.

Henry, however, sat as straight as a
stick, both hands on the reins, offering
merely a half smile as they approached.

She instantly felt glum. *Why can't he
be more like his sister?* she wondered

as they passed by. *Isn't he happy to see me?*

Mamma had once told her, *"Dat loves us, even though he doesn't say it."*

"Like Henry?" Grace blurted aloud now, recalling the way he'd asked her to marry him, not saying he loved her even then.

In that painful moment, the disappointments of the past months caught up with her. Was this the reason she'd awakened the morning after Henry proposed with so little joy about their coming union? Had she subconsciously known she was headed for a cheerless marriage . . . like Mamma's?

For sure and for certain, she'd made excuses for herself—for Henry, too, initially thinking her ho-hum feelings stemmed from her disillusionment over Mamma's leaving. But she knew there was far more to it. And seeing Henry just now and the way he'd looked right through her triggered an onslaught of suppressed feelings.

Somehow she'd managed to overlook his shy nature from the first date on, hoping that in time he might open his heart. Plenty of men were like that, including Dat. Yet the way she felt right now, it was hard to think of living out her years with a husband like her father. *Hard . . . if not impossible.*

Grace stubbed her toe as she turned into the driveway. In all truth, she found not a speck of pleasure in the thought of being engaged to Henry Stahl. If anything, she was panicked by it.

chapter

thirty-two

Washday in Ohio fell on the same day as back home, though here Lettie had no access to a wringer-washer or a clothesline. For that reason, she offered to pay Tracie Gordon for the use of the inn's automatic washer and dryer.

"I wouldn't think of charging you," the younger woman said. "You just help yourself whenever you're ready. There's an iron and ironing board in there, too, if you need them."

Lettie had assumed the facilities would be in use to wash the inn's soiled linens and towels. But later, while sorting her own clothes, she discovered from the housekeeper that she was the only weekday guest. The tidy little laundry room was all hers.

Once her washing was folded and pressed, she returned to her room and smoothed down her hair at the middle part. Then she bathed and chose a clean dress and matching apron.

She'd felt queasy all morning—a bad case of nerves. Samuel, being a recent widower, might be too grief stricken to welcome a visit from her. She had no way of knowing how things might turn out between them. They'd cared so deeply for each other. But that was long ago.

Lettie hoped her second car trip down to Fredericksburg would not be in vain. The drivers here were as expensive as in Lancaster County, but that wasn't the only reason she hoped she might find Samuel Graber at home this time.

Her heart felt like it might beat right out of her chest as she stood waiting beside the front room window for her ride. For weeks her emotions had been nearly raw, yet as she pondered what she was about to do, she felt more vulnerable than heartbroken. Tears slipped from her eyes, and the tree-lined street became a shimmering stream.

How will Samuel receive me?

The afternoon sun cast a gentle light over the narrow street as the driver parked two doors away and opposite from the house belonging to Samuel. Lettie spotted a man pulling weeds in the front yard, and her breath caught in her throat when she realized it was indeed Samuel.

Dressed like an Englischer, she thought, reminding herself to breathe.

His fancy attire wasn't the only thing that had changed since their courting days. His face was somewhat fuller, his light brown hair peppered with gray on the sides.

She paid the driver and stepped out of the van. Her pulse raced as she made her way up the street, feeling her weight on the sidewalk as she took each step approaching the front yard. Once again she admired the overall attractiveness of the place, and she prayed for courage.

I'm this far. . . .

Meanwhile, Samuel moved up to the front porch, unaware of her as he pinched off dried blossoms from the begonias in matching pots. She stood quietly at the foot of the steps, suddenly too bashful to announce herself.

Ach, what have I done?

Just when she'd thought she might simply retreat, he turned and saw her there—an unexpected sight to be sure. She was, after all, wearing her Amish garb, her hair in the traditional bun.

"Hullo, Samuel," she said, offering a smile.

He squinted and straightened. Then, suddenly, his eyes grew wide and twinkled in recognition as a smile spread across his face. "Lettie? Is it you?"

She smiled back, nodding. "Jah, 'tis."

"Goodness, what a surprise!" His laughter rekindled so many fond memories. "Well, for Pete's sake!" He stood back and appraised her.

"Nice to see you again, Samuel." She felt slightly more confident now that he seemed so delighted.

He apologized for having forgotten his manners. "Please . . . won't you come inside?" He motioned toward the door, holding it for her.

"Denki." She let the word slip.

In the house, she inhaled slowly . . . deeply. *Here at last.*

"Make yourself at home," he said, a curious smile on his face.

She looked around, taking in the comfortable room. It had the look of a small library or perhaps a den, as she'd heard some fancy folk call such a room. Plenty large enough for two upholstered chairs—one a soft green, the other eggshell in color—with an oak lamp table between them. The chairs were situated facing a small glassed-in fireplace, and books, dozens of them, lined the shelves, one side reaching to the ceiling.

Samuel waited till she was seated before he moved the decorative pillow from his chair and sat down, too, still simply beaming. "Goodness, how long has it been?" he asked, his eyes fixed on her. "Twenty-some years."

"At least." But she knew precisely. A girl never forgot her first love.

He leaned back. "What brings you to Ohio? Business or pleasure?"

My visit with you, she thought.

Her mind—no, her heart—was whirling. So much to say. "Well, I'm in the area for several reasons," she managed to respond, embarrassed at his keen attention.

"You've come alone?"

She nodded. "This trip, jah."

"You must still live in Bird-in-Hand, I assume?"

She said she did. "I married Judah Byler," she added quickly.

"Judah?" He glanced at the ceiling, as if trying to place him. "Why, sure . . . I remember now. He was kind of a reserved fellow, wasn't he?"

She nodded only slightly, wanting to change the subject . . . needing to. "I heard of your wife's passing from Sarah, when your sister was visiting in Bart some weeks back. I'm so sorry to hear it."

He thanked her, saying that Emmie's passing was something of a blessing, because she'd suffered for so long. Then he went on. "Well, I'll be . . . I had no idea Sarah was back there. When was this?"

"In March . . . she came to see a relative's new baby."

"Ah yes, our grand-niece." He
scratched his head. "Guess I failed to
even send them a card. Emmie handled
that sort of thing, you know." He chuckled. "I've got so much to catch up on."

"Have you lived in Fredericksburg
very long?" she ventured.

"Three years now," he said. "I'd always wanted to own a welding shop,
and when this one came up for sale—
less than four miles away—I snatched it
right up." He rose suddenly, going to his
books. "Here's another one of my
dreams come true," he said, waving his
hand at the shelves of books. "Would
you care to see some of my favorites?"

"Poetry?"

"Is there anything else?" He laughed
and the sound brought her joy. "Emmie
used to say my poetry books were my
Bible, but that was only a joke." Still, he
was obviously attached to his fine collection of Browning, Frost, Dickinson,
and several other poets she hadn't
heard of.

He brought Alfred Lord Tennyson t⸍

her and ran his finger down the list of po-
ems on the first page—"Audley Court,"
"The Beggar Maid," "The Blackbird,"
"The Charge of the Light Brigade." . . .

" 'A hundred summers! can it be?' "
he quoted from "The Day-Dream."

Oh, she was sixteen again . . . shoo-
ing flies away from her face as she sat
high in the haymow, listening intently to
the rhythmic sway of his voice, the mes-
merizing way he had with each stanza
and measure of phrase. As if he were
born to read poetry to her and to her
alone.

"Emmie said I was a dichotomy—part
grease monkey, part rhymester." He
glanced toward the window, surely
thinking of her just now. "Not sure where
she ever heard that."

"Rhymester?" Lettie asked.

He nodded. "Guess it's strange, but I
never wrote a poem for my late wife.
Wasn't much good at it, I guess."

He was, after all, more an interpreter
of poets, she remembered, though he'd
tried his hand at rhymes.

"I once wrote a decent one, though,"
he said quietly. His gaze found her. "It

was the day my father told us we were leaving Lancaster County."

She sighed, heavyhearted now at the prospect of hearing what she knew he was about to say.

"I wrote the poem for you, Lettie." He rubbed his hands back and forth on the arms of his chair. "I had no way of knowing how to get in touch," he said. "No one seemed to know where you'd gone, or why you'd left."

"I was out here, in Ohio . . . came with my mother to help my father's very ill aunt." She took a long breath. "But that wasn't the only reason we came, Samuel."

She'd imagined this very moment for more than a month—had even practiced her words. Somewhere in Samuel's dining room, a clock was ticking. And out on the pretty porch the wind chime tinkled, the sound ever so haunting as it drifted through the window screen.

Samuel's face was pensive now.

Ach, how I loved him.

Pursing her lips, she tumbled over the waterfall of the past. "The reason I'm here is to make a confession. One I should've made years ago."

Seeing his furrowed brow, she paused and felt the distance of their years apart.

"Lettie?" He leaned forward, his hands on his knees. "What is it?"

She swallowed hard, willing herself to find the courage. "Truth is, I never should've left you, Samuel. Not without tellin' you the truth."

His fingers fidgeted on the piping along the edge of the chair.

"Ach, but I was so deceitful. And I have paid dearly for it. And . . . I'm ever so sorry."

He frowned tenderly. "Whatever you have to say . . . please, feel free to say it, Lettie."

Samuel had always made it easy for her to speak her mind. Her heart. "I had a baby," she said softly. *"Ours."*

He sat motionless, eyes wide. "We . . . have a child?"

She bowed her head, staring at her folded hands. "It was wrong of me not to tell you." She was afraid she might cry. "I was nearly five months along when Mamm and I went to Kidron to stay . . . where I gave birth."

"Oh, Lettie, I wish I'd known."

She shook her head, drawing a shallow breath. "It was never my idea to keep such a secret—or to give up the baby." She pulled a hankie from her sleeve. "Ach, this has weighed on me for so long."

His face was drawn, pale. "Who else knew?"

"Only my parents at first." She sighed heavily. "And of course my great-aunt. Then, much later, I confided in my closest sister, Naomi, but she passed away several years ago." She told him how she'd stayed then at the same inn she'd chosen this visit, having the baby there.

"A boy or a girl?" he asked tentatively.

"Mamma hired an Amish midwife, and together they decided it was best, all round, that I wasn't told. I never even got to see or hold the baby," she said sadly. "Honestly, though, I had a strong feeling I'd birthed a son."

"This is all so shocking." Samuel's face was filled with angst. "You see, Emmie and I always wanted children.

Very much so," he said quietly. "We yearned for our own, but Emmie wasn't well for much of our marriage. And now you say that I had a child all along." He pressed his fingers against his temples. "And I missed it all, all the growing-up years."

"I know, Samuel. I know. . . ."

She'd heard of Samuel and Emmie's childless marriage from Sarah, who'd revealed the sad news when they walked together at the barn raising. "This is one of the reasons why I came lookin' for you," she said. "My heart broke for you, Samuel, when Sarah said you'd lost your dear wife . . . and you'd never had children."

He glanced at the window, eyes blinking as he seemed to calculate the years. "Our child must be close to twenty-four by now."

Brushing away tears, she nodded. "Born April twenty-ninth that year."

Six days later than Grace's own birthday . . . and only two days from the anniversary of Naomi's passing. Tears slid down Lettie's cheeks.

His eyes probed hers. "Do you have any idea where he or she might be?"

She explained that she'd hoped to find the midwife while in Kidron, with no success. "I wanted to find our child first, before coming to see you."

A way to attempt to bridge the chasm between them, she'd realized. Oh, but their unresolved parting had taken its dreadful toll on her. And after stumbling upon Samuel's sister, Lettie had purposed in her heart to find both Samuel and their child, to set things right. During the long nights of wandering, she'd prayed for both her child and for Samuel. Deep in thought, she'd wished for a way to find their child, but had no idea where to look. Aside from Kidron, Ohio.

"That was very thoughtful of you . . . and generous, too," he said.

"Well, I'm still searching for the midwife—anyone who might know something, but I'm discovering there are many hurdles." Lettie closed her eyes, reliving the questions that continually plagued her. *Does my child know how much he or she was loved? Is my son or daughter happy? Healthy?*

"I would have helped you raise the baby . . . would have married you." Samuel's voice was strained. "That was my intention, Lettie, you must know. But I was young and my father moved us away in a failed attempt to keep his wayward son in the church," he said. "Poor excuses, I know, but I was under my father's roof then."

She understood. "I, too, was under the control of my parents." A little sob escaped. "Ach, Samuel, believe me, I wanted to keep the baby, but my parents—*my mother*—forced me to give the child away."

He shook his head sadly.

"A private adoption was arranged by a local doctor after the midwife took the baby away . . . that day."

"I'm so very sorry," he said. "What you went through . . . alone."

"It was a closed adoption, too, which is why this has taken much longer than I first expected. I immediately began making contacts after seeing your sister

Sarah." She paused. "I have no idea how long it'll take."

Samuel grew silent again, unquestionably lost in a blur of musings.

A lengthy silence prevailed; then he rose and went to stand near the bookshelves. "I took advantage of you, Lettie . . . when we were young. I apologize for that."

"We both knew better."

He walked to the window, his hands in his trouser pockets. "I'd like to help with your search," he said. "But I'm tied to my work here. Perhaps I can at least assist with your travel costs."

"Mighty kind of you, but that's not necessary, really." She thought of the money she'd withdrawn for the purpose of supporting her search. "Besides, my husband would not approve."

His eyebrows rose. "Judah didn't accompany you to Kidron, then?"

"It's lambing season." She gave her best excuse, not wanting to admit to having kept Judah in the dark about the trip. And the bigger secret—her child out of wedlock. "Well, I've taken up enough of your time." She rose and made her way to the door.

"Please, Lettie, let's stay in touch." He followed her outside to the porch. "How can I contact you?"

She mentioned the inn. "But I won't be there much longer. So it's best if I contact you, all right?"

He nodded and smiled sadly. "I appreciate your coming." He touched her elbow. "I'm sure you've considered this, but you have to realize there's always the possibility our child doesn't wish to be found."

"Such news could turn a person's life upside-down, for certain," she agreed. "Might find it horribly upsetting . . . even reject the notion."

"And . . . what if he or she doesn't know about being adopted? It's a terrible risk."

"Jah, 'tis." Overhead, the wind chime was surprisingly still. "And I can't be gone from my family indefinitely." She was needed at home, for gardening and canning . . . and for the fall wedding season.

For Adam's wedding. And for Judah.

Oh, how much she had to share with her husband. He wasn't the easiest to talk to, but he was a good man, and he'd weathered her ups and downs through the years. Judah had no knowledge whatsoever of the baby she'd conceived with Samuel—her cherished secret.

I owe Judah an apology, too. . . .

"Well, I really must be goin'." She moved toward the steps.

"I'll look forward to hearing from you," he said. "Be safe, Lettie."

She turned to wave. Then, seeing her driver parked across the street, she hurried to the van, breathing more freely now. She'd accomplished what she'd come to do.

The first of many difficult steps.

———

That night Lettie dreamed of Judah and saw his dear face once again. He was carrying a wee lamb in his arms, giving it a baby bottle to spare the lamb's life.

Your father's such a gentle shepherd, Lettie had once said at the table in front of all of them, even though he was truly considered a sheep farmer. Adam had nodded, looking right quick at Grace.

When she awakened, she felt the familiar pangs of homesickness. Yet her long journey had just begun. She would search for her firstborn child, the newborn taken from her much too quickly. Torn away from her . . . out of her life.

She wept for the infant she'd lost. Mamm had deprived her of laying eyes on that sweet bundle—*"the sinful result of forbidden love,"* she'd said so many times Lettie believed she was, in fact, consigned to hell.

"I must forgive Mamm, too," she said, rising to meet the day. "And Daed."

There were times when she honestly wondered if her husband and children would even want her back . . . if they knew her secret. And if she didn't return soon, there'd be dire talk of the *Bann,* too. She could easily fall into despair thinking about all that her family must be struggling with now, in her absence. And not just the amount of work left over from her leaving. No, there must be a terrible sense of rejection and the anguish of not knowing where she was or why she'd want to abandon them.

Yet, on the other hand, Lettie felt strangely relieved, as if a very heavy burden had been lifted from her. Not allowing herself to dwell on bleak thoughts, she opened the window and welcomed the warm May morning, a breeze catching the curtain, making it flutter.

I've come this far!

On a tree branch nearby, a jenny wren chirped happily. Then, moving away from the window, Lettie gathered up her clothes and began to pack to the cheerful song of the little bird. She was determined to locate the Amish midwife. Somehow, she would.

A favorite verse of Judah's came to mind—one from the prophet Isaiah, in the Old Testament. *And the Lord shall guide thee continually.*

Bowing her head, she asked God to do just that.

chapter

thirty-three

Grace could hear the muted sound of voices coming from the Singing as she slipped around the back of Deacon Amos's barn and leaned hard against a tree trunk facing the cornfield. The bark was still warm from the sun, fair as this Lord's Day had been. Yet the day had also been a difficult one.

Sighing, she gathered her wits. She'd exited the barn without Henry, who had been milling about with a group of singles—fellows who were not yet engaged or seriously courting anyone. Surprisingly, Yonnie Bontrager had been among them. *Surely he and Becky will pair up, like usual,* she thought, glad for this moment of respite behind the barn. There, where the ministerial brethren sometimes came and stood in a cluster, hashing out church issues and whatnot.

Pressing her hands against the tree's rough bark, she soaked up the quiet. It was impossible not to contemplate the thorny evening ahead of her—ahead of *them.* She'd glanced at Henry several times as they were singing with the rest of the group, pondering how best to do what she knew she must. She'd waited too long already, and she wondered what he might think of her when all was said and done.

Henry has no passion for life, she thought. *Nor for me . . .*

She stared at the night sky, letting her gaze drift over the wide expanse of stars and the blackness beyond. With all of her heart, she'd wanted their relationship to be mutually affectionate. And she had waited for him to make the first move toward marriage, all those months after they'd become serious . . . yearning for his marriage proposal. To think all the while Mamma had been silently suffering her own relationship problems.

The stars seemed much farther away this night, and she found herself reaching up and pinching her fingers to frame an especially bright one. Some of them were six million light years away, she'd read in a school book. In that moment, surrounded by the majesty of God's creation, she felt ever so small.

Ach, my wants and wishes seem petty just now.

She willed herself to be content with her soon-to-be lot, since breaking up with Henry Stahl would mean certain Maidelhood.

"A reserved man can be hard to live with," Mamma had said. Remembering bolstered Grace's courage. Mamma would be in favor of her breakup with Henry.

Just then, she heard voices coming from the side of the barn. Right away she knew it was Adam and his fiancée, Priscilla. Grace leaned to peer around the tree and held her breath to listen.

"You *were* gawking at me," Priscilla spouted off. "And your face was none too approving."

"Aw, now, Prissy . . ."

The sound of sniffles traveled to Grace. "You must not like the color of my dress," Priscilla continued. "Is that so, Adam?"

"Never said that."

She heard rustling now, like one of them was pacing in the tall grass a few yards from her hiding place.

They're arguing like this . . . over a dress? She wondered if Adam had endured other such sassy encounters.

Grace had recently seen her sister, Mandy, with a new beau, Becky Riehl's cousin. Mandy had seemed so comfortable, even joyful. In fact, this very night after the singing portion of the gathering was through, Grace had noticed several other blissfully happy couples . . . talking face to face, smiling and laughing.

Grace shook her head, annoyed at her brother for putting up with such an outspoken girl. Adam deserved better.

Then and there, the thought of so many lacking relationships weighed on her, and she hurried away from her spot to find Henry before she lost her nerve.

More than a half hour later, Grace was still waiting for Henry. He was certainly taking his time. Was he discussing fieldwork with the other fellows, perhaps? She'd considered simply leaving and

walking home, but she made herself
stay put right near the barn door.

Dozens of couples streamed out from
the Singing as the night progressed.
And such a lovely evening it was . . . still
mild from the balmy day. Mandy and her
beau strolled out through the open barn
door, laughing and holding hands.

Waiting with as much patience as she
could muster, Grace noticed Yonnie
Bontrager walk through the door by
himself. How peculiar it seemed, since
she was accustomed to seeing him with
Becky. Glancing over her shoulder, she
looked for her friend, having seen her
earlier in the long line of girls. But Becky
was nowhere around.

Unexpectedly, Yonnie turned and
looked at Grace just then. A smile
spread across his face, and his eyes
caught hers if but for a moment. Then,
still smiling, he gave a nod and turned to
make his way toward the lane. *On foot,
like always,* she thought, still surprised
he was alone.

Quickly, Grace dismissed his gaze
and too-broad smile, and she wandered

toward Henry's open buggy, more than ready to have the evening behind her.

————

Heather clicked the safety latch on her mother's bracelet, then slid it up her arm. Eyes woozy from hours of thesis work, she went out the door, pleased at having written five new pages. A break was well deserved. She was beginning to feel confined and was curious about a funky little coffee shop she'd spotted the other day, so she decided to venture there. *Hopefully it's still open. . . .*

Her dad had left another voice mail, saying he wanted to see her. "To get your input on several ideas swimming in my head about that farmhouse we're going to build," he'd said, laughing. "I'm coming your way in a few weeks, once I wrap up this project. Okay with you?"

His coming might not be such a bad idea. That way she could ask him to bring some of her more casual dresses and skirts, since not a single pair of jeans fit right anymore. Of course, with summer coming, she could just invest in a few shorts and tops at the outlet malls, which were as plentiful around here as eggs in the Riehls' hen house.

And, too, these past few days observing Andy and Marian Riehl interact with their large family made Heather wonder if maybe she shouldn't try to gently level with her dad—tell him the real reason why she'd run away.

———

Grace drew in a small breath when at last she saw Henry coming out through the barn door, glancing from side to side. *Looking for me,* she thought, suddenly sad.

She would not enjoy another Singing for a long time, she was quite sure. Why would she care to attend the cheery gatherings when, in all truth, she would feel anything but cheerful?

"Henry?" she called softly from where she stood near his buggy. "I'm here."

To think she was about to inflict on him a pain similar to that Mamma had inflicted on Dat. Cringing, she knew it was not wise to ride with Henry tonight—even for one last time. No, she must speak to him now and let him go home alone.

"Henry . . . I'd like to talk to you," she said, her throat husky as she moved toward him.

He nodded and motioned for her to get into his open carriage.

"No, I mean here," she said, her body tense. "Do you mind?"

He shrugged.

"Can we walk that way . . . toward the cornfield?" she asked, feeling strangely forward as he fell into step with her. "Over yonder."

She wondered if he might ask what was on her mind, but as was typical, he left it to her to take the lead. Yet now instead of experiencing her former melancholy, she was nearly encompassed with anger.

"It's not right," she said suddenly.

He turned, studying her in the dim light of the quarter moon. "What ain't?"

She paused to consider her words. "Our engagement." She took a few more steps before she stopped and faced him. "Maybe we moved too quickly," she said more quietly.

"You're not makin' sense, Grace."

Unsure of herself now, she did not want to sound ungrateful . . . or even unkind. "I shouldn't have said yes to your proposal, Henry." She looked at the sky. "Ach, but this is ever so hard."

"Wait—you're sorry you said you'd marry me?" His voice was tinged with resentment.

She nodded slowly and looked beyond his shoulders.

His face fell, and she felt horrid. Henry was a good, dependable man. She hoped her rejection would not lead to bitterness. She knew too well how the emotion could fester and eventually overtake a person.

She recalled their first dates, the slow-paced buggy rides long into the night—how he was content to be silent for as long as an hour at a time. Once she'd turned to him and asked, *"What're you thinking 'bout?"* and he'd said simply, *"You, Grace."*

She'd thought it an endearing, even a tender thing to say. But his inability to express anything more made her certain, without a doubt, that Henry Stahl did not possess what she longed for in a husband.

"I honestly believe we made a mistake," she said. "And I'm so sorry to say it."

He didn't attempt to change her mind, nor did he offer a good-bye kiss on her cheek. He merely bowed his head for a moment, then took a slow, deep breath. "All right, then," he said, turning away. "If this is what you want." And without another word, he headed back, climbed into his buggy, and drove away. Grace followed with her eyes until the horse and carriage were two black silhouettes on the road.

"Good-bye, Henry," she whispered, half wishing he had put up a fight for her.

Walking home by the shimmer of moonlight on Deacon Amos's silo, Grace felt a strange kinship with the night's stillness. Contentment came so quickly it surprised her, reassuring her that she had done the right thing for both Henry and for herself.

chapter

thirty-four

The next morning, once the washing was hung out across the clotheslines, Grace asked her brother if he'd mind returning the gift Henry had given her. "Please, will ya, Adam?" she pleaded when immediate opposition registered on his face. "You don't have to say one word to Henry 'bout the clock—I'm not askin' for that."

While she had no regrets, she truly felt weary. The bold action would surely lock the door on any hope of future reconciliation.

Adam's face scrunched into a tight frown. "Ain't becoming of you, Gracie."

"Well, it's the hardest thing, I know that."

"So think about what you're doin', then."

She sighed. "I have, Adam. And . . . I

expect Henry will be waitin' for the clock."

"Then you must've had words last night."

"Only mine."

Adam shook his head. "I hope you at least apologized. It wasn't fair to say yes if ya weren't certain."

"Jah, you're right. And I was as kind as anyone could be."

He grimaced. "Then so be it." Her brother followed her upstairs and took from her room the most beautiful chiming clock she'd ever seen, carrying it down to his open buggy. Lifting it high, he placed it gently inside, then looked back at her. "I can't change your mind?" he said. "No parting words to give Henry some hope, just maybe?"

"This ain't some snap decision, Adam," she said. "I've been a-ponderin' it for quite some time."

"Well, then, if you're mighty sure." He gave her a tender smile, pushed his straw hat forward slightly on his head, and made one leap up into the buggy.

Grateful for her brother's support, grudging as it was, she said, "Denki for makin' the delivery." She was relieved Adam did not despise either her or what she'd done.

"Consider it done." Adam waved, then picked up the reins and clucked his tongue. And old Willow, *bless her heart,* moved forward, pulling the carriage down the driveway to the road.

———

Heather politely refused Becky's invitation to run an errand midmorning, again using her thesis as an excuse to stay in her room. She glanced out the window, waiting until Becky had hitched up the horse and buggy and left before she ventured from the house to her car, hoping to slip away unnoticed.

She wanted to drive over to her father's land and poke around there. How glad she was that her dad was pulling out of his initial grief. Or so it seemed. A breeze shuffled the leaves in the nearby maples, and she noticed a fragrant aroma coming from Mill Creek, to the south. She'd walked along the wide stream at dusk several times, musing on her decision to abandon her summer plans to escape her grim diagnosis.

Now, as she drove the short distance, she noticed a van parked in a narrow lane, an Amishwoman and her young children filing in while an older man in jeans and a striped shirt stood near. Was he the driver? She'd heard from Marian Riehl of Mennonites and others making a living driving the Amish. She found it fascinating that a people who were prohibited to own or drive cars were permitted to pay others to drive them places. Another riddle of this Plain culture.

When Dad's land came into view, she pulled onto the shoulder and parked. Getting out, she walked to the passenger side of the car, leaned against it, and stared in awe. This was the perfect place for her dad to recover from his great loss.

And mine. She realized how very lonely she had been since her mother's death. Yet she felt powerless to stop pushing would-be friends away—a life-long pattern.

"At least I'll have an idyllic spot to return home to, when I want to visit Dad," she muttered, making her way across the fertile green field.

Imagine Dad growing potatoes . . . She walked the perimeter of the acreage, thinking again of her mother. Forever missing the only person she'd ever opened up to fully.

Enjoying the breeze on her face—the sky was such a profound blue—Heather realized her mother would be happy if she could see her now. "She'd be ecstatic that I've come here," she said aloud, thinking ahead to her appointment with the alternative doctor.

And, looking across the field to the farmhouses dotting the land, Heather felt as if they were all inviting her inside . . . as if she were being made welcome in this rural, back-roads place. Here, where dairy cows roamed free from constraint, munching leisurely in deep pasture grass, and where field crickets sang a familiar refrain each evening. Once she'd nearly lost her breath to the beauty of the moment as she watched a giant red sun drop gradually over faraway hills.

A subtle yet potent anticipation stirred within. And for the first time since arriving here, she wondered if there was something to Becky's talk of Providence. Had she been led here by an unseen hand?

Heather smiled at the thought, surprised by a sense of hope for the future. *Whatever it may bring.*

———

While refilling Jakob's coffee cup, Adah glanced out the kitchen window. After a full morning of doing laundry, Grace was presently down near the springhouse, weeding her herb garden. *Working her heart out.*

How she loved the little plot, and she could just imagine the lively flavors in their salads, come June.

It seemed like just yesterday when she'd helped young Grace make the first plantings of chives and thyme and other herbs. Lettie had been there, too, looking on and encouraging them in the process. Grace had marveled at their herb garden springing to life year after year, with many varieties reseeding themselves.

Presently, Grace stopped hoeing to look at the sky, and Adah realized anew the incredible strain on her granddaughter of late. All the energy it took to attempt to hold the family together—she was doing a fine job of it, too.

Grace wants to find her mother and bring her home. . . .

Adah had awakened with a bad dream in the night, wondering if it was an omen of sorts. She hadn't wanted to go into much detail with Jakob, but sitting here at the table now, she felt she should ask her husband if she was making a mistake by keeping the Ohio letter hidden.

———

Grace saw Mammi Adah coming out the door, waving to her. Briefly, she considered confiding in Mammi about Henry; then she thought better of it. If Mamma were here and knew of her decision, she would surely agree that letting Henry go was the right thing.

"You're out here early," her grand-mother said, bringing her own hoe.

"Wanted to get a head start on the day."

"Ach, you sound like your mother— she says the same thing. . . . I mean—"

"It's all right. I understand what you meant." A knowing look passed be-tween them, and Grace stood tall and stretched her back. "I spoke with Dat privately this morning, out in the barn. He's agreed, though reluctantly, that I can leave to look for Mamma once lambing's over—that is, if the market lambs are fast gainers."

"Well, someone ought to look for her, I s'pose." Mammi nodded slowly.

"Dat also says I mustn't go alone in my search, though."

"Sensible enough." Her grandmother leaned on her hoe, her expression thoughtful. "So . . . who do ya think might go with you?"

"I really haven't gotten that far yet," Grace admitted. "There's a little time to think on that, what with the lambs still comin'."

Mammi reached into the folds of her

dress to remove a slip of paper. She held it out to Grace, her eyes bright with tears. "Sounds like you might be needing this."

Grace accepted the paper and opened it, startled to see the address for an inn in Kidron, Ohio. "Is this . . . ?"

"Jah . . . the address where your mother and I stayed in Ohio all those years ago. I talked to your Dawdi 'bout it, and he agreed you should have it." Mammi paused a moment, then added, "We both hope it leads you to her."

She was surprised by the sudden change in her Mammi's attitude. "So you don't mind anymore?"

Mammi gave her hand a quick squeeze, her eyes still brimming with tears. "If you're successful, perhaps your mother will be home in plenty of time for wedding season. Or sooner . . . hopefully." She stooped again to return to weeding around the chives.

Grace felt sure that was possible. How hard could it be to find someone in Ohio Amish country anyway?

Judah cradled his newest lamb as he squatted in the hay. He kept his distance from the ewe for a time as she rested from the birth. New life had been springing forth almost daily now, and he was mighty grateful for so many healthy lambs.

He'd gone for another walk earlier today—pushing away the underbrush with his arms to make his way through a less-traveled path in a wooded area near Mill Creek. This time, he did not flail and lash out but rather offered a simple prayer that Lettie might know, somehow, that he loved her.

Stroking the lamb in his arms, he considered Grace's eagerness to begin her search. And he could kick himself for relenting. *Where will she look?* He had no idea himself. The rigid stipulations he'd put on the whole thing were his saving grace, because not a soul would be willing or able to leave family and farm chores behind to accompany Grace next month.

Yet what if she does find Lettie? The possibility nagged at him. Not that he didn't want his wife to return—with everything in him, he did. But he longed for Lettie to come home on her own, not due to pleading. Nor because of Grace's attempt. Judah wanted the bride of his youth to decide to come back because she loved them . . . loved *him.*

In his mind's eye he pictured Lettie walking up their driveway, the worn brown leather suitcase in hand. She might simply slip into the house unnoticed, before any of them began to stir, just as she had gone away in that dreadful darkness while they'd slumbered so soundly.

And wandering down to the kitchen, ready to greet a new day, Judah would see her there, back where she belonged, and the words locked away for much too long would tumble at last from his lips.

Epilogue

Tonight the rain was a mere drizzle as I went out front to sit on the porch swing. Soon, though, it started making down harder, splashing on the railing . . . and at times, onto me. Still, I stayed put in Mamma's spot, curling up there, pulling my bare feet beneath my long dress. Creating a shelter, of sorts. And, ach, how I needed it!

I couldn't help thinking of Becky's short visit here earlier today, when she shared how befuddled she was over their Virginia guest, Heather. The young woman has suddenly become distant and even looked to be crying one afternoon, according to Becky, who wonders if she is heartbroken or maybe ill. Now I knew that must have been the woman I saw crying and running down the road that day. Honestly, as Becky described the way she isolates herself most of the time, I couldn't help feeling sad for the girl called Heather.

But knowing Becky and her family, surely they'll draw her out in due time.

I told Becky about my own growing eagerness to go looking for Mamma. I asked her what *she'd* do, but it's awful hard for a person to know something like that. Becky looked all thunderstruck and said, "Oh, Grace . . . your family needs you here now more than ever." Of course, it wouldn't do for both Mamma *and* me to be away—least not till after lambing season, like Dat suggested. I'm glad he's agreeable, but I heard all too clearly the hesitancy in his words. If only he hadn't made it near impossible for me. 'Twill be nothing short of a miracle to find someone to accompany me.

Yet find someone I must, for all our sakes—Dat's especially. Who would've thought Mamma's leaving would get the best of him, putting him flat on his back?

Something must've happened while he slept away the days. There are times now when he'll utter more than five words in a row, as if he regrets being so quiet with Mamma. And so it seems good can rise out of turmoil and disappointment. So many feelings we've all experienced since Mamma's leaving. All's forgiven on my part, but I know I'll be offering up a prayer for a forgiving heart yet again tomorrow . . . and the next day. I only hope Mamma doesn't turn silent on us again, after her one and only phone call.

Mammi Adah's reaction to the whole thing continues to bewilder me. For sure and for certain, I'm thankful to her for giving me the address of the Ohio inn. But why should I suspect Mamma might have gone there? And why doesn't Mammi Adah seem surprised by my mother's need for a secretive journey?

The way Mammi Adah stares at me sometimes—it's unnerving, to say the least. I can't help thinking she might know why my mother would wish so hard for something she didn't have here in Bird-in-Hand. What would compel a forty-year-old wife and mother to rush out into the world like that?

Mammi says it's human nature to

wish for more than we have. The thought convicts me, if only briefly, when I think of Henry's and my brief betrothal . . . and my failure to go ahead with the wedding. Was I wrong to hope for something more? Truly I don't think so. These past few days since we've parted, my heart is at peace with what I did. If I am to live out my life as a Maidel, then so be it.

On the porch, the wind suddenly gusted, and the rain became a real downpour, forcing me inside, lest I "catch my death," as Mamma used to warn—back when things were a bit calmer under our roof. Yet even then, there was a charged atmosphere, a buildup to our present storm.

Retreating to my room, I wrapped up in a cozy afghan and enjoyed looking at Becky's recent drawing of three hummingbirds. I traced the outline of the smallest one and imagined it coming to life, hovering near Mamma's feeders out back. I'd always wondered why I was so keen on these delicate birds, and now I thought I knew. It was much more than their freedom of flight; it was their persistent search for the sweetness that sustained them.

I found myself reciting a stanza from a poem Mamma had taught me from one of the McGuffey's Readers.

Quickly, I opened my dresser drawer and reached for the journal presented to me on my birthday. Filled with an unexpected sense of hope, I wrote the beautiful words from "April Day."

The very earth, the steamy air,
Is all with fragrance rife!
And grace and beauty everywhere
Are flushing into life.

I held my pen and again studied my friend's lovely drawing. Becky's ongoing friendship is ever so dear.

Eventually, I dressed for bed and then brushed my hair. Mandy called softly from across the hall, and I hurried to meet her—going and sitting on her bed for a while, before time to outen the lanterns. Together we joined our hearts in earnest prayer for our mother, just as we do each and every night, waiting not so patiently for her return.

Acknowledgments

Creating a new series is always a special beginning—the joy of the fresh slate of characters and their circumstances. *The Secret* is not based on any particular true story or life event shared by any of my Amish friends or Plain relatives. It is rather the collective story of countless women who have given up a child at birth to adoption, either willingly or otherwise. Lettie Byler's heartrending journey, and her daughter Grace's response to it, is particularly dear to my heart as an adoptive mother.

During the writing of this novel, numerous people offered their assistance and encouragement. Their input is so essential that they really deserve their own paragraph!

My ongoing thanks to my husband, Dave, who loves the brainstorming process as much as I do. And to our daughter Julie, who lives and breathes my first drafts and is, thankfully, not reticent to point out embarrassing mistakes!

I offer heartfelt appreciation to my outstanding editorial team and reviewers— David Horton, Rochelle Glöege, Julie Klassen, Ann Parrish, and Jolene Steffer.

Thanks also to my clever cousin Kendra Verhage, an artist in her own right, for naming the Bylers' beloved mare, Willow, during Thanksgiving last year—so much fun! And to her sweet mother, my auntie Judy, who offered prayerful support during the final weeks of my writing deadline.

To my astute and ever helpful consultants in Lancaster County—both Plain and English—your prompt responses still astonish me and are a great blessing. Also, many thanks to Barbara Birch, proofreader extraordinaire. And to John Henderson, as well as the Mennonite Information Center and the Lancaster Historical Society.

To Carolene Robinson and Sandi Heisler, dear friends and medical consultants, your insight and knowledge are vital to this series. Thank you!

For the faithful prayers and quick feedback to title ideas, I send not-so-cyber hugs to Dave and Janet Buchwalter, Debra Larsen, Donna De For, Bob and Aleta Hirschberg, Iris Jones, Jeanne Pallos, Barbara and Lizzie, and to my own little grand-girls, who say the sweetest prayers. And, last, though he should be first, I give my love to my dear dad. Your prayers are precious!

All honor and praise to our heavenly Father, Creator and ultimate Mender of broken hearts, without whom no story would be possible.

DATE DUE

DATE	ISSUED TO

DEMCO